The Magpie's Daughter

by

Margaret Gregory

Cover designed by msgdragon
Cover images:
© Can Stock Photo Inc. /WMI_Photography
and Pixabay

Also by Margaret Gregory

TYMOREAN TRUST SERIES:
Book 1 - Power Rising
Book 2 - Great Ones
Book 3 - The Return to Earth
Book 4 – Earth Mission
Book 5 – Alien Contact
Book 6 - Invasion

ATAPI SORCERESS SERIES:
Prequel – Korvu: The Beginning
Book 1- The Wild One
Book 2 – Atapi Sorceress

Maeven - Dragon Thief

THE THIRD GENERATION SERIES:
Book 1 - Wanda: From Bad to Worse
Book 2 - Wanda: Choosing Crime
Wanda – Early Days (anthology) Book 1 and 2
Book 3 – Wanda: Risking Life to Live
Book 4 – Erin: The Forcing of Wisdom
Book 5 – Wanda: A New Life Part 1 – Hidden Secrets
Book 6 – Wanda: A New Life Part 2 – First Mission
Book 7 – Wanda: Full Circle
Book 8 and 9 – Erin: The Call
Book 10 - Royal Favour
Book 11 - The Serpent's Shadow

For permission requests, address the request to the author c/o
Permissions,
TAT Indie Publishing
PO Box 2728
Rowville, Victoria, 3178
www.tatindiepublishing.com.au

Andrea, called Andy, heard the whisper with disbelief. "What do you mean - the night's takings are gone?"

Kay, the junior waitress sidled closer to where Andy Cappell was rinsing dishes and stacking them in the dishwasher. She glanced over her shoulder.

"Just that. The Boss finished bagging it and left it in his office while he spoke to Joe and got his coat. He went back and it was gone. He's calling the police."

Andy had no chance to comment. Just then, the rest of the staff on clean-up walked into the kitchen, followed by the manager, Nigel Talliver. She wiped her hands and turned to listen.

Talliver repeated what Kay had just told her, but he added some unsettling news.

"I'd like you all to stay back. The police would like to question you and find out if anyone saw anything."

Andy did not mutter her disapproval as many of the others were. Instead, she hoped to keep a low profile. She had past dealings with the police and she was hoping that whoever came, did not know her by sight.

"All of you, keep on with your work, you'll be called in turn," Talliver instructed.

The crowd dispersed. Andy went back to rinsing dishes, subconsciously listening for the police to arrive.

Joe Saddler, the Head Waiter, summoned Andy just as she started the dishwasher. The police had not been there long. They must have summoned her first. She followed Joe to a corner near the entrance.

"Miss Cappell, keeping out of mischief, I trust?"

Andy recognised the Senior Constable, but couldn't remember his name.

"Of course," Andy retorted, forcing a grin. "How can I help you?"

The officer turned his attention back to the robbery. "You can tell me what you were doing about twelve-thirty this morning."

"Washing dishes," Andy answered immediately. The officer made a note in his book.

"Did you look at the clock?"

"I didn't have to," Andy told him. "That's my job. I scrape and rinse the dishes that come back from the tables, stack them in the dishwasher and put them away when they are clean."

"Did you take a break at any time?"

"I had to go to the ladies, once," Andrea admitted tartly. "Other than that, the furthest I went was from the sink to the dish hatch."

The questions went on for a further ten minutes, then "We are going to want to get prints from all the employees, you'll need to see Constable Yelland at the front desk."

Andy stood up. "How come?" She asked, putting one hand on her hip.

"The door to the office was forced," the officer told her. "We've found some prints."

Andy turned and walked to the front desk. All she could see of the constable was her hair.

"Andrea," Yelland greeted with no trace of friendliness.

"Yeah," Andy copied her tone.

"What have you been up to now?" Yelland asked.

"Nothing," Andrea protested.

"I hope you haven't moved into your old man's line of work."

Andy scowled. "No I haven't! I work here, and I don't need you and your mate implying I'm dishonest. I'm not!"

"We are not implying anything," Yelland said calmly. "We just need to eliminate you as a suspect."

"Suspect! Yeah."

Andy could tell how the woman's mind was working. "All I've done is climb things – misdemeanours, that's all."

"How high were you when you overdosed your friend?"

"I didn't do it!" Andy snapped, her face turning red with suppressed anger.

The constable's glance said what she didn't voice. The incident she referred to was on her record. The police believed that she had given her one and only friend a nearly lethal dose of drugs. The girl survived, fortunately, but because the police found drugs in her locker at school and in her room at home, they had blamed her. Especially since she had been high on something that night too.

"Can I go back to work now?" Andy asked when all ten of her fingertips were black.

"So long as you stick around a while longer. We may need to talk to you again."

"I'll be in the kitchen." Andy stalked off.

While Andy was trying to look busy finishing off her chores, two strangers walked into the kitchen and began looking in all the cupboards, and under benches. She assumed they were detectives and watched them without making any comments.

Finally, they asked her about the contents of some locked cupboards.

"The chef and his offsider have their own equipment. They each have a cupboard to lock it in," Andy explained.

"Who has a key?"

"They do. I'm not sure if anyone else does."

"Where is the silverware kept?" the other man asked.

"Out to the right of the serving hatch, with the clean table cloths and stuff."

"Can you show us?"

"Sure, I've a pile of it to put away."

Andy hefted the heavy basket of cleaned cutlery.

"How many sets of cutlery are there?"

"Some nights there seem like thousands. I have no idea," Andy told him.

"Thank you, Miss…"

"Andy," she supplied.

The two men nodded at her and went back to the front of the restaurant. At least they were not treating her as a culprit.

The police were still present an hour later. Andy had finished her jobs and really wanted to get home. She went to her locker to fetch her clothes to change into to go home.

"Miss Cappell, we would like to talk to you again, in the manager's office."

Andy jumped and turned around. Roberts, that was the constable's name.

"What for now?" She didn't need this aggravation. The officer said nothing. He followed her to Talliver's office.

"Andy," he greeted with no trace of friendliness. "The police found this in your locker."

He indicated a bundle on his desk.

"One of the table cloths?" Andy asked. "I don't know how that got there. It wasn't there when I arrived for work!"

After a moment, during which her boss just stared at her, Andy's tired mind realised what was being implied. "Hey!" she protested. "I didn't put it there! It could have been anyone. I don't have a lock on my locker because I never have anything valuable in there!"

The manager had then proceeded to unroll the tablecloth and reveal a full four piece setting of the restaurant's silver cutlery.

Andrea had felt her mouth drop open in surprise and when she spoke it had been in a squeaky voice.

"Mr Talliver, I did not put that in there!"

The policemen questioned her further while Talliver remained quiet. His arms were crossed and he was watching her.

However they had already ascertained her movements that evening and night and none of the other employees could possibly have seen her near the lockers or the office.

The police were finally satisfied and left taking the rewrapped bundle with them.

Andy began to leave but her boss called her back.

"Call back in the morning for your cheque. We won't need you from tomorrow."

"You're firing me? That's not fair. I haven't done anything wrong!"

"I no longer require your services," Talliver stated.

Andy stared at him but his face stayed set. Angry, Andy stalked from the office, went and changed from her uniform, then stomped from the restaurant to begin walking home.

It normally took Andy half an hour to walk from the restaurant in Williamstown to her mother's house in Newport, but she was too wound up to sleep so she kept walking.

Chapter 2

Andy heard an insistent voice and woke from a doze. She felt a cold breeze on her face and looked around. She could see lights everywhere and blue and red ones below. Then she looked down and saw the cars slowing down as the passed her perch and the police car. The voice was coming from an annoyed officer.

"Lady, come down from there!" he was calling. "Come down before you fall down."

Andy rested her head on the wire cable, "Dammit!" she told herself, recognising where she was. She was astride the safety railing on the Westgate Bridge. Pedestrians were not even meant to be on the bridge.

Andy climbed down easily and was grabbed by the officer.

"What were you doing up there?" he demanded.

Andy had no answer for that. "I don't know," she told him. "I don't remember getting there."

"You will have to come with us to the station."

"Alright," Andy agreed, knowing she had no choice. She tried to shrug of the officer's grip, but he kept hold of her. His partner was making a report about her over the car radio.

"Have you been drinking?" she was asked.

"No," Andy said.

"Are you taking anything?"

They were talking drugs. "No."

Andy allowed them to help her into the back of the van, and she spent the short drive in a state of tension, hoping the reeking, snoring drunk on the other seat would not wake up.

It was quickly apparent that they did think she was drunk or on drugs because firstly they asked to take a breathalyser test and then requested her permission to take a blood sample. She was finger printed for the second time that night and advised that she would receive a summons to appear in court on account of her being on the bridge.

The worst part of the whole affair was having her brother, Martin, called out to take her home. It was like she was still a child and not almost eighteen.

Martin Cappell was twenty-five, fair when his sister was dark, but with the same facial structure. He wasn't a big man but at five foot six, was still four inches taller than his sister.

He arrived at the station looking like he had been roused from bed and had dressed hurriedly. He didn't hide his displeasure at being dragged out in the middle of the night to deal with a delinquent sister.

Martin never once looked at her directly. Instead he listened to the trouble she was in, agreed to take her home and make sure she attended the hearing in two days' time. In the course of the conversation he casually let slip that his sister had done things like this before.

Andy was seething at her brother's condescending manner and although she wanted to hit him, she knew it would be a mistake to do it in a police station.

As soon as Martin was driving away from the police station, Andy began an angry tirade, letting out all the things she had not said in the hearing of the police.

"You don't know what you do half the time" Martin jeered in retaliation. He turned his car into their street and added, "I have seen you going into and out of places and you don't know that you've done it!"

"Liar," Andy said angrily. "It's only been twice! Anyway, you're no saint yourself! I know what you get up to, you sanctimonious prig."

"You've been caught four, or rather five times now!" Martin continued with a sneer. "I don't get caught!"

"Yet, you bastard!" Andy retorted.

Andy would have liked to be the one to inform the police of her brother's illegal activities but she had to admit he was diabolically clever in covering his trail. She had also learned, years ago, how vengeful he was. She simply didn't dare tell on him.

At home they separated without further conversation. Andy flopped onto her bed without bothering to undress and fell into an uneasy doze.

The house was quiet when she woke again, at well past her normal rousing time. Memories of the previous night returned and further sleep was impossible. At least she wouldn't have to face her brother, by now he would be at his day job, acting as the by the book, law abiding county sheriff. He would be out finding ways to book unwary drivers for parking even an inch out of line.

After changing into fresh clothes and eating a hasty breakfast, Andy decided to face going to get her final pay cheque. Fortunately, it wasn't her boss that she had to speak to but his assistant. He handed over her pay envelope without comment. Normally her pay went into her bank at the end of each fortnight, but this time it was a cheque. She cashed it at the bank on her way home.

Andy arrived back home and walked through to the kitchen, intending to make some lunch. She didn't expect to see another woman there, acting as if she belonged.

"What are you doing here?" she greeted her brother's girlfriend rudely.

It was obvious from Merryl's attire of bathrobe and a towel around her hair that she had stayed the night.

"I live here now!" she smiled silkily. "Martin and I are engaged."

"I knew he had no taste!" Andy replied taunting. "Stay out of my room!"

"Keep out of mine, bitch!" Merryl replied in kind.

Andy stalked past the other woman and went into the lounge room to watch TV for a while before returning and finding something for lunch.

Mid-afternoon, Andy heard Merryl leave the house and decided to snoop in her brother's room again. He wasn't due back for another two hours. She began her snooping with careful thoroughness. It wasn't her intention for him to even suspect that she had been there. Her previous visits had gone undetected. This time though, her timing was out.

"What are you doing in here?" Martin roared, startling Andy into turning around.

There was no safe answer to that question. She ducked as he charged towards her but this time she wasn't quick enough. His full weight landed on her and drove the breath from her lungs.

Andy fought for breath as her brother pounded her back with his fists.

"Martin!" Merryl said sharply. She wasn't concerned that Andy was getting hurt; she simply didn't want her lover killing his sister so they would have to cover it up.

Martin didn't want to kill her yet either, he punched her once more then stood up.

"Get out of here before I kick you!" he said hoarsely.

Andy finally managed to breathe. "I'll get you for this!" she threatened weakly.

Martin laughed at her as she crawled slowly from his room, unable to stand and walk. "You'll get worse if I catch you in here again."

He turned to Merryl and smiled at her. They walked down the passage together, ignoring Andy.

Andy pulled herself onto her bed, slowly and painfully. She didn't try to move further until she heard Martin and Merryl leave the house. Then she walked slowly to the kitchen to find the supply of painkillers.

"I'm not staying here a day longer!" Andy muttered to herself. "Martin will just have to lose the bond money!" She spared no regrets about that.

On her way back to her bedroom, she collected some clothes from the laundry and an old backpack from the dusty hall cupboard.

There were very few personal items that she wanted to take. After clothes, the remaining space was filled with two water bottles and some tinned food that didn't need cooking. She added a cup, plate and cutlery and a can opener as an afterthought, then grabbed an old mobile phone, that had been Martin's, from where she'd hidden it. He didn't know she had it. He'd cracked the screen and so thrown it out before buying a newer one with the latest apps and features.

Once she'd got a new SIM card, she'd found it still worked, not that she had anyone she wanted to call. Still turned off, that went into a side pocket of the pack, with its charger.

She pushed the pack into her wardrobe and lay down to rest until after dark when she knew that both Merryl and Martin would be out until the early morning hours.

Andy took another dose of painkillers and shoved more into a pocket in the backpack. She walked carefully to the nearest bus stop, trying not to jar her back. An hour and a half later she was at Southern Cross station, which she still thought of as Spencer Street. However she was too late for the trains she wanted, so she found an unobtrusive corner to curl up in and try to sleep. An interrupted doze was all she managed because her body was used to being awake at that hour.

In the morning she brought a ticket to Ballarat. Relieved to be gone at last, Andy slept most of the way.

She was fully awake when she arrived at Ballarat Station and quickly found the location of several backpackers' hostels; one was quite close to the station. When she was finally shown into a room, she breathed a sigh of relief. It felt good to be away from her brother.

She joined other guests in the communal kitchen for lunch. As she prepared baked beans on toast, she began chatting to two young men her own age. They were openly friendly and didn't expect more than casual details about her. She decided to join them on a bike tour around Ballarat the following day.

Andy had no idea she was being followed as she rode around Ballarat, enjoying being a tourist. Colin and Michael were pleasant company and it was possible to forget her aching back and her brother. When she returned to the hostel tired and elated, all she wanted to do was sleep.

She awoke early and had breakfast in an otherwise deserted kitchen. Then she used the unoccupied female showering facility and revelled in the warm water. She considered her plans for the day. A visit to the Laundromat that she had seen the previous day had to be a priority. It opened early and was not far away.

As she sat waiting for her washing machine to finish, a rough looking man came in with a bundle of clothes. She glanced at him before turning her attention elsewhere. The man made her feel uncomfortable and she didn't want to start a conversation with him. Instead she studied her surroundings and felt glad for the presence of the security cameras.

Colin and Michael found her again at lunch and invited her to join them when they visited Sovereign Hill. This time they were on foot but it was again a thoroughly enjoyable afternoon.

Andy thanked providence that she had woken early and gone for a walk to loosen up her stiff muscles. She returned just as a police car pulled up outside the hostel. A shiver of apprehension made her walk quickly to the side entrance of the hostel and run up to her room. Her belongings were all in her pack so she only had to grab it, but voices in the stairwell made her dive into the empty room opposite and lock the door.

Curiosity caused her to press an ear against the door in an effort to hear what was going on. Her slightly guilty conscience had made her assume the police were after her for missing her court appearance, but it didn't mean they were in truth. The voices were indistinct, so the best she could do was stay as quiet as possible and watch for the police car to leave. The window in this room overlooked the main street and she could just see the rear of the parked police car. While she waited, she opened her pack and felt down the side to where she kept her main supply of money. Something hard and lumpy, that she couldn't identify, met her questing hand. She unpacked her bag enough to see what it was.

She pulled out what appeared to be one of the hostel's striped pillowcases. It clinked softly, and Andy found it contained one and two dollar coins, along with a proportion of the tokens that she had used at the Laundromat in lieu of coins. She looked at it as if it contained a live snake. It was obvious what she was staring at, but how it had got into her pack was not. The coins were stolen but there was no way that she dared take them to the police. She remembered the things found in her locker at work and wondered if she was going mad. Maybe Martin was right! Maybe she did do things without remembering - and forcing those money boxes at the Laundromat would have been simple if she had wanted to do it.

Her mind argued with her conscience but greed lost out to common sense. She shoved the bag of coins under the room's unmade bed.

As soon as the police car left and it seemed to have stayed for a very long time, Andy grabbed her retied pack and departed the hostel by the rear door. No one paid special attention to her and the few she met were still chatting about the visit of the police.

At the train station, Andy tried to buy a ticket on the afternoon train to Albury, but it was fully booked. The station master suggested the Greyhound bus and she was able to book a seat on the bus leaving at 4pm. With five hours to wait, Andy booked through her pack and went to the nearby gardens to find a quiet spot to wait.

Chapter 3

"Hey! What are you doing up there!"

The angry male voice startled Andy, rousing her from a doze, and for a moment she couldn't recognise where she was.

"Can't you read the signs? No climbing the trees!"

Sure enough, she was up a tree, but Andy couldn't remember getting there.

"If you don't come down right now, I'll call the police," the uniformed groundsman threatened. He was an elderly man, but he still looked physically strong.

"All right," Andy muttered, not wishing to give the man a chance to carry out his threat.

She climbed down carefully, feeling her bruised back protesting.

"What did you climb the tree for?"

"I really don't remember doing it!" Andy answered but not unexpectedly the man snorted in disbelief.

"Stay out of the gardens! If I see you back here I will call the police!" The groundsman warned her.

Andy was only too happy to agree, it was time she was heading back to the bus. As she walked, she thought about being up the tree and shivered. She really couldn't recall doing it and that had begun to scare her.

No one seemed to be paying any attention to her as she boarded the bus and hours later no one seemed interested when she alighted from the bus and began trudging with her pack back towards the river. The Murray River separated Albury, NSW from Wodonga in Victoria. She recalled seeing what might have been a park as she crossed the river and this was her destination. She hoped to find a secluded spot to sleep for the night, which being warm wouldn't hurt her. The morning would be soon enough to get a feel for the city and she would need to find a bank. A lack of money was her major reason for sleeping in the open. By the time she found a suitably isolated spot by the river, she was more than ready to sleep.

Albury came alive around her as she walked to wards the city centre. She actively sought work with any business that looked like they could use an unskilled worker. A lack of references was her major problem, not helped by looking as if she had slept in the open in her clothes. After a second night of sleeping out and a second day of walking around the town, she finally met a woman who was willing to let her sweep floors. The wage she offered was low but she offered a room to bunk in and breakfast as compensation.

Andy was happy to work hard and keep a low profile. In fact she so pleased her new employer that she was asked to do more little chores around the woman's shop, things that the old woman was finding harder and harder to do herself.

Two weeks passed quietly, and Andy began to feel more secure. Thoughts of her brother haunted her, as she wondered if he cared that she had gone. In another couple of days she would be eighteen and her brother would no longer be her legal guardian.

"Another one!" Mrs Haddie commented to herself as Andy entered her kitchen for breakfast.

"Another what?" Andy asked as she collected the cutlery and plates to set the table. A job she had offered to do to help her host.

"Oh, another robbery. That makes the tenth business to be broken into in as many days. The police think the same person is responsible for all of them. Probably some young drug addict. They have a rough description."

"What places has the thief hit?" Andy asked curiously.

Mrs Haddie mentioned two that she remembered, but did not notice that her boarder has suddenly gone very still.

It might be coincidence, but both the places were businesses where she had gone seeking work. Andy forced herself to continue laying the table but her mind was only partly on what she was doing. The front page of the local daily paper was face up on the table and she gathered it to read. The break-ins were the major story and people were asked to look out for a young dark haired person of about her height. It was also noted that the crimes were committed by someone expert at picking locks.

Mrs Haddie's delicious bacon and eggs tasted like cardboard. A lump of irrational fear settled into Andy's stomach. All ten places were places she had visited. She couldn't be doing it. Surely if she was up half the night she would be tired in the morning? Surely if she was robbing these places she would find all this money in her pack? The coincidence was so great that she was desperately afraid she was doing things she couldn't remember – like the tree climbing in Ballarat. It was time to leave – to go somewhere else.

The dark car parked outside Mrs Haddie's shop was ordinary enough but Andy felt suddenly afraid. Instead of returning there with the shopping she had done for her employer she continued on another two blocks to the house. The bags and the change were placed at the back door and Andy ran into the unlocked bungalow. The few loose items were thrown into her pack and the bag was secured roughly. As she began to walk down the drive to the street, she saw the same dark car drive past and stop. Andy backed away and looked for somewhere to hide.

"You must be mistaken," Mrs Haddie was saying. "Andy is a hard worker, very polite, very helpful. I've been letting her sleep in the bungalow."

"Do you mind if we take a look in there?" the policeman asked.

Andy was watching through the leaves of a large tree that grew over Mrs Haddie's roof. The man had a badge pinned to his shirt pocket.

Mrs Haddie seemed reluctant to agree, but the policeman ignored her dithering and strode towards the bungalow as if expecting her permission.

He glanced inside and commented matter-of-factly, "It appears as if she has gone!"

"Oh, dear!" Mrs Haddie brought her hand up to her chest. "I sent her off to do some messages for me."

"When would that have been, Mam?"

"Just after I opened the shop, about nine thirty" Mrs Haddie looked upset.

The policeman helped her back to the house, and then noticed the groceries near the door.

Andy was glad they had been found; she didn't want to lose Mrs Haddie's good opinion.

The conversation was muffled by the roof for a time.

"She is simply wanted for questioning, that's all Mam. She may be able to help us clear things up. We don't believe she is dangerous. If she returns, just ask her to come and see us or you can give us a call. Would you like a lift back to your shop?"

Andy stayed huddled on the roof for a long time after the policeman had gone. Mrs Haddie, the dear old thing, might believe that 'wanted for questioning' was nothing more than being helpful but Andy had no such delusions and she knew nothing that would help the police. If she went to them or they found her, there was still the matter of the missed court appearance in Melbourne. It was a pity, but she would have to leave and she couldn't risk staying to say goodbye.

Before she left her hiding spot, Andy considered the best way to get to the bus depot. She decided to risk catching the local bus to the centre of Albury and walking the final way to the depot. If she booked her pack in early again, she would be less noticeable.

The local bus ran right past Mrs Haddie's house and shop and in the time she had been there she had learnt the timing of the busses. Andy allowed just enough time to reach the nearest stop before climbing down from the roof. She hoped that the drivers had not been told to look out for her.

It was a relief when she finally reached the Greyhound depot and bought a ticket to Broken Hill. With her pack booked through, she went to the adjoining coffee shop for an early lunch. When she returned to the depot, two uniformed police were talking to the booking clerk, but it wasn't the one that had served her. Andy slipped into the ladies room and waited in there until nearer twelve o'clock when the bus was due to leave.

There were no problems when she presented her boarding pass, no sign of police, and no sudden hand on her shoulder. Andy hoped that the police had lost her trail. The ticket had been purchased using a false name – Martina Chappell.

Chapter 4

Coming into Broken Hill, Andy had noticed a number of motels and caravan parks. After collecting her pack, Andy walked to the nearest van park and booked the cheapest onsite van for three nights. The hire fee took most of her remaining ready cash so she knew she would have to get to a bank to withdraw from her account and risk having her movements traced.

Andy followed the same pattern that she had in Albury and began canvassing the town, looking for work. On the second day, late in the afternoon, she became aware that she was being followed. The woman she spotted was dressed in jeans and a t-shirt, similar to what she was wearing herself, but was a bit too far back to be recognised.

Anger grew in Andy and she decided to try and get behind the woman and follow her in turn.

Her attempt began when she went into the nearest shop, which happened to be a jeweller's salon. She positioned herself so that she could watch the window as she browsed a watch display.

The woman caught up, glanced inside, saw her and moved on.

Andy let the shop assistant show her some of the least expensive watches but declined to like any of them. Outside the shop she went to the edge of the road and glanced up and down the street as if she planned to cross over. In the process, she spotted the woman and began walking in her direction. The woman began to walk away but glanced back frequently. After about five minutes, the woman ducked out of sight, probably to let Andy pass her.

Instead, Andy ducked into a narrow laneway between two houses and then into a tree that overhung a fence. She waited and was rewarded by seeing the woman pass by below her, looking worried and trying to see into all of the gardens that she past. When she finally seemed to give up and began walking purposefully away, Andy followed her.

In time the woman went into the Broken Hill Hotel. Andy found a place outside to watch and wait. Her vigil was rewarded. Half an hour later she recognised her brother, neatly and casually dressed, emerging from the hotel accommodation entrance. He was accompanied by the woman, now dressed in a flowing yellow skirt and white blouse but without the dark wig. Andy had not recognised her with the wig but her follower had to have been her brother's fiancé, Merryl Street.

"Bastard!" Andy thought to herself, immediately assuming that her brother was up to no good and his target was herself. She watched them drive off in a taxi before the impulse to repay her brother became irresistible.

Andy walked openly to the accommodation door, felt in her pocket as if for a key, but actually pulled out something much more useful. The little picklock would open almost any lock in her skilled hands and in a moment she had the side door opened and was inside the accommodation wing of the hotel. She strolled along the passage as if she had every right to be there and went down to the main desk to ask if her brother was registered there. The clerk confirmed that he was but did not give a room number. However there was only three keys missing from the board and she studied the numbers as she asked the clerk to call her brothers room. As anticipated the call was unanswered so she said she'd be in the bar and try later. By a roundabout route that bypassed the reception desk, she went upstairs intending to examine each of the three rooms in turn.

In the second room she entered, she was rewarded. The luggage was instantly familiar as were the jeans and wig thrown over a chair. Andy locked the door behind her and began to search quickly through her brother's bags.

When she found three hundred dollars hidden under the baseboard of one case she took it without a qualm. In another part of the case was a set of ID cards with her name but Merryl's bewigged face. Andy took the one that was a driver's licence. There was nothing to indicate that Martin was having her followed and then robbing the places that she had visited. It was time to go.

The jewellery store robbery was on the morning news when Andy was having breakfast. The details were similar to those for the spate of robberies in Albury. She listened intently; the police had no suspects yet. A nasty idea occurred to Andy and on the way out of the caravan park for the final time she made a call from the payphone at the entrance.

When she stepped away from the phone she had a smug smile on her face and was certain that the police would be paying her brother a visit. Her amusement lasted as she walked into town and then she was distracted as she began to walk through a used car yard. If she were to buy a car, with cash, it might be one less way by which her brother could trace her. Two cars were unlocked and she took the opportunity to sit in each and pretend she could afford to buy them. They were priced way beyond her means but at least her legs had a rest. Reluctantly she emerged from the second car and continued looking.

Two car yards later she found what she needed in a small, older model car for a thousand dollars. She put a deposit on it and went to the bank to withdraw the balance from her account. The fake ID had proved to be extremely useful for the drivers licence claimed her age to be twenty, not almost eighteen.

Three hours later she drove carefully out of the car yard and back to the local shopping centre. Her first attempt at parking consisted of driving into an empty parking bay at the far end of the lot where she would be able to drive out again. After returning to the car with a small supply of groceries, she visited the opportunity shop opposite the supermarket and found some other useful items. Then, feeling very pleased with herself she headed out of town on her way to Adelaide.

It was curiosity that made her turn off the main road at a signpost that said Cooper's Crossing. Her father had lived there when he had first come to Australia from England. That was before he moved to Broken Hill and married.

The open desert country was so different to anything that she had ever experienced. It seemed like her car was the only car in the world. She stopped for a break in the shade of a lone tree on a slight rise and could see for miles. For the first time in days she felt safe, convinced that at last her brother could not guess where she was.

The solitude was a relief too, as she ate some of the food she had brought from Broken Hill. She almost choked as she suddenly laughed whilst drinking some water. Was her brother still trying to explain himself to the police in Broken Hill?

The good mood lasted until she tried to start her car again and found it wouldn't. That's when she began to be afraid. Then she remembered the phone she had shoved into her pack. She had charged it back in Ballarat, and hadn't used it since then. However, when she tried to call directory assistance to get a local number for a garage, she had no signal. With a scowl, she shoved the useless thing back into her pack.

Andy stayed with her car, hoping that someone would come along. By nightfall, she would even have welcomed her brother. As the night deepened and the day's heat gave way to the chill of the desert night, Andy retrieved the blanket that she had bought in the op-shop from where she had stashed in the boot and wrapped it around herself. Finally she crawled into the back seat and tried to find a comfortable way to sleep.

The sun was well above the horizon and the temperature was beginning to climb when Andy spotted the dust cloud in the distance. She watched it approach and prepared to attract the driver's attention.

Chapter 5

Andy grabbed her pack from the seat beside her as the car stopped in the town of Cooper's Crossing.

"I can't thank you enough for giving me a lift" Andy spoke to the couple in the front seat. "I hope I'll be able to repay the favour sometime."

"If you are ever out near Murrawindi, call in," the woman, Julia Cullen invited. "Jim can always put an extra pair of hands to work."

"If I am ever out that way, you certainly could put me to work." Andy promised as she scrambled out of the car. "Though if my car can't be fixed, I'll be relying on shank's pony to get around."

Jim Cullen gave a polite smile but Julia grinned broadly and waved at Andy who had stepped back away from the car. Andy returned the wave, thinking how she had come to like Julia Cullen in the short half hour that it had taken to reach town from where her car had died.

They had dropped her at the garage, but being Sunday, it was closed. The town didn't look like there was much activity at the best of times. Well, there was no harm in knocking, just in case someone was around.

When there was no response to her knock, Andy surveyed the town. The Cullen's had suggested that she make enquiries at the Pub or, failing that at the flying doctor base. Either of those places would be able to contact the garage owner Emma Patterson.

The traffic in the street was nonexistent as she crossed over to try and find the hotel. Finally she spotted the round brewery advertisement on the roof of one building and headed that way.

The hotel looked to be shut too but when she tried the door, it opened, so she slipped inside. There was no one in sight.

"Is anybody here?" she called loudly from just inside the door.

A few moments later, a woman bustled into view, looking surprised to see her there.

Andy forestalled any comments about the bar being closed by speaking first.

"Hello, I was wondering if you could help me find a mechanic."

"Well Emma runs the garage, but she would be out on her property today." The woman had a name tag with Nancy on it. Andy deduced she was Nancy Buckley, the proprietor's wife.

"Fair enough, it is a weekend." Andy said thoughtfully. "Will she be in town tomorrow?"

"I expect so," Nancy told her as two men walked into the bar area. "Oh, Vic, this lass needs a mechanic."

"Car broke down?" Vic commented, stating the obvious.

"Yes, about half an hour back down the road." Andy admitted ruefully. "The Cullens were nice enough to give me a lift this far. I only stopped the car for a short break but I couldn't get it going again. I tried everything that I could think of, but then I'm no expert so it might be something quite simple."

"We could give Emma a call" Vic suggested.

"I'd hate to drag her here for a five minute job." Andy said aloud. "It can wait until tomorrow, it's not going anywhere."

The second man, who had been silent until then spoke up.

"I could go out there with you and take a look at it? If you would like me to."

Andy turned her attention away from Vic and surveyed the rough looking character. He seemed friendly enough.

"Would you?" Andy was somewhat surprised by the offer, but then she was unused to the helpful friendliness of the locals here. She half expected some sort of catch to the offer, but at the same time her city-bred suspicious nature didn't really like leaving her car unattended.

"I'm Luke Mitchell," the man introduced himself, putting out his hand for Andy to shake.

"Andy Cappell," she took the proffered hand and shook it.

"When would you like to go?" Luke asked, looking intently at Andy.

"Now?" she suggested tentatively, and Luke nodded.

Andy headed for the front door, but Luke forestalled her.

"Back way," he told her indicating the direction with a gesture of his head. He led the way through to the back of the hotel as Andy automatically took notice of her surroundings.

There were two horses cropping the grass at the rear of the hotel, one was saddled, the other only had a bridle on it. When Luke began to cross over to the horses, Andy suddenly realised how they were going to get back to her car. She tried to hide her surprise at this unexpected mode of travel.

Luke noticed that she was still carrying her bulky pack and suggested that she leave it with Vic Buckley, the proprietor of the hotel. Though reluctant, Andy saw the sense of it. She would have enough trouble just staying on the horse!

Nancy had disappeared when Andy took her pack back in but Vic was behind the bar getting ready for the evening trade. He agreed to mind it for her and lifted it behind the bar.

Andy didn't want to admit that she had never been on a horse before. She watched Luke effortlessly mount the unsaddled horse and hold the bridle of the other horse ready for her. She approached the horse with trepidation and wished that she could use a nearby stack of empty beer kegs to help her mount. No one had ever accused her of being afraid to try something new so she put on a bold face. She managed to get up on her second attempt, in a totally graceless fashion, but the horse was well trained and Luke was holding it firmly so it only shuffled a bit.

She watched Luke carefully and imitated his commands and motions to get the horse moving. She let out a little sigh of relief as her horse began to follow its mate. Just as she began to breathe more easily and think that it wasn't going to be too bad, the horse began to trot down the road, evidently taking its cue from Luke. Andy took a deep breath and devoted her entire concentration to staying in the saddle.

Her car seemed to be exactly as she had left it and amazingly she managed to make the horse stop next to it. With relief, she dismounted and handed the reins to Luke who walked both horses into the shade of the tree. He dismounted with the ease of much practice and she felt she was walking with an exaggerated wide legged gait and tried not to.

The shade had not moved around to where the car was parked yet so the car was very hot to touch and the sun had caused the interior to feel like an oven. Andy carefully unlocked the door and opened it wide to try and let the hot air out and the faint breeze in.

Fortunately, Andy thought, it was an automatic, so she could try and start it without having to sit in the car on the burning hot seat or touch the equally hot steering wheel. The motor turned over but didn't start. She pulled the bonnet cord and wrapped a handkerchief around her hand as she lifted up the bonnet.

Luke returned at that point and began checking things under the bonnet, beginning with the water and oil and progressing to more mechanical things. Every now and then he would ask her to try starting it and finally it did.

"What did you do?" Andy asked, greatly relieved. Her knowledge of mechanics was virtually non existent.

"I just checked and fiddled with everything that I could. It may have been a loose connection or a vapour lock in the fuel line. Get the car back onto the road and I will ride back to town after you."

"I really appreciate your help, Luke," Andy thanked the man as she dragged the rug off the rear seat and positioned it over the seat she had to sit on. She wished she could do something similar for her hands which had to touch the hot steering wheel.

Andy drove the car forward, and almost got bogged in a soft sandy patch. Luke had watched as the car wheels had begun to spin and was about to come and off to help when the car wheels found enough traction to reach the hard gravel of the road.

Andy drove slowly and watched as Luke retrieved the horses and mounted the saddled one this time. When he had caught up to her, she accelerated to a moderate speed that the horses could maintain. After about fifteen minutes the car died again and she let it roll to the side of the road and pulled the bonnet cord again.

"I ought to shoot it" Andy said in disgust as Luke lifted the bonnet up for another look.

Andy looked as he again fiddled with wires, hoses, plugs and other parts.

Luke suddenly asked "Do you know Frank Cappell?" He turned to see Andy's surprised expression.

"My father's name was Frank!"

"Was?" Luke queried.

"Yeah, he died in gaol." Andy said without a trace of regret.

"Not that it made much difference to us," she went on, "I think the only time he spent with my mother was when he conceived Martin and me and for nearly a year when I was nine."

"I'm sorry to hear that he's gone." Luke sounded sincere. "I liked the old cuss. He was a decent bloke, even if he couldn't stay out of trouble."

"Keep his mitts off other people's stuff you mean!" Andy corrected. "I hardly knew him."

She wanted to end the subject but Luke continued.

"You'd be from Melbourne then. You are a long way from home."

"I don't know how you knew, but as far as I'm concerned I'm not far enough! I'm trying to find somewhere isolated enough and far enough away that my brother will leave me alone. We had a terrific disagreement and I simply can't stand that woman he brought home to live with him. Will I try to start it again?"

Luke nodded and the car started on the second attempt.

"Hopefully I will get to town this time," Andy grumbled. "It's a heap but it was all I could afford. I will get the garage to check it anyway."

Luke's expression seemed to indicate his agreement but he said nothing, simply mounted his horse again to follow her.

This time the car did make it to town and Andy parked it outside the garage. Luke continued to the hotel and Andy walked that way after locking the car. Locking it was a habit but if someone wanted to pinch it they wouldn't get far and there was certainly nothing of value to pinch from it. Her mind turned to the idea of buying Luke a drink to thank him for his trouble. In fact she was extremely thirsty herself.

The front door of the pub was locked so Andy went around to the back following the sound of angry voices which ceased abruptly as she entered the area of the main bar. Vic and Nancy, who had seemed so friendly before, now looked at her as if she had just crawled out from under the woodpile.

"Why do I get the idea that I am no longer welcome?" she asked bluntly eyeing first Nancy and then Vic. The couple glanced uncomfortably at each other but neither seemed to want to speak.

"Well?" she challenged them. Finally Luke Mitchell answered her question.

"Sometime earlier today, someone robbed the till!" he said quietly, without sounding accusing.

"You can't think I did it!" Andy demanded, but she had gone noticeably pale. It was obvious that whilst nobody was actually saying it, that the Buckley's were thinking it.

"The money was found in your bag!" Luke continued.

"That's crazy!" Andy said looking at Luke. "If I was rotten enough to rob this place, I wouldn't stick around and I wouldn't leave my stuff where every sticky beak could go through it. I don't need to stay here and take this. I want my bag!"

"Jack took it!" Vic finally spoke up, awkwardly.

"Jack? Who the hell is Jack?" Andy demanded, but she reckoned she could guess correctly.

"Jack Carruthers is the local policeman." Luke informed her.

"And just where does he hang out?" Andy asked, trying to hide her anger.

"Just up the road a bit" Like supplied.

"Right!" Andy said determinedly and turned to walk from the room.

"I'll come with you if you like" Luke offered.

"Thanks Luke, but I won't need you. I appreciate your help with my car and I was going to buy you a drink by way of saying thanks but some jerk took all my money. This won't take more than a few minutes to clear up." Andy stomped from the room and headed for the main street. She had only gone a short way when her own inner doubts surfaced.

"Perhaps I really did it?" a pernicious inner voice insisted.

"Perhaps Martin is right when he says I do things and don't remember?"

Andy tried to pull herself together.

"No! I saw him in Broken Hill and Merryl was dressed like me!"

"But how could he know you were here?" the pernicious voice reminded her.

Andy purposefully squashed her doubts and concentrated on her conviction of innocence. She lengthened her stride towards the building with the police four-wheel drive parked outside.

The front door was open and when Andy walked in the policeman was behind the front counter talking on the telephone.

He glanced up when he heard her enter.

"Yes, Vic, she's here now, thanks" Andy heard him say.

Jack Carruthers terminated the conversation but before he could speak Andy started.

"What right did you have to look in my stuff without my permission and walk off with it?" she demanded forcibly but not loudly.

"I was investigating a crime" Jack was on the defensive, realising that Andy had a point. He wasn't going to argue that it had been Vic who had looked and found the money.

"Maybe I am not completely correct, but it was my belief that you need a warrant to search personal possessions or that I had to have been charged with something first," Andy insisted.

"So you are a lawyer are you?" Jack wasn't feeling comfortable but it wasn't obvious. He could argue the point with her if he chose.

"No, but I am not some hick from the sticks. I have had an education, I can read and I do watch television. I am not completely ignorant," Andy said derisively. "I want my bag and everything I had in it."

"I need to ask you a few questions," Jack said calmly, reverting to routine.

"Questions be damned!" Andy said angrily but she was trying to hide her fear. "Why does everyone assume that just because I am a stranger in town, I'm the criminal?"

"No one is assuming that!" Jack stated calmly, hoping to sidetrack Andy from her accusations. "It is simply that you were around during the period that the money could have been taken. I'll also be talking to Luke Mitchell. No one is accusing him either!"

"They said at the pub that the money had been in my bag! They looked at me as if I was a thief."

"Why don't we go into the next room and you can tell me why it wasn't you!" Jack suggested in a friendly manner.

Andy didn't look deceived, but after a long considering stare she agreed with ill grace. Logically he did have to investigate and she had been there.

There were two chairs and a desk in what was obviously Jack's office. Jack sat in the one behind his desk and indicated that she should make use of the other. He found a pen and a sheet of paper.

Andy waited for him to begin, and rubbed her forehead where she seemed to have the beginnings of a major headache.

Firstly she was asked for her name and address and her reason for being in town.

She gave her name, her Melbourne address but admitted that she no longer lived there. The third question was more difficult to answer but she finally told him what she had told Luke Mitchell and added that it had been curiosity that had prompted her to turn off from the road to Adelaide.

"What an understatement" Andy thought to herself, but it would definitely not help her case to elaborate on her stays in Ballarat, Albury and Broken Hill or mention the trouble in Melbourne.

"How did you get here?" Jack asked as if the answer wasn't really important.

"Train, bus and car" Andy didn't intend to volunteer any information.

At that point the phone rang and Jack turned his attention to the caller. His replies were brief but Andy began to feel alarmed.

"Yes, Jim...When was that?...How much?...Yes, I'll make inquiries... Yes, I'll be in touch."

Jack hung up the phone, and Andy sensed a hardening in his manner.

"Vic mentioned that you had car trouble," Jack's tone wasn't quite as friendly now.

"Yes, Luke Mitchell was kind enough to offer to help me get it here. It is a heap but it was all I could afford."

"Had it long"

"About two weeks" Andy lied as she forced a grin.

"Vic also mentioned that the Cullens dropped you off when your car broke down.'

"Yes, I thought it was pretty decent of them."

Jack didn't miss the note of caution in her voice now.

"Jim Cullen is missing some papers from his wallet," Jack began, but he waved Andy to silence when she opened her mouth to butt in. "He had it down between the front seats. You didn't happen to notice any loose papers on the floor at the back did you?"

Andy looked at Jack for a few moments before answering.

"How much does he reckon I pinched?" Andy asked carefully, it was obvious she was on the right track.

"He wasn't accusing you" Jack told her. "He was just covering all possibilities. He has misplaced about eight hundred dollars."

"It probably slid under his seat!" Andy suggested and looking squarely at the policeman added, "I didn't see it. I didn't touch it!"

"You did have a lot of money in your bag" Jack commented.

"Yeah," Andy muttered. "Mine! Five hundred of it I got out of my account, three hundred I got off my brother! It may seem a lot but it is all I have left anywhere and I have to make it last until I can find a job."

Andy wasn't stupid. She knew how it was looking. Someone had lost a wad, she had one.

"Tell me what you did after the Cullens dropped you off." Jack changed the tack of his questions, not sure if he believed Andy or not.

Andy told him carefully and exactly in terse statements what she had done since arriving in Coopers Crossing right up to the time she entered the police station.

She added her observation that she hadn't seen anyone else around except Luke and the Buckleys.

Andy's eyes met those of Jack Carruthers, almost daring him to disbelieve her.

"I'll get your statement typed up and then you can go, though I would appreciate it if you would stay around town a few days to help clear this up."

Jack wondered if he was making a mistake, but this woman

wasn't acting like she was guilty.

"How long will that take?" Andy asked, feeling uncomfortable and it wasn't just the headache. Though she wasn't going to admit it, she suffered from claustrophobia and this room even though it had a window, felt like it was closing in.

"Can I come back later?"

"I'd rather you waited" Jack watched for her reaction.

"Well in that case, can I type it up in exchange for a glass of water?"

Andy wanted out but she didn't want to have to come back.

Jack agreed to her offer and suggested that she work in the outer office, which had no files of confidential information. He showed her where the typewriter was and gave her some paper before going out the back for the drink of water.

He half expected her to be gone when he got back but instead she had already started.

Andy reckoned that the water hardly touched the sides of her mouth as it went down, it wasn't enough but she decided not to ask for more – getting her statement typed so that she could leave was more imperative. The water was enough to make her sweat and it was stuffy in the police station in spite of the fans.

Jack Carruthers found something to keep him occupied in the outer office as he watched Andy typing. He was impressed by her speed; he would be taking much longer.

Andy carefully read over what she had typed before handing it to Jack Carruthers. When he had finished reading it through he invited her to sign it if she was happy that it was correct.

"Can I have my bag and money?" Andy asked, eager to be gone.

Jack reached under the counter for her bag and handed it to her.

"I'll just be keeping the money until I check the numbers on the notes with the bank." Jack informed her.

"Then you had better give me a receipt for it," Andy told him tartly, restraining herself from saying anything more.

While Jack organised the receipt, Andy made a point of checking the contents of her bag. The subtle insult was not lost on the policeman.

The urge to get back outside was so strong that Andy practically snatched the receipt from Jack's hand and didn't quite run out the door.

Jack grabbed his hat and car keys from a shelf near the door, intending to go after her. He wanted to get the registration number of her car so he could make some further enquiries about her. He stopped, stunned to find her sitting on the veranda of the police station leaning against the wall.

"I suppose you are wondering why I am sitting here," Andy said with no hint of the aggressiveness that she had displayed inside.

"From the way you took off, I thought you would be half way to Broken Hill by now," Jack said with commendable nonchalance.

"Wrong direction!" Andy said with half a laugh. "The simple fact is, I have no where to go. You've got all my money, and I doubt that I would be welcome at the hotel even if I would want to go back there. My car...well I would be an idiot to drive it before I get it checked over. I can't even pay to have that done at the moment. What the hell am I supposed to do?"

Jack Carruthers was at a loss for a solution. He was relieved when Luke Mitchell appeared, having heard Andy's remarks.

"You can stay with me if you want to," Luke invited, and added for Jack's benefit, "I knew her father a long time ago."

"I seem to be in your debt, Luke," Andy told him as she stood up, wanting to get away after discomforting the policeman.

"I will need a statement from you too, Luke," Jack reminded him, "I'll come and see you later."

Luke shrugged an affirmative and began walking back towards the hotel.

When he entered, Andy refused to go in until Nancy Buckley came out and apologised for her earlier mistrust. Inside, she chose to sit in the furthest corner possible and chose only to drink water. It was all she felt like and she only barely realised that she needed it but she didn't realise how close she had come to being dehydrated.

Jack Carruthers had driven past Luke and Andy as they walked to the hotel but only Luke had noticed. He stopped outside the garage and made a note of the registration of her car and its description. He glanced into the interior and saw nothing amiss.

Something caught his glance as he turned from the car. The side door of the garage was not closed properly. Jack strode over to look more carefully. The lock had not been forced, so he pushed it open without touching the handle. In the light from the open door, nothing seemed to be amiss inside but he entered and walked slowly around. The money drawer was open and empty. He could not tell if anything else had been touched. He would have to contact the owner, Emma Patterson. When he left, he ensured the door was locked.

Back at the station he put into motion what he considered a routine enquiry about the car and the money that he had found in Andy's bag. He expected to be able to confirm the woman's innocence. There was no way he could have anticipated the bee's nest he had shaken.

In fact, Andy had no idea of the heap of trouble brewing for her either. It was only that Jack was called away later to attend to a problem on one of the nearer stations and didn't get back until morning and then before the report reached him he was called out to search for a missing child that delayed matters. The delay gave Andy some warning of what was to come.

Chapter 6

Luke was camped on the property of a man for whom he was doing odd jobs. Andy had accepted the offer to share his camp, but if it hadn't been for the circumstances she never would have agreed. She ignored the whispers that followed her as she left the pub with Luke. She really didn't care what those people thought, but she was wondering if she was walking into trouble. Luke was still a stranger, even if he had been a perfect gentleman so far.

Andy offered to help with the camp chores, but Luke insisted that she was his guest. Instead she found a shady spot under a tree and sat and watched as he walked around the camp with an easy grace.

It was not hard to doze off in the warmth, and when she awoke sometime later, it was to see Luke walking up from the trees, carrying a water filled billy.

"What's down there," she asked.

"A small waterhole," he told her. "It is deep enough to swim in."

The idea of a swim appealed to Andy, but again she wondered if it were wise – when she was alone with a stranger. Luke seemed to divine her thoughts.

"I'm about to start cooking something for dinner, it will take a while. If you want to go and cool off I will call you when it is ready."

Andy decided, nodding in reply to his comment. She stood up and walked off in the direction Luke had returned from. At the pool, which appeared to have been made by damming a small creek, she squatted on the side for a while, listening to see if she had been followed. After long moments of silence she moved behind some bushes and stripped to bare essentials and walked into the pool. The water was delightfully cool on her hot skin which had probably got sunburnt. When she emerged, feeling refreshed, she sat in the sun to dry, dressing again just before she heard Luke calling.

It was dark and becoming cool, Andy felt replete after eating Luke's surprisingly delicious meal. She was sitting hugging her knees, gazing into the fire. Luke was lying on the far side of the fire, resting easily on hip and elbow. He hadn't bothered her with questions for which she was grateful.

"When did you meet my father?" Andy asked suddenly looking over the fire at Luke.

Luke thought for a while before answering.

"About twelve or thirteen years ago, I was on the outskirts of Gosford and he was just out of prison."

"I'd have been about six or seven then" Andy thought aloud. "He actually came home for a year after that stint in prison. I loved him and followed him around like a shadow. I copied everything he did, trouble was I was too young to realise that picking locks was illegal, to me it was fun. I was with him the day he was arrested."

Andy stopped talking but her mind recalled that day vividly, it was the worst day of her life.

The policeman had thought to teach her a lesson and had put her into an unlocked cell for ten minutes but it had been enough to give her claustrophobia ever since.

When Andy drew her mind back to the present she was surprised to find another figure squatting in the fire light.

"Lo, Luke"

The figure was an aborigine, the first she had ever seen close up. She simply stared.

"Hello, Dougie" Luke returned the greeting warmly. "What brings you?"

"Nothing much. Brought Sarah in to see the doctors." Dougie replied speaking better English than Andy had expected.

"Dougie, meet Andy" Luke introduced.

"Lo, Andy" Dougie spoke to her.

"Hello," Andy croaked back, glad of the darkness that was hiding her blush. She was embarrassed by her assumption of superiority.

"Never seen a black person before?" Dougie asked with a slight chuckle.

Andy blushed more furiously.

"No, not this close. I didn't mean to be rude!"

Dougie laughed unaffected by her apology. "City Fella?"

"Isn't it obvious?" she replied, and they laughed more at the chagrin in her voice.

Thinking that the two men might want to talk and deciding that she had enough of the day she rose and said "Goodnight."

She headed for the tent that Luke had offered to her to sleep in but she went in only long enough to grab a blanket and her pack. She curled up outside, next to the tent and used her pack as a pillow and was soon asleep.

The birds woke Andy before dawn and lying there enjoying the freshness of the morning she became aware of movement around the fire and the sounds of someone making tea.

When she tried to move she became aware of the stiffness of her muscles from riding the horse the previous day and that brought back everything that had happened then. She groaned and decided it was time to get up. By the time she had taken a necessary walk behind some bushes and had a sketchy wash at the waterhole, the tea was ready.

Andy accepted the mug of tea with many thanks but it had only barely cooled to drinkable temperature when she heard a car approaching. It became identifiable as the policeman's car when it came closer.

Andy experienced a few moments of panic before resolutely turning to tidy up her belongings. She was aware that Dougie had reappeared and was waiting with Luke and watching Jack Carruthers drive the final distance to the camp. Andy kept herself apart from the others as Jack got out of his car but she was close enough to overhear the conversation.

"The two Lovatt boys are missing again, this time with their cousin Stephen Linden. The Lovatts have searched their place but will check again now that it's light, however one of the hands thought he heard them ride off on their bikes very early this morning. The Lovatts have done it before, but Stephen has to be found. He is on twice daily medication."

Dougie was ready to go at once and joined Jack in the police car. Luke quickly doused the fire and went to saddle his horse. Jack queried Andy's intentions.

"Well I won't be much help searching for the kids as I don't know the district. I'll probably walk back into town and see about my car.

And I will stick to the main road so you don't have to come looking for me!"

There were no objections so Andy was left on her own at the camp.

After an hour of walking Andy began to realise that she had either misjudged the distance back to town or her own stamina, but there was nothing else to do but keep going. The crudely fashioned sunhat that she wore was making her head sweat and she wished she had a bigger water container. It was late morning when she reached the turn off to the town tip.

There was a sign pointing to town, three kilometres further on.

The trees on the side road provided some shade where she could rest a while. As she sat she wondered idly if the three boys had been found. An apparently unrelated thought occurred to her as she recalled the fascination some of her city bred playmates had for rubbish tips. Would country boys be any different?

The tip wasn't far down the road; a quick visit would be her contribution to the search.

Andy followed the road to the edge of an old quarry and continued along a rough track that slowly wound down into it. Andy concentrated on her footing; she heard what she at first thought was shouting but dismissed it as some sort of unfamiliar bird noise. Then she rounded a bend with bushes growing thickly and found three bikes leaning against the quarry wall. The track beyond that point was too rough even to wheel the bikes.

She heard the voices again and tried to hurry faster but the track was eroded by water and mini rock slides and it made anything faster than a slow walk hazardous.

About twenty metres from the bottom, Andy slipped and slid half of the distance. She crawled to her feet, bruised, scratched and filthy.

The childish voices were more urgent and Andy saw two small figures well out onto the pile of rusting and rotting junk, waving and yelling to get her attention. She walked on to the bottom where the junk started and looked for the safest path to the boys. There was no way for her to hurry as the junk, carelessly dumped, was too unstable for anyone but a lightweight to traverse. The last thing she needed was to slip in between the rust junk and become trapped herself. There was no question of not proceeding, and by the time she reached the boys she had collected countless more scrapes and cuts.

The boys were frantically trying to open a discarded fridge. The outside showed the marks of their unsuccessful attempts.

"Who's in there?" she asked looking around for something else to try prising the door with.

"Tommy, Miss" the elder of the two boys whispered. "We can't get him out."

Andy reached for a flat piece of metal as she asked "How long has he been in there?"

She attacked the closing mechanism with the sharp corner of the metal. It began to give, but not enough. The boys watched anxiously.

"He's been in there ages, miss."

"Use those pipes of yours, there and there" Andy instructed, continuing to apply pressure to the catch. "Push down hard."

It took the combined effort of all three of them to open the door and it rose with a whoosh.

Andy grabbed it before it fell shut again.

"Hold it up," she told the boys as she reached in to see if the third child had a pulse. He did but it was weak and the boy wasn't breathing.

As she lifted the boy out of the fridge, a piece of pipe fell into the chamber. It must have been pushed in through the almost rotten sealing stuff around the fridge door. The boys let the door close so Andy could put Tommy onto it.

She began EAR at once, but it was a long five minutes before the boy seemed to be breathing on his own. As she listened to the ragged breathing, she asked the other boys their names. They were Billy Lovatt and Steven Linden.

"We have to get Tommy to a doctor" she told the solemn boys. "I will carry him but you might have to help steady me."

Andy was grateful to the boys as her greater weight threatened to dislodge junk into new resting places. She breathed a sigh of relief when she finally stepped off the junk and had to lay Tommy down to catch her own breath. Too soon for her aching muscles, she lifted Tommy up again and began to pick her way back up the washed out track. Tommy was still breathing but neither deeply nor regularly.

When she reached the point where the bikes had been left, she placed Tommy in the shade. Her mind recalled the lack of any shade further up and she doubted that she had the strength to carry him all the way to the trees near the main road.

"Bill? How long will it take you to get up to the top and cycle to town or home to get help?"

Andy deliberately used the more grown up form of Billy's name. He was the younger of the two brothers.

Billy swelled up importantly and assured Andy that he could be home in twenty minutes.

"Get going! We have to get the doctors here as fast as possible."

"Step?' Billy quizzed his cousin, but Stephen shook his head, declining to ride with him.

"I'm not feeling very well!" was all he said.

Billy accepted that and began to push his bike back up to the top of the quarry.

Stephen watched his cousin until he disappeared over the lip of the quarry and then turned his attention to the woman who had arrived in time to help them.

"Will he be all right, miss?"

"I don't know, Stephen," Andy admitted, unable to give a positive answer. The boy was looking awfully pale and scared. "Who put the pipe in?"

"I did, and I tried blowing air in there until it got too hard."

"I think you did the right thing. What little air you put in may have made the difference." Andy told him approvingly. "Without that I might have arrived too late. What was he doing in there any way?"

"He was pretending to be Dracula in a coffin," Stephen said in a small voice, no doubt aware of how close to a coffin the old fridge had become.

Andy didn't comment. She figured that the boys wouldn't need her to lecture them and she was in no way amused by the morbid imaginations of small boys.

It seemed to take forever for help to arrive. Andy had been watching the time and trying to estimate when help would come. She was relieved to hear Stephen shout down to her from the lip of the quarry when he saw the ambulance arriving. She had sent him up to wait for the doctors and was in fact glad that he had been out of the way. Tommy had stopped breathing again, twice, and she had needed to recommence EAR. For the past ten minutes she had been maintaining the process, timing her breaths with Tommy's attempts to breathe in.

Stephen hurried ahead of the three adults he was leading down the track.

"They're here" he said excitedly.

The leading man was obviously a doctor but he didn't stop to introduce himself. The woman was a nurse; her name badge read Kate Standish. She quickly slipped an oxygen mask onto Tommy's face and gave a brief smile as she edged Andy away from Tommy. Andy was only too glad to leave the boy's care to the experts and moved to where she could see the others approaching. The third member of the group carried a rolled up stretcher and was probably the driver of the ambulance. As Andy watched the nurse adjust the regulator on the oxygen cylinder, she became aware of more people approaching. The man with Jack Carruthers was, she guessed, Tommy's father because his attention was on the unconscious boy.

Andy walked out of the way, wondering if she had the energy to climb back up to the top. She wasn't aware of Jack Carruthers until he spoke next to her.

"What happened" he asked, causing her to jump slightly.

"He was stuck in an old fridge and his friends couldn't get the door open again." she told him as she turned to face him. "That one, over there, on the top of the pile."

Andy pointed, and Jack scanned the heap until he saw it. He began to walk over to the junk.

"Sergeant, I don't suggest you try to climb over there. The junk is too unstable for anyone to climb on, particularly if you weigh more than those kids."

Jack walked back to her, thinking that he was seeing the real Andy Cappell, not the frightened, angry, woman who seemed to try to bluff him.

"Is that how you came by all those scratches?"

"Most of them, but they're nothing. I've had worse." Andy dismissed her injuries.

The doctor had organised Tommy Lovatt onto the stretcher which was now being carried by his father and the ambulance man back up the track. Kate was walking beside it carrying the oxygen tank.

Stephen, still looking pale was walking slowly behind them.

"Tom!" Jack called to the doctor who turned back on hearing the summons.

Andy protested, but Tom Callahan examined her scratches.

"You'll need to come back to the hospital and have those scratches and cuts cleaned. When did you last have a tetanus shot?"

"Um, ages ago" Andy squirmed at the thought.

"Come on then, you can ride back with Jack" he told her firmly. "It looks like you have been out in the sun too much as it is." He had noted the signs of sunburn and he suspected dehydration.

Andy shrugged dismissively, but she was glad she wouldn't have to walk back to town. Now she only had to climb back up the hill. She followed Jack back up the track, and only an inborn stubbornness kept her going. They caught up to Stephen who was sitting in a heap on the path, unable to walk any further, Jack lifted him and carried him the rest of the way.

Andy reached the road but felt her legs turn to jelly and her vision become grey. She stumbled a few steps and sat down to catch her breath.

She felt a gentle hand on her shoulder and as her vision cleared she saw Tom Callahan squatting down beside her.

"You did well keeping Tommy alive," he said quietly as he checked her pulse. "Keep breathing deeply for a while."

"I don't think I could have done anything if Stephen hadn't had that bit of pipe pushed in. He said he managed to blow some air into the fridge." Andy told him, between breaths. "The credit should go to him."

"It was lucky that you went there," Tom commented, intending to give her the credit she deserved even if she was not claiming it herself. "What made you think to come?"

"I'm a city brat. Some of my friends were fascinated by such places. I thought that country kids might be too – it was just a vague hunch."

"Can you stand?" Tom asked then, and he helped her up, suggesting that she drive back with Kate in the RFDS station wagon.

Andy nodded to indicate she could walk on her own and went with deliberate effort to the white car with the RFDS emblem on the door. Tommy Lovatt was being lifted into the ambulance and Stephen climbed in after him. Andy didn't bother to wonder why. Billy Lovatt and his father were climbing into Jack's four wheel drive.

Andy was quiet during the drive back to town. She answered Kate when she was asked her name but didn't feel like talking because her head was beginning to pound and ache. She was also feeling nauseous, because of the smell that was clinging to her clothes. No wonder Kate had the windows open fully.

At the hospital, Andy was put in the charge of another nurse, a cheerful blonde who led her to an examination cubicle and instructed her to change into a shapeless white gown. While Andy was doing that Annie fetched a jug of water and a glass which she put within Andy's reach.

"You are to drink as much of that as you want," Annie told her. "Now, let me look at these scratches."

Annie had a basin of cool water and proceeded to wash the cuts and scrapes. When Andy's skin had dried, she began to gently cover them with antiseptic cream. She noted the fresh bruises on Andy's arms and legs and asked about them.

"I slipped down the hill a bit," Andy admitted. "The edge of the track crumbled."

"You are lucky you didn't break anything. Do you hurt anywhere else?"

"I think I scraped my back a bit, but my clothing would have got the worst of it."

Andy said truthfully, but regretted the admission when Annie looked at her back and gave an exclamation of shock.

"You have a whole batch of new bruises on your back," she commented without mentioning the obvious signs of many almost faded older ones. "I will see what we have to rub on them."

Andy stiffened, realising that the bruises her brother had given her could not have completely disappeared even if her back had no longer felt tender. She waited for Annie to ask about them but she didn't.

Annie returned with a doctor and she introduced him as Doctor Standish. The first thing he did was to prepare the tetanus injection. Andy turned away and tried not to flinch as the needle went in. An involuntary "ouch" escaped her. She breathed deeply a few times to settle her stomach and tried to ignore the acute discomfort at the injection site.

Standish began to question her about her medical background and Andy answered as honestly as possible, aware that Annie was noting down her answers.

Then he examined the treated cuts, commenting that none would require stitching but a few needed to have dressings put on them. Then he considered the bruises on her arms and legs before asking her to let him examine her back.

He asked how her back felt and Andy admitted it was sore from her tumble.

"How was it before you fell?" he asked carefully.

"Okay," Andy said tersely, not really wanting to discuss the old bruises.

"How did you get all that old bruising?" he asked directly.

Andy looked away from him and shrugged.

"Are they the reason why you left home?" Geoff Standish asked on a hunch.

"One of many," Andy said in a small voice.

"You should have reported the assault to the police," he advised her.

Andy laughed as if the idea was ludicrous.

"No way! It was my fault any way. I was poking around where I knew I shouldn't have been."

"That isn't a reason to treat anyone that roughly," Geoff insisted. "Who was it.?'

Andy shook her head, "It's no matter. I left and it's simpler to just keep away."

"Did you tell your family?" Geoff asked.

"I only have a brother," Andy said without humour. "And we are definitely not friends!"

"Was he the one who hit you?"

Andy refused to answer and Geoff drew his own conclusions. There wasn't anything he could do unless she co-operated. He would however write his observations and suspicions into his medical report.

"If you are feeling better you can go," Standish advised her. "Try to keep out of the sun and drink plenty of fluids and try to get a hat and some sun cream. You look like you've got fairly severe sunburn. You obviously aren't used to being out in the country and you will have to be careful to avoid dehydration. So finish off that jug of water before you go. Annie mentioned that she will be able to find you some clean clothes."

Andy nodded obediently and continued to drink the water. She was not in a rush to go anywhere.

Andy asked Annie how to get to the garage from the hospital as she dressed in the borrowed clothes; her own were in a plastic bag on the floor beside her. She thought it was past time to see about her car and implied as much to the blond nurse.

That might have been her intention as she walked out the back entrance into the small hospital garden, but as soon as she saw the big old tree she had an uncontrollable urge to climb it. With a quick glance to check that no one was watching, she climbed it with amazing agility. The bag of clothes was no handicap either as she settled herself onto a thick bough that was hidden from sight by a dense screen of leaves. She had no fears about falling and there, alone and well above any wandering people, she relaxed and let the slight breeze through the leaves lull her to sleep.

A dog yapping at the base of the tree woke her several hours later. For a moment she was disorientated, but she remembered climbing the tree and smiled to herself. She was pleased that she remembered and amazed that she had slept so long.

Her amusement quickly vanished as she climbed to a lower branch and saw through the less dense leaves, the police car parked at the hospital.

"Why should I be worried?" Andy asked herself. "I haven't done anything. I haven't!"

The dog moved away and the garden became quiet. Andy was about to climb down when she heard voices, getting louder.

"If you see her, Tom, just tell her that I need to talk to her again." Jack Carruthers was saying. "I've cleared up the matter with the Cullens and I need to know if she has any idea about the man that was seen entering the pub after her."

"If I see her, I'll tell her," Tom Callaghan promised, but as Jack seemed distracted he asked, "Was there some other problem?"

Jack didn't answer immediately.

"I've got detectives from four cities wanting to interview her," he said finally. "I have to find her again before my superior comes from Broken Hill. He was annoyed that I didn't keep her in custody."

Jack Carruthers moved off and Andy watched until the police car was driven away.

"Dammit! I haven't done anything!" Andy swore aloud, oblivious that someone might hear her.

Some one did!

Chapter 7

Tom Callaghan was returning from walking Jack to his car. He had mixed feelings trying to relate what Jack had told him about the girl with his own impressions. Then he recognised Andy's voice coming from the tree.

"Andy?" he called softly. The slight rustling from the tree stopped suddenly.

Andy looked down and saw Tom Callahan looking up at her, but she made no move to come down.

"Why are you up there?" Tom asked.

"I wanted to be alone!" Andy answered after a while.

"You heard what Jack said?"

"Yes."

"Jack has been wasting his time looking for you."

"He only had to look up!"

"He seems to have cleared up some bother you were in."

Andy made a rude noise and Tom knew she had heard all the conversation.

"Do you want to come down and talk about it?"

"No! Talking would be a waste of time."

"Why?"

"I have a fair idea what they think I have done and no way to prove that I haven't."

"Come down," Tom invited. "Perhaps I can help."

"I doubt it!" Andy disagreed, but she climbed down with an ease that impressed Callaghan.

"Who taught you to climb?" Tom asked, changing to a different subject.

"My father! He used to be a steeplejack. I like climbing; I have a good head for heights."

Andy paused and laughed. "My brother gets dizzy standing on a chair! I got into the habit of finding something to climb when I wanted to avoid him. When I am really riled up I sometimes don't remember getting up somewhere. I did this time. And I don't get claustrophobia up trees."

"I'm on my way to the base, do you want to come?" Tom invited.

"That's a little too close to the Police Station, Doc, for my current peace of mind."

"Jack didn't tell me to turn you in just to let you know that he wanted to talk to you."

"I don't really want to go and talk to him. He's quite nice as policemen go, but ..."

"But what," Tom prompted as they started to walk towards the doctor's car.

"Every place that I stayed since I left Melbourne has had robberies. Everyone has been somewhere that I went to for some reason. I can't remember robbing anywhere, I have never wanted to rob anyone, but it could have been me. The robber was an expert at picking locks, so am I; my father taught me when I was too young to know it was wrong. My brother claims that I do things that I don't remember doing but I do often find myself up somewhere without remembering getting there. How can I be sure I am innocent? How can they? I've been in trouble three times for being where I shouldn't. Jack said he should have had me in custody – I don't blame him, but I wasn't joking about having claustrophobia – I can't stand being locked in."

Tom could see her trembling. He felt sure she was telling him the truth. If she were guilty, she would have run away when she had the chance.

"If you co-operate with Jack. I'm sure he will be reasonable." Tom advised her. "You impressed him this morning."

Andy lapsed into silence as Tom drove to the RFDS base.

"Perhaps you should drop me at the police station," Andy suggested as they neared town.

"Have you eaten since breakfast?" Tom asked, ignoring her suggestion. He caught Andy's small headshake.

"I'll see that you have a snack first, and then you can talk to Jack." He sensed Andy relax a bit.

At the base she was introduced to Clare the radio operator and saw some of the people she had met that morning. They all smiled at her. Clare was happy to act on Tom's request for a snack for Andy. A messenger brought some sandwiches from the snack shop in town.

Tom Callaghan let Andy share his office as she ate and waited until she finished before asking questions. He had obviously read Standish's report on her condition. He didn't ask about the old bruises, but about how she got on with her brother.

"How is Tommy Lovatt?" Andy asked instead of answering.

"Recovering," Tom Callaghan assured her. "I asked about you and your brother."

"I don't want to discuss my brother!"

"You don't sound like you get on well with him," Tom commented.

Andy barked a laugh.

"Ok. You asked! Since Mum died we have co-existed. My bastard of a brother fought to become my legal guardian. I'm sure you think that was a brotherly gesture and he can be positively charming when he wants to be, but he is a bastard. He hates me. I hate him! Now that I am eighteen, he can go to hell!"

"Why does he hate you?" Tom asked quietly.

Andy shrugged. "Probably because when our deepest desire came true and our father came home to live with us I became his favourite. I could follow him everywhere, no matter where he climbed. Martin couldn't, and he couldn't seem to win Dad's approval. It was a long time ago."

A gentle knocking could be heard.

"Come in," Tom invited, and Clare poked her head around the door to Tom's office and apologised for the interruption.

"Do you have your key for the file cabinet? Mine doesn't seem to want to open it."

Tom felt in his pocket, rose and went out to the outer office. Andy followed and watched as Tom tried to open the offending drawers – and while others tried.

Andy spoke up without thinking – "Can I try something?"

Everyone stood back and let her in.

There was a gadget in her hand that she kept hidden, but within moments the jammed lock was open.

Among the voices of approval was one that wasn't.

Andy stiffened before turning.

"I'll take a look at that gadget!" Jack Carruthers insisted. His gaze fixed Andy like a hawk on its prey.

Andy returned the look defiantly, not wanting to part with something that had been a gift from her father. Everyone's eyes were on her as she passed the small tool to the policeman.

It was obvious that Jack knew what it was.

"I'll keep that," he said very officially, watching her for a reaction.

Andy tried to act casual, as if she was unconcerned by the fact that the policeman had found a burglars picklock in her possession. Somehow, she didn't think that Jack Carruthers was deceived.

"Let's go back into my office," Tom suggested quietly. Curious glances followed the trio.

Jack followed Andy back into the little office. She felt like a rabbit with a fox breathing down its neck. Though she considered it a hopeful sign that Jack hadn't immediately insisted she go back to his station.

"I've been looking for you all day," Jack sounded annoyed.

"I was at the hospital!" Andy said very meekly. "I climbed a tree and fell asleep."

Tom nodded to indicate that the statement was true and Jack squashed his rising anger.

"Jim Cullen found his money!" Jack told her, and noticed the look of relief in her eyes.

"I also checked the numbers on the money you had," Jack was watching Andy closely.

"Some of it was stolen."

The relief vanished and Andy looked pale.

"That can't be," Andy protested. "Stolen from where?"

"A second hand store in Albury."

Her mind wondered why her normally clever brother had kept stolen money in his room. If she hadn't stolen it, would the police have found it and what about the fake ID's? He may have intended to plant it on her, like the money in Ballarat. How could she implicate her brother without making things worse for herself? She couldn't – damn Martin.

Jack wondered what was passing through the woman's mind.

"What was the story about someone entering the pub after me?" Andy managed to say. "Was he about five-six, blond and slightly built?"

"Did you see him?" Jack asked, he remembered her saying she'd seen no one.

"No."

"Who were you describing?" Jack asked. For a moment he was sure that she wouldn't answer.

"My brother!" Andy said. "I hoped to have given him the slip."

She dared not suggest he might have robbed the till at the pub.

"Perhaps we had better discuss this at the station," Jack suggested in an official tone.

Only Tom noticed that Andy went tense.

"Ok, I want this matter cleared up."

Andy kept her face averted from Jack's as she stood up to leave the room.

"A moment. Jack?" Tom requested.

"I'll wait outside!" Andy promised.

"Jack, she heard you say that there were other charges in the wind, and told me she hadn't done anything. She is afraid that you will have to lock her up – I believe her when she said she suffers from severe claustrophobia," Tom said quickly.

Jack nodded, and without further comment turned to go after Andy.

When he couldn't see her in the outer office, he hurried outside. Once again he was surprised to see her waiting on the outside steps for him. She looked frightened but came with him quietly, though she didn't speak at all on the short trip to the police station.

Andy preceded Jack into the same room where they had spoken before and sat where Jack pointed. He went around to the far side of his desk and placed the confiscated picklock on the desk in front of him. He gave her a long penetrating stare. Just when he had managed to convince himself that this woman was innocent, she produces that illegal little tool and demonstrates her skill with it – what was he supposed to think?

"Do you have any idea how much trouble you are in?" Jack asked her seriously.

Andy was looking down at her hands and hunched herself down in the chair.

"No."

"Do you?" Jack repeated. This time Andy nodded.

"You are trying to convince me that you are innocent – perhaps you can start by explaining why you had that." Jack pointed to the tool.

"It was my father's," Andy said. "It's all I have that was his. It's more like a good luck charm to me."

Jack shook his head, "You will have to do better than that."

"I can't. You can think what you want but I haven't robbed anyone." Andy didn't consider taking money from Martin as robbery.

"Well then, why do I have police from Ballarat, Albury and Broken Hill wanting to talk to you?" Jack asked her.

"I can guess," Andy admitted. "In Ballarat, I found a pillowcase full of coins and Laundromat tokens in my pack. I'm sure I didn't rob the place! I left it under the bed in the room opposite where I was bunked and scrammed."

Jack was curious at her phrasing, "I'm sure I didn't rob the place." To his mind, it suggested that she had doubts.

"And Albury?" Jack prompted and he saw Andy squirm as if embarrassed.

"I didn't rob anyone!" she repeated defiantly.

"What did you do?" Jack asked.

"The first two nights after I arrived by bus, I slept down by the river. I spent the first two days walking around looking for work."

"Why did you run away?"

"Because the police came and spoke to the old lady I was working for, and I couldn't prove that I knew nothing about the robberies. It was too coincidental that every place that I went into asking for work was later robbed. My brother keeps telling me that I do things that I can't remember doing later. I have to believe him because several times I have found that I've climbed someplace and I can't remember doing it. But if I was robbing the places I should have had all the money, but I didn't."

Jack looked unconvinced.

"And I didn't want to talk to them because I've had some minor run-ins with them in the past."

Jack nodded, knowing that she had failed to appear at a court hearing in Melbourne. He decided not to mention that yet.

"Then what?" Jack probed.

"I came to Broken Hill. The same sort of thing started happening," Andy began and went on to tell how she had been followed by a woman dressed like her and how she had in turn followed the woman and seen her brother and his girlfriend, but not how she had gone into their room at the hotel.

"Then I decided to withdraw all my savings and buy a car. I left Melbourne to get away from them; I don't know how they kept finding me. I don't know how he could have followed me here. It was a spur of the moment decision. I was heading for Adelaide."

Jack had been taking notes and when Andy stopped, he took the opportunity to catch up before asking more questions.

"Are you implying that your brother is trying to frame you?" Jack asked her then.

"I wish I could," Andy said reluctantly, she would only make it worse by trying.

"Why would your brother want to frame you?" Jack insisted. "Do you have any proof?"

Jack glanced up and saw that someone else had quietly entered the room, he was about to stand up in respect to his superior but the other waved him down. It was a tacit command not to mention his presence.

"If I knew why I would be laughing!" Andy said unhappily. "And, no, I can't give you proof. There is nothing that I would like better than for someone to prove that he is not the model citizen that he claims to be."

"Do you know that he's not?" Jack asked.

"Know, yes, and again, prove no." She stopped herself saying that she didn't dare.

Jack shrugged. "Well then, unless you can give us something concrete to act on, it's just speculation. Now, as things stand, I am going to have to keep you here. There is someone coming from Broken Hill to talk to you and take you back so that the detectives from Albury and Ballarat can talk to you."

Andy slumped further into the chair, if it weren't for the sunburn her face would have paled. She certainly felt sick.

"All right, I did go into Martin's hotel room in Broken Hill," Andy finally admitted. "I found a black wig and the clothes that the woman I followed was wearing. It had to have been Merryl following me. I know she saw me in the jewellery shop when I was hiding from her."

"That is hardly conclusive," Jack told her.

Andy squirmed in her seat, fighting her well ingrained fear of trying to tell on her brother.

"Oh, all right, I went through Martin's stuff and found a pile of false ID's with my name and a dark wigged Merryl's face, in his case. I also found three hundred dollars in there and I took that. It had to be the money you said was stolen. The other five hundred was what I had left over from buying my car."

Jack looked up at his superior to see if he wished to say anything.

"Sergeant, if I promise not to leave town, could I stay at the pub?" Andy pleaded.

Jack wasn't given the option to consider it.

"I'm afraid that won't be possible, Miss Cappell," a voice from behind her stated.

Andy jumped visibly, and almost fell out of the chair twisting around to see who had spoken.

"Who are you?"

"I'm Detective Chief Inspector Hayley, Broken Hill CIB," the newcomer informed her and went on to add, "I have a warrant for your arrest on two counts of robbery."

Andy knew she was cornered.

"I didn't do anything!" she protested futilely, hoping he had just arrived.

Hayley closed the door behind him and walked to the chair that Jack had hurriedly vacated.

"You are under arrest for the robbery of Smiths Jewellery store and for the robbery of money from Martin Cappell, which you just admitted to."

"I didn't rob the jeweller's. It had to be Martin, he had…" Andy stopped speaking abruptly. Whatever she said would damn her …

"I haven't got anything more to say," Andy said trying to sound defiant. "When I get to Broken Hill you had better arrange some legal counsel for me! I won't sign anything either."

"This attitude won't help you!" the Chief Inspector told her coldly.

Andy looked away from him deliberately and remained silent.

Hayley began to read Jack's notes and his hand reached out to touch the picklock.

"I see you haven't mentioned skipping out and missing your court appearance for your escapade in Melbourne." Hayley commented as he put the rough statement down.

"Let me explain how things look to me! You decide to run away to avoid the hearing. Your brother, who was your appointed guardian, was responsible for seeing that you got there. When you went off he had to try and find you; then, because you resented his efforts to make you see sense, tried to frame him for your crimes. We had an anonymous call claiming that he had robbed the jewellers. We paid him a visit; he was very polite and even let us search his belongings. He explained that he was in town trying to find his sister and was afraid that she was doing the robberies and wanted to help her. He was more than a little angry with you."

"My brother hates my guts," Andy blurted out. "And he is not my guardian anymore! I'm eighteen now!"

"Yes, indeed!" Hayley said thoughtfully, looking at her closely. "How long have you had a driver's licence?"

Andy didn't know what to say, so she said nothing. She only had the phoney one that she had taken from her brother's case. If she admitted that, then they could add driving without a licence and using false identification to her list of crimes. He probably would anyway. It was her word against Martin's and if she was accused of robbing Martin, he had obviously talked his way out of the trouble she'd tried to make for him. She slumped miserably in the chair.

"Magpie Cappell really trained you well," Hayley said changing his tone. He spoke conversationally to Jack Carruthers. Andy glanced up, having the sudden notion that she knew this man.

"This woman's father was Frank Cappell, a notorious jewel thief and burglar. He could climb anything and open any lock. He was nicknamed 'Magpie' because he loved shiny things like jewels and coins, and because he often broke into houses through high windows. It seems that one of his children has begun to follow his footsteps. It is fortunate that the other did not."

Andy looked away, trying not to breakdown and cry.

"You have a lock up here, Sergeant?" Hayley asked, all business again.

At Jack's nod he continued.

"Miss Cappell can spend the night there – we'll be returning to Broken Hill in the morning. I hope she will be more cooperative when we get there."

Hayley nodded to Jack and he took Andy's arm gently and when she stumbled to her feet, led her through to the back of the station. He was aware that his superior was following.

Andy stumbled along, acutely aware of where she was going. Panic and nausea were rising within her at the thought of being locked in a cell.

Jack could feel that she was trembling and wished there was another choice. He really couldn't make up his mind about her. Before, when he was convinced she was bad, she risked herself to help the kids, but then she does something to make him wonder again.

He recalled what Tom Callaghan had said about her suffering from claustrophobia, and was impressed by her lack of hysterics, but when he opened the cell he could feel resistance building and felt she was about to baulk.

The Chief Inspector sensed it too, and as she tried desperately to pull away from Jack, he grabbed her other arm, and with practiced ease, held her against the wall, quickly frisked her and pushed her through the door.

"You are not nine years old anymore," Hayley commented as he closed the door.

Andy stumbled forward from the momentum of the push, and as the door closed, fell in a heap on the floor, trembling violently. The detective's words finally penetrated her brain and belatedly she recognised the policeman who had tried to teach her a lesson so long ago. The memory drove her deeper into despair.

She forced herself to stand up and then ran to the door; it was securely locked. Her fists pounded on the solid metal door but she only hurt herself and made little noise.

Already she felt the temperature in the cell getting hotter, and the air getting less and less, her breathing grew ragged and she tried to gulp in enough air to breathe.

She must have passed out for a time, because Andy woke and found herself curled up on the floor. The memory of her predicament returned to her and she felt herself gulping for breath again, but something was different now. She could actually feel a slight breeze on her face and it helped her to quieten her breathing. Then she caught a glimpse of a crack of light next to the door. Her feet took her to the door, which moved as she pressed her fingers into the gap and pulled. She was outside as soon as it was wide enough for her slender frame and running.

Her momentum was halted with painful abruptness by something catching the neck of her shirt.

Chapter 8

"You are so predictable," a hateful and familiar, sneering voice whispered in her ear.

Andy recognised her brother's voice and struggled to free herself, but he had too firm a grip.

"Martin, you toad, let me go!" Andy insisted.

Martin laughed and gripped one of her arms.

"Not until you thank me properly for letting you out," he insisted.

Andy struggled again, futilely. Her arm hurt.

"Thank you, Martin for letting me out!" she spat at him.

"Not good enough," Martin said nastily.

"If you went to the trouble of letting me out shouldn't we get going before the police see us?" Andy tried to side track her brother.

"No rush," he said with assurance. "They've all gone to the pub for a feed."

Martin was enjoying watching his sister growing angry, and he was ready when she aimed a kick at his groin. He twisted so she missed and in return squeezed her arm harder.

"Enough," Andy pleaded, and the pressure eased slightly.

"I expect you to be grateful for my letting you out," Martin advised her. "Very grateful!"

"I am very grateful."

"Grateful enough to do something for me, to do exactly as I ask you?"

"What do you want me to do?" Andy asked suspiciously.

"Yes or no?" Martin insisted, ignoring her question.

"No!" Andy decided and felt the pressure increase back to painful.

"Yes or I push you back in that cell and jam the lock."

Andy had no choice and Martin knew it. She did not want to go back into the cell and right now she would agree to anything that would get him to let her go.

"Alright, yes!" Andy capitulated.

"Much better!" Martin said easing his grip again. "Now, do you remember what I used to do to you when you told on me?"

Andy nodded with an involuntary whimper.

"Well, you are going to help me do something and it's not even illegal. However if you don't do exactly what I ask, I will hand you back to the cops. I have made sure they have enough evidence to put you away for twenty years. But, that will only be after I give you a thrashing you will never forget. After that little stunt you pulled in Broken Hill, you had better give me no reason to get angry with you. Believe me, it won't take much."

"I'll do whatever you say," Andy promised and Martin was satisfied that he had her so scared that she would. He eased his grip but didn't let her go. He forced her to walk to a clump of bushes, behind which was a gap in the fence and presumably how he had reached the police station from his car.

Andy breathed a bit easier as they moved away from the police cell. She knew what her brother was capable of, and now that she wasn't so petrified her mind was beginning to work again. Martin wouldn't go to the trouble of releasing her unless he was desperate. That meant that in spite of his threats she had some leeway. He wouldn't try to hurt her too much until she had done what he wanted of her.

"What's this all about then maggot-face?" Andy asked again. She was gripped tighter.

"I need you to get into somewhere for me," Martin admitted. "Merryl was going to help me but she changed her mind."

"So your whore came to her senses and walked out on you?" Andy taunted.

Martin gave her arm a savage wrench. "Don't try to annoy me, Sis. I'm giving you a chance to share in some money."

"Only because you have no choice!" Andy replied accurately.

"Dad left us a legacy," Martin told her, knowing that he would have her undivided attention.

"I intercepted a letter to you from him. He expected you to share it with me. He left it in his eyrie, said you should be able to work it out but we'd have to work together to find it."

Andy smirked; Martin would only share as a last resort. She wondered why he was so desperate.

"Two hundred and fifty thousand dollars is what he stole on his last job. It was never found. He was arrested out near here at an old wheat silo. The police supposedly searched it thoroughly but never found it. But Dad liked to climb, so he would have hidden it very high, no hurdle to you, but it would be a dark enclosed place – where you wouldn't go. His eyrie! Am I right?"

"I thought he was only making that place up," Andy gasping for breath as Martin pushed her almost to running speed. She tried to recall a conversation of almost nine years ago. The place that actually came to mind was not a wheat silo but a tallish building in Broken Hill. A building her father had taken her to once before he was arrested that last time and before their mother had moved to Melbourne.

Her father had talked about where he used to hide, but somehow she had reached the conclusion that the place no longer existed; that he had found a new eyrie. Well, if Martin thought he was on the trail...

"Yes, it was one place you wouldn't have the guts to get to!" Andy taunted. "Like when he took me on that chase across the roof tops of Broken Hill."

Another painful wrench on her arm told her she had touched him on a sore spot.

Andy hurt too much to talk any more as she had to keeping walking fast. She was looking out for Martin's car, hoping she could break free when he opened it.

After ten minutes they slowed next to an unfamiliar car with an airline sticker on the back, obviously a hire car. When Martin released half his grip to open the car door Andy gave a compulsive heave and broke free. She dove under his arm and began to run. She was lighter, faster and more desperate. Martin gave chase, he only had a rough idea of the town's layout, but he thought that she was heading out of town. When he saw a cruising police car he slowed to a walk and kept his sister in sight – he smirked when he saw her dive into a garden to avoid being seen.

It was beginning to get dark, as Martin began to walk back to his car. He had marked the place where Andy had hidden, and the police car had gone past her. It was about to pass him and he was aware of the scrutiny of the two policemen. They were from Broken

Hill, unlikely to guess he wasn't a local. Martin turned into the next house and bent over as if to check in the letter box, then sauntered to the door. The police car kept going. Martin came out of the garden and began walking more swiftly.

He reached his hire car and quickly drove back to where he had last seen his sister. He stopped outside the house and checked the garden, Andy had gone. Returning to his car he drove slowly out of town and was rewarded by seeing a slight stumbling figure walking along the edge of the road.

Martin pulled up beside the person, jumped out and grabbed his sister before she could elude him again. He slammed her against the car; there was hate blazing in his eyes.

"I warned you!" he snarled.

Andy couldn't help whimpering; she knew she had pushed him too far and knew what he was capable of when he was this angry. She trembled in his grasp.

"Turn around!" he said with deliberate menace.

When she didn't move, he threw her around and punched her hard; three, four, five times.

"Get in the car!" he ordered, raising his fist as if to strike her again.

Andy obeyed slowly, fumbling with the door catch and not looking back at him.

Martin slammed the door behind her and threw himself into the driver's seat. The car tyres screeched and skidded on the gravel as he took off.

By the time he reached the centre of the town his anger was under control. He was sure of his credibility with the police, and equally certain that his sister had none. If she wasn't going to help him, she was not going to be let free either.

He parked outside the police station; there were no police cars parked there and when he walked up to the door it was locked. Out of the corner of his eye he saw the far rear door of his car opening slowly and silently. In spite of his own mood, he smirked. His sister was acting so predictably. Whenever he had bested her she always ran and hid.

Martin ignored the open door and instead waved down the police car that was approaching.

He explained who he was and explained that he had seen his sister walking along the road as he drove into town – she was in his car now.

"It appears not, Sir," one policeman remarked, and Martin pretended to notice his open door.

The police observer spotted Andy in the light from a street lamp as she ran down the road.

"We'll handle this, Sir. Wait here!"

The driver returned behind the wheel and drove quickly towards Andy.

Martin waited, hiding his smirk. He wanted to be sure that Andy was caught and after this, all the police would be certain of her guilt and his innocence.

Andy heard the car and dived between two houses. The observer jumped from the car and slammed his door, continuing the chase on foot as the driver revved to drive quickly around the next block.

Martin heard someone approach.

"Mr Cappell," Chief Inspector Hayley greeted, recognising the man standing outside the police station.

Martin returned the greeting with no trace of fear or guilt. He adopted a concerned, worried manner and repeated what he had told the other policemen.

"She's run off again. I can't seem to get through to her anymore," Martin added, still peering down the street.

"I understand that she is now legally an adult and responsible for her own actions," Hayley commented neutrally.

Martin looked startled, he had forgotten that Andy had just had a birthday, but the notion worked in his favour.

"Are you suggesting that I keep out of this and let the police handle her?" Martin suggested. It was what he wanted them to say.

"Where are you staying tonight, Mr Cappell," Hayley asked instead.

"I – ah – at the hotel I expect," Martin acted hesitant, and then added, "It looks as if your men have lost her. Perhaps I had better help you look."

He sighed realistically. "She has probably climbed a tree or onto a roof. That's what she has usually done when I can't find her."

Hayley considered the information thoughtfully.

"Why don't you go and arrange for a room at the hotel before it closes, and come and see us in the morning?" Hayley suggested.

The Chief Inspector couldn't tell if Martin Cappell was relieved or reluctant to go. He simply gave another long look down the street, nodded and returned to his car. He drove slowly down the street towards the pub."

Martin had no intention of staying in the room he arranged, but he paid for it in advance as if he were. It was a precaution in case the police checked on him. He would have to hope that his sister was caught – he had something to do, something his own life depended upon.

Time was running short, thanks to Merryl deserting him and Andy refusing to help. At least, his sister would not be able to beat him to the money.

Martin slipped out to his car an hour after the hotel closed, and after the old man who ran the place had found an excuse to check on him and bring up some towels. There were no signs that the police were still looking for his sister, no flashing lights or car sounds. He breathed more easily as he drove out of town on the road that led to the old wheat silo he had mentioned to his sister. Her comments made him certain that he had been correct in his deductions.

In the boot of his car he had a length of rope and when he stopped at the silo he took it out and tied one end of it around his waist. He grabbed a small torch from the car and shoved it in his pocket. He was glad that the sky was clear and the half-moon gave him some illumination, but even more relieved that it wasn't any brighter.

The thought of what he had to do scared him as almost nothing else did. But his life was at stake and he had no one to help him. At least at night he wouldn't be so aware of how high he was climbing but the faint light would show him where to place his hands. Once he was inside, the darkness wouldn't bother him.

Martin threw the loose end of the rope over the lowest rung of the ladder and used it to help him scramble up. He was in excellent physical shape. Once on the ladder he felt himself trembling, but being determined to continue, didn't realise that the ladder was loose. He dared not look down so he counted the rungs as he climbed. When he estimated that he was halfway or about twenty metres up he felt the first ladder end and he had to reach up a bit higher to feel the start of the next section. He had to untie the rope from around himself or he would be unable to go higher.

Martin had gone two rungs on the second ladder when it tore out of the wall and dropped with him on it. One leg became wedged, up to his crotch, behind the top of the lower ladder.

Only some roosting birds heard his scream and when he stopped they quit their screeching and settled back to sleep.

Chapter 9

Andy clung to the tree trunk, aware that the two police cars were prowling around the streets looking for her. The flashing lights reflected of the walls of the buildings.

She stayed very still; the tree wasn't that big and if she moved, it would too. It was just as well it was dark too. In the daylight, there would not have been enough leaves to hide her.

Now that she had stopped, her back hurt where Martin had hit her and the rest of her body ached; particularly her wrenched shoulder. Her legs were tired from running and tears stung her eyes.

Time lost all meaning as she clung to the tree. When the flashing lights had not been around for a time and even the noise from the pub had quietened, she considered coming down, but she didn't know where to go. And with her mind so wrapped in pain, misery and despair, she wasn't even aware of people walking below her flashing torches onto rooves and up trees.

Sometime later, Andy climbed down from the tree. Her movements were slow and totally lacking her usual grace. Her numb mind wasn't paying attention to where she was going.

A slight sound brought her to awareness and she looked up from the ground and saw the policeman from Broken Hill walking towards her.

An instant of stunned recognition caused panic to take control of her legs. She dodged around him and dived low under his futile attempt to grab her.

In spite of his bulk, Hayley wasn't slow. He caught her in a few steps, unintentionally grabbing her already wrenched arm. His subordinates and Jack Carruthers were already moving in.

Hayley was not expecting Andy to fight him, she wasn't the fighting type; no more than her father had been. He was prepared for her to try and twist free and try to keep running. The very last thing that he was prepared for was for her to suddenly fall, so he was in no sort of position to catch her. She fell heavily, landing on her knee and wrist. There was no way he could have known that her shoulder had already been partly dislocated, and as he grabbed it the bone wrenched fully out of place. It was the pain of the dislocation that had caused her to black out.

Andy realised that she was on the ground, dirt fortunately, not concrete. She hurt so much that she couldn't move. Her first thought was that she had fallen from the tree, then she heard sounds around her and tried to get up, thinking that her brother had found her again. A firm but gentle hand held her down.

"Don't hurt me again, I'll do whatever you want," she whimpered incoherently, but the voice that asked her if she could stand wasn't Martin's.

Andy didn't answer, she simply tried to push up with the arm that hurt least, but the wrist wouldn't bend. She sank back to the ground.

Gentle hands helped her to her feet, but her right shoulder throbbed in time with her head, her left wrist and knee hurt like hell as she tried to keep her weight on her right leg. When she tried to walk, her left knee couldn't take her weight and she grabbed what was nearest to stop from falling. When she felt the urge to be sick, she couldn't even twist her head.

"Help her to the car, Jack," Hayley instructed mildly, as if he hadn't just had his clothes fouled.

"I will meet you at the hospital; I don't think that you will have any trouble with her this time."

Jack nodded stiffly, he hadn't been reprimanded for letting her escape, but he blamed himself. He might have been in trouble if Hayley himself had not personally frisked her before locking her in the cell.

Hayley had reminded him, quite forcibly, that the woman was a criminal and should be treated as such.

Jack found it hard to be rough with her. She might be a thief but she wasn't evil. He supported most of her weight as she hopped to his car and he fitted the seatbelt when she simply collapsed into the seat.

He kept glancing at his passenger as he drove to the hospital; she appeared to be asleep and didn't answer his attempts at questioning her. Concerned, he used the radio to call the RFDS base and have them alert the hospital to be ready for him.

Kate Standish waited by the gurney at the ambulance entrance as Jack drove in. She helped Jack place his passenger there and they pushed it into the examination room. Kate had recognised Andy, as did her husband Geoff when he arrived moments later.

"What happened, Jack?" Geoff asked the policeman as he began his examination, firstly for indications of concussion.

"She was running away from us. When she was caught, she fell."

Geoff continued his examination, and found swelling around her right shoulder. He cut away the clothes to see the area better. He continued on, finding that the left knee and wrist were also swollen.

He spoke softly to his wife mentioning his findings and adding, "We'll need to take x-rays."

Geoff began manipulating Andy's shoulder to get it back into place. It finally slipped back into place with a snap.

Andy opened her eyes and saw the doctor who had treated her that morning. It felt like days ago.

"Sick," she croaked.

Geoff glanced at Kate and she produced a bowl and helped Andy who was struggling to sit up. She was trembling violently as Kate supported her and was unaware that Jack was being firmly removed from the room.

As Andy sat up, Geoff continued cutting away the clothing. He was planning on checking out the bruising she had received that morning and when the fabric was out of the way he frowned. Kate glanced where he was looking and saw as he had five massive contusions.

Geoff continued his examination with even more attention to detail. Finally he handed Kate a gown for Andy before leaving the room.

Geoff went over to Jack Carruthers who had been joined by a stranger, immediately introduced as Chief Inspector Hayley.

"What have you found?" Hayley asked immediately.

Geoff didn't answer straight away.

"What is the nature of your interest in my patient?"

"I have instructions to take her to Broken Hill as soon as she is fit to travel," Hayley informed the doctor in an official tone.

"Her right shoulder was dislocated, there is swelling in her left knee and at the left wrist. As far as I can tell, nothing is broken. There is the possibility of concussion. I will know for sure after we take some x-rays."

Geoff paused, considering his next words carefully before proceeding to say what might be considered accusing the police.

"When I saw her this morning, I found evidence of healing bruises on her back, extensive bruising. She had acquired more from her fall this morning. However there are now five massive bruises forming on her back and others less noticeable on her front."

Hayley's head snapped up.

"Bruises? May I see them?"

"Later, if she permits you to. We are just about to take her for x-rays. I will have to keep her here at least overnight."

"She is my prisoner, doctor, I will have to be allowed to maintain a guard," Hayley insisted in turn.

Geoff quietly absorbed the implication of the comment.

"Very well," he agreed. "Excuse me."

"Bruises, Jack" Hayley looked at the Sergeant thoughtfully.

Jack felt uncomfortable, wondering if he was being suspected. His worries were settled almost at once.

"Neither Sanders nor Reilly have been near her and I know you have a soft spot for the woman. So what are we missing here, Jack?"

"The brother?" Jack suggested.

"The fine, upstanding, concerned guardian," Hayley mused. He recalled what he had read in Andy's statements. "She implied that he might have been in town yesterday, but he makes out that he just arrived. She claims that he is not what he seems but won't give us proof. She doesn't like him ... Jack, go and see if he is still at the pub."

Jack went at once to obey the request.

Hayley waited where he was until he became aware of a commotion further down the passage. He followed the voices. Andy was struggling against Kate, Geoff and the x-ray technician. They were trying to get her to stay lying down on the table. She had been fine until the restrictive machinery had surrounded her.

Hayley walked in and added his strength so that the technician could apply some restraints to keep her from moving. It didn't help; Andy was trembling too much for a good X-ray, and still trying to get free.

Geoff settled the matter by prescribing a fast acting sedative. Once that began to have an effect, the technician was able to get to work.

Andy couldn't control her reactions but when the sick feeling in her stomach began to subside and the walls seemed to move away, she relaxed into sleep.

The area around her was dark, but a subdued light was coming from further away – an illusion of distance.

The memory of her panic returned but it did not paralyse her. She remembered the pain, but it had dulled. Her right shoulder was strapped up, her left wrist and knee bandaged.

Thoughts of the events of the past days came into her mind, along with the hopelessness of her situation. She was certain that her brother had engineered the mess she was in and used his knowledge of how she'd react to ensure she walked into his trap. But why had he done it?

Martin had always dominated her, took malicious delight in doing so. Whenever she tried to break free, well she knew how vengeful he could be.

Was all of this because she had run away? If that were all, why would he bother?

Thinking that she was at last alone, Andy gave in to tears of hurt, frustration and helplessness. Deep in her heart she wished that she dared to take the major step of informing on him.

Hayley sat back quietly, listening. He had relieved the second of his men an hour ago and had been mentally reviewing the case against her. He was trying to think of any avenues of investigation he may have missed.

Hearing the misery in the quiet sobs threatened to soften his habitual hardness. The woman was a criminal, like her father. Yet he couldn't forget the child, was it nine or ten years ago, crying incoherently after being in a closed but unlocked cell for ten minutes, then screaming and clinging to her Daddy when he was to be taken from her again. It had seemed an excellent lesson at the time.

Frank Cappell had not been a violent man. He was a habitual criminal with a curious, if twisted, sense of moral values. Climbing and thieving had been a compulsion with him but he had never been vengeful towards those who had nabbed him. He had always accepted that they had their duty to do. He had never failed to help a mate in trouble either, or expected to be repaid.

Hayley wondered if similar compulsions drove this child of his. She was very like him and so unlike her brother.

There did not seem to be any flaws in the evidence against her. Her fingerprints were all over the items in her brother's case and she had been caught on the security film at the jewellers. That film had shown a white object falling from a pocket when she had pulled out a handkerchief to wrap some rings in. The object had had been found and was a student ID card with her details and fingerprints on it.

Something nagged at him.

Years ago he had come to dislike having to arrest Frank Cappell. He felt a similar reluctance now, and as little option.

Hayley thought about what Andy had told Jack Carruthers, how she had stopped short of actually accusing her brother of anything. His associates had so far found nothing to suggest that Martin Cappell was anything but an honest citizen.

Andy could have been telling the truth, but she might also be a very good liar. If she was convinced that her brother had reason or opportunity to frame her - why wouldn't she do anything more than hint?

As Andy dropped back into sleep, Hayley pondered how she could have got out of the cell. There had been nothing in her clothes or left in the cell that she could have used to pick the lock. Jack still had her burglar's tool – and where had she acquired those bruises?

Andy awoke when the nurse came in with breakfast and her medication.

"How do you feel?" asked the cheerful Annie.

"Everything hurts" Andy said miserably. "And I am not hungry!"

"Have your medicine and you will probably start to feel hungry in a little while."

Annie helped Andy to take the tablets and then helped her shuffle slowly to the toilet and back into bed.

"Now," Annie turned serious. "The doctor insists that you eat something and drink as much as you can!"

Andy nodded without enthusiasm then answered with distaste the questions she was asked about how her system had functioned. When Annie had marked her chart and departed, Andy lay back against the pillows and closed her eyes. She seemed to be paying no attention to anybody, and certainly made no attempt to look when Jack Carruthers came in to replace his superior and the two men conversed quietly for a few moments.

Hayley didn't go far; he went in search of one of the doctors and found Tom Callaghan.

"How soon can I take Miss Cappell out of here?"

Tom had just begun to read Andy's case file and quickly finished scanning the rest along with Geoff's recommendations.

"We want to keep her in here until later today," Tom advised the policeman. "The x-rays show no breaks but we want to make sure there are no delayed signs of concussion and that her insides are functioning as they should. We also want to make sure that she has some more rest."

"I'll come back later, then," Hayley nodded to the doctor.

Hayley chose to walk back to the hotel for a late breakfast and to see if he could have a chat with Martin Cappell. When he arrived he spoke to Vic Buckley, but neither the proprietor nor his wife Nancy had seen their other guest that morning. Vic told him which room was being used by Cappell.

Decisively, Hayley strode up the stairs and knocked on the door of room seven. There was no answer and when he tried the door it was unlocked. He pushed the door open carefully and looked around. The bed didn't look slept in, the pile of towels was still piled neatly on the end of the bed and there were no signs to even indicate that the room was occupied.

Hayley checked the room carefully, found nothing at all and walked back down the stairs thoughtfully.

When he was finishing his coffee and Vic came over to chat, Hayley mentioned his finding. Vic obliged by telling him that Cappell had booked for one night only and had paid in advance. Hayley nodded as if the matter was unimportant and allowed Vic to chat on about other things until he excused himself to return to work.

At the police station, Hayley examined the door of the cell closely. Last evening he had assumed that Andy had managed to pick the lock somehow. In the daylight he could find no indication of a forced entry or exit on the lock of the cell. He made a note to get the lock examined by an expert.

In the station itself, one of Hayley's subordinates was minding the front desk.

"Any reports?" Hayley asked.

"None, Sir," Riley reported crisply.

"We need to look out for the car driven by Martin Cappell," Hayley told the Sergeant. "It was a hire car of some dark colour. See if you can find the registration and a description and put a call out for it to be reported if seen."

"Over the air to everyone too?" Reilly suggested.

"Yes," Hayley said thoughtfully. "Just in case he has headed bush, but I don't think he is the type to rough it."

Chapter 10

"How do you feel?" Tom Callaghan asked Andy a short time after lunch.

"Like hell!" Andy said deliberately, knowing Hayley was listening.

"Any nausea, headache, blurred vision?" Tom continued.

"A bit of a headache still," Andy admitted truthfully.

Tom checked her eyes and how they responded.

"What about the shoulder?" Tom persisted.

"Unfortunately better than I wanted it to be. It's just aching. Ditto knee and elbow."

"Nothing was broken," Tom told her. "If you take things easy, there is no reason to keep you here."

"Yeah, Yeah," Andy muttered, wondering if the police would let her take things easy.

"Where did you get the extra bruises on your back- five of them?" Hayley asked Andy after Tom had finished quizzing her.

Andy refused to answer or to look at him.

Hayley let his breath out as a hiss.

Perhaps this wasn't the time to question her about her brother – but as things stood – unless she could give him some evidence of her brother's guilt, she would go to gaol for a long time. He couldn't advise the withdrawal of charges without evidence or something strong enough to create doubt.

"What will I do when the last lot of pills wear off?" Andy asked Tom, ignoring Hayley.

"I will organise some pain relief," Tom promised. "Do you need anything else?"

Andy looked mutely at him then said softly, "A cure for small closed in places?"

Tom looked thoughtful and nodded.

"Annie will help you get dressed," Tom told her. "Luke Mitchell brought your pack in."

"If you see him, give him my thanks," Andy requested.

Tom watched Andy disappear behind a privacy screen with Annie, before speaking quietly to Hayley.

"She's very tense and that isn't helping her shoulder," Tom told Hayley. "What will happen when you get to Broken Hill?"

"I intend to recommend a low security detention centre – I am aware of her claustrophobia. Can you prescribe a mild sedative?"

"I would want to know that she is able to have it when she needs it," Tom said directly.

"I'll make sure it is organised," Hayley promised neutrally.

"I won't be sorry to see the last of Coopers Crossing!" Andy said to Annie, trying to sound calm as she walked back to the main part of the room.

Annie carried her pack and then went to fetch a wheelchair for Andy to use as far as the hospital entrance.

"If you are wheeled in, you have to be wheeled out," Annie said with a grin which Andy found infectious. Her scowl turned to a faint grin which only lasted to the door out.

Andy allowed Annie to help her out of the chair and Hayley to help her into his car. His grip was surprisingly gentle.

"If you give your parole, the trip at least will be more comfortable," Hayley told her as he sat in the driver's seat.

Andy glanced at the policeman, his look was uncompromising. She nodded, not trusting her voice, not really trusting herself.

Hayley concentrated on driving for a time and his passenger showed no signs of wanting to break the silence. Finally, he decided to ask some of the questions that were bothering him.

"Your brother isn't a very nice person, is he?" Hayley deliberately phrased the question to put Martin Cappell in a bad light.

Andy turned to look and Hayley, but was wary.

"I thought you considered him Mr. Congenial," Andy accused.

"I am beginning to have doubts."

"Oh, really? How come?" Andy said sceptically.

"One or two things," Hayley didn't go into details.

"Well, whether he is nice or not depends on who you are," Andy said carefully. "I have no doubt that he has been very polite to you!"

"And if I were you?" Hayley suggested, not sure if she would answer.

"You'd guard your back!" Andy said quietly. "If you were sensible you would have as little to do with him as possible."

"What hold does he have over you?" Hayley asked.

"Nothing!" Andy denied. "He was my guardian, that's all. I had no choice but to stay with him."

"Nonsense! Why did you run away from Melbourne – to get away from him or from your court appearance?"

Andy didn't choose to answer.

"As things stand now," Hayley explained, "You are likely to be in jail at least ten years. Why would you endure that for him?"

"I didn't rob the jewellers or anyone else!" Andy insisted. "You can't possibly have any evidence to prove that I did."

"What about the money that you took from your brother?"

"That doesn't count!"

"He insisted that charges be laid."

"One crime doesn't rate ten years."

"You'll have a criminal record."

"Some people think I have already," was Andy's sour reply.

"Why confirm it?" Andy went quiet again. Hayley tried another tack.

"I think your brother is afraid of you! So he's trained you to be afraid of him."

"No way!" Andy retorted without thinking. The idea was ludicrous. The only thing he was afraid of was heights and she so rarely got the better of him and never for long.

"He couldn't afford to let you run away from him, or else why bother to follow you? He must feel that you would get the better of anyone else so he had to come himself."

Andy clammed up, this conversation was getting dangerous. She did not want to discuss Martin.

Hayley let the silence continue for a while.

"If you are being abused there are people who can help you, even if you don't want to talk to us."

"What can they do?" Andy found herself asking and Hayley was suddenly sure he was on the right track.

"A safe place to stay, counselling to help you deal with it."

"I am dealing with it!" Andy interrupted, but stopped saying anything more.

Hayley ignored the sudden withdrawal.

"You are enduring it, you shouldn't have to. What if he is doing the same sort of thing to other people?"

Andy looked to be thinking, which indeed she was. Her brother was never slow to hit back at her but somehow she never thought him to be the type to do it to anyone else. He always put on a controlled manner and even when he ran into arguments in the course of his work, he kept his temper.

Hayley didn't interrupt her thinking, but was pleased to see her considering his remark. She may not want to act on her own behalf, but if someone else was being victimised…? Just one more way she was like her father.

"You weren't running from us last night, you were running from him – weren't you? How did you get out?"

"The door was open."

"And?"

"I ran."

"And then?"

Andy clammed up.

Hayley counted to ten slowly.

"Why don't you like your brother?" Hayley asked, trying to approach the matter from a different angle.

"He doesn't like me!"

Hayley wondered if he should tell her that he had proof that the cell door was forced from the outside. It occurred to him to wonder why Martin Cappell had been so keen to have his sister caught after she had escaped, if he had been the one who released her. There was no proof that he had except a gut feeling. Andy might have an accomplice somewhere.

"Your brother booked a room at the hotel last night, but he didn't sleep there and he was supposed to see us this morning."

Hayley couldn't see the expression on Andy's face but she didn't seem surprised.

"Your brother's fiancée has returned to her job in Melbourne!" Hayley commented.

"The bitch finally came to her senses and walked out on him," Andy muttered smugly.

"What makes you think that?"

"She is a prostitute; she wouldn't want to return to her job if she was still willing to let Martin support her," Andy snorted.

"Your brother can open locks too, can't he?"

"Yes ..." Andy started to say more and realised that she had been tricked.

"I will tell you what I think, and this is off the record. You tell me if I am wrong," Hayley said carefully putting his thoughts together.

"I think that your brother forced the cell door open. I think that you were wanting out so much that when you saw the door open, you didn't think, you just ran. I think Cappell was waiting for you, caught you and tried to make you do something. You refused, he got angry and hit you on the back but you escaped from him."

Andy seemed to shrink into the seat but didn't say his guess was wrong.

"I did freak out," Andy admitted in a small voice. "Reminding me of your little lesson when I was a kid simply made things worse. That had more effect than you could have anticipated. I discovered that I couldn't stand being locked in and I never stole from anyone because I was not stupid enough to think I would always get away with it. Dad was the smartest person I knew and I think you know how often he was caught."

"Hmm," Hayley thought to himself. "That is another matter."

"Why did you take money from your bother?" he asked aloud. She had admitted doing that.

"He owed it to me!" Andy snapped, without explaining.

"Did you expect to get away with that?"

"That was a private matter!" Andy insisted. "He had no right to bring the police into it!"

"But he did..."

"Yeah, but there is something I don't figure." Andy said thoughtfully. What she meant was – something she was amazed the police hadn't thought of.

"If I hadn't said that I had stolen money from Martin, how could you prove it? This is off the record. I did go through his stuff but you only have his word that money was taken. I did actually take three hundred dollars from him. It was hidden under a false bottom in his case. That amount which turns out was stolen from Albury. The other five hundred that I had was what was left of what I withdrew from my account when I bought my car. They were all new so maybe the bank has a record of what numbers they gave me. You should be able to check how much I withdrew and how much my car cost and the odd amount that I gave as a deposit was all I had left on me…"

"You will give us permission to check your account details?" Hayley asked mildly.

"Yes," Andy agreed, sure that it would help her case.

"Anyway, when Jack checked my stuff in Coopers Crossing, that's all I had. Now I left the bank and walked back to the car yard it was about twelve when I drove out of the yard. I went to the supermarket and an op-shop. The receipts for what I bought are in my wallet.

It was about one or one thirty when I left town. I intended to head for Adelaide but decided to come here when I saw the turn off. I stopped about five and got stuck out there overnight. The Cullens picked me up about nine thirty and I told Jack the rest. Anyway, if I had three hundred dollars stolen from Albury and three hundred stolen from Martin, and five hundred from my account, it doesn't add up. I didn't know you were after me until after Jack had confiscated my money, so I couldn't have hidden it and why would I? And I know from the news that more than just cash disappeared from the jewellery store so where is the rest of it? I assume that you checked my car and pack and all. So if I took it where is it?"

"You might have an accomplice," Hayley suggested an obvious answer.

Andy hadn't considered that. "You'll have a hard time proving something that doesn't exist."

Hayley wasn't yet prepared to agree with her, but about the money she had a point. It was something that he hadn't considered.

Andy looked away, convinced that Hayley wasn't going to consider her argument.

"You have a valid point," Hayley admitted after some moments of silence. "I will check what you have said, but you will need to make a formal statement. We cannot drop the charges against you without some definite proof and we may have to delve into your relationship with your brother to get it. Are you willing to discuss that? You have hinted things about him, are you willing to give us anything concrete to work on?"

Hayley risked a glance at his passenger. In an instant she had gone from challenging to scared. Whatever was between her and her brother ran deep.

"I will be asking for an eight day remand in custody," Hayley told her. "The accommodation is almost like a motel room. It shouldn't be too bad."

"Except I won't be able to leave!" Andy said very softly.

Hayley heard her but chose not to respond.

"You will be safer there than out on the streets," he pointed out instead and saw Andy nod, an unconscious sign of agreement.

"One final thing, if you make a statement – tell the truth, the exact truth – even if it makes things look blacker for you. I will endeavour to prove your theory, but if you have lied about anything and we can prove it, it will throw doubt on everything you say. Think about it!"

"I will," Andy answered very quietly.

Unexpectedly, she no longer saw Hayley as an implacable enemy. He did seem to care that she might be innocent, but could he find proof that she was?

Chapter 11

Andy heard Hayley's mobile phone ring, but didn't pay it any attention. The policeman said nothing that would tell her what the conversation was about. Instead she kept her eyes closed and pretended to be asleep. It was better than Hayley's too probing questions.

When the car slowed and did a U-turn, she kept her left eye open to watch the scenery but didn't dare ask where they were now going. After a while she dozed off, waking again with a start when the car came to a sliding stop.

What Andy saw first was the old triple wheat silo and the abandoned freight station next to it. A moment later its significance dawned on her. By that time Hayley was halfway out of the car looking up.

Andy tried to follow his gaze but couldn't see, so she opened the door for a better view.

"Stay in the car!" Hayley ordered. His mind was clearly on this new situation.

Andy ignored the order. She wanted to see what had attracted the policeman's attention.

A number of crows were circling around the silo and it was obvious what was attracting their attention.

"Martin!" Andy said flatly, identifying him by the clothes he was wearing. "He must have been there since last night. He usually doesn't wear the same clothes two days running."

She was oblivious to the fact that she had just admitted seeing her brother the day before.

"You are sure?" Hayley asked and was surprised with the vehemence of her reply.

"Yes! Let him rot up there!"

She was too busy enjoying the sight of her brother's predicament that she was unaware that Hayley was coming around to her side of the car. Before she knew what was happening, Hayley had handcuffed her left wrist to the door handle of the car. She jerked her wrist in surprise and then again in frustration.

Hayley walked across to the metal ladder that went to the top of the silo. There was a rope dangling from the bottom rung which was about seven feet from the ground. He tested it with his weight and the ladder began to give.

The trapped man did not appear to be moving.

Hayley strode back to the car to use the radio to call the flying doctor base.

"Broken Hill Police Mobile to Victor Charlie Charlie..."

Andy only half listened to the terse description of her brother's plight. He was really too far up to see properly but she guessed that a section of the ladder had broken loose and dropped down, trapping Martin at the top of the lower section. She didn't try to hide the smirk on her face and didn't care if her escort disapproved of her attitude.

The voice on the radio indicated that the Nomad, the flying Doctor aircraft, would bring out ropes and rescue equipment. Andy was already considering how they would have to go about freeing her brother, it wouldn't be easy. They might even need her to help. The idea gave her an urge to climb the silo – and an equally strong but much more dangerous urge to gloat at her brother.

"Have you any idea what he was trying to do?" Hayley asked her curtly.

"Raiding bird's nests," Andy replied sweetly.

"You are in enough trouble already, don't make it worse," Hayley reminded her.

"How can it be worse?" Andy snapped at him. "I didn't make him climb up there. I'm not stopping you from helping the brainless idiot. Why don't you ask him?"

"Did you know that your father was arrested out here?" Hayley changed tactics.

He watched his prisoner closely for a reaction.

"Martin said something about that. Did you arrest him that time too?" Andy sounded accusing.

"Yes," Hayley recalled. "We searched this whole structure and didn't find anything. Is that what your brother is after?"

Andy dropped her hostility.

"Yes," she sighed. "He told me he'd intercepted a letter from Dad to me. It was about a legacy he had left for us in his eyrie. He had said we would have to work together to get it. I hate dark enclosed places, he hates heights. Dad used to live here for a time, he was the only kid game enough to climb to the top. I'm surprised Martin got as far as he did."

"Do you think this is Frank Cappell's eyrie?" Hayley asked, interested to know the answer.

Andy was thoughtful.

"Perhaps, it was once. I was only eleven when he died and I grew up in a city. I pictured a tall building with a nest on top. I thought it was only make-believe!"

"Stay here! There used to be another way up inside."

"I can't exactly go anywhere," Andy muttered in disgust as she watched Hayley stride towards a door at the base of the nearest silo.

After the policeman had disappeared inside, Andy studied the silos. The three silos were touching each other and she assumed they were separate inside. A narrow enclosed catwalk ran across the points of each of the three structures and had a small hut perched at one end; the end into which Hayley had disappeared. The rusted remains of the conveyor system which had fed the grain into the silos, showed just under the catwalk. She just had to climb it!

Andy had forgotten her sore shoulder, knee and wrist. In fact, without stopping to analyse her actions, she was unwrapping the bandages about her knee and wrist. She shoved the fabric into her pocket and began to fumble with her belt. There was a two inch piece of rigid wire hidden in the casing.

There was a loud noise, like a gunshot and then another. She glanced at the silo, her brother hadn't moved. For the life of her, she didn't know if Hayley carried a gun. If he did, who did he shoot? Or who shot him?

Andy fumbled more urgently to get the wire free and open the handcuff. Being attached to a car, in the open, was far too exposed for her liking, especially if her sudden flash of intuition were true.

Martin must have had a very strong incentive to climb up there. Something like the threat of death or torture. He thought there was money up there, so it must mean that he owed someone a lot of money. If that someone was here and had shot a policeman, he or she would be dangerous and may start threatening her. There would be no denying the family likeness between her and her brother.

As soon as the wire was free, she had the handcuffs unlocked. There was no sign of Hayley; that made Andy uneasy. If he had shot the unknown person, he would have come out to request back up – wouldn't he?

Andy had to admit to a grudging respect for the Broken Hill policeman. He wasn't the kind to compromise. What would he do if she went in there and he had everything under control? Would he be as unimpressed as Jack Carruthers had been when she had opened that dratted drawer? She would just go and peek.

Andy ran with only a slight limp to the door through which Hayley had disappeared. She stopped, just outside and listened. There were sounds of junk being thrown around and a male voice cursing and swearing. The language was really foul and it certainly wasn't the urbane Hayley.

Keeping to the thin bit of shade to the left of the doorway, Andy poked her head into the opening. It wasn't completely dark inside, as rays of brilliant sunshine shone in through holes in the roof. The place didn't cause her to feel the debilitating panic.

The sound seemed to be coming from the next silo in; the three structures were apparently not separate. Andy crept forward cautiously, keeping in the shadows but close to the bright areas. She came to the gap between the first two silos.

In one patch of light, over to her right, she saw Hayley. He was lying awkwardly and very still. Movement caught her eye and for a moment a man was visible in another patch of sun. He threw something unidentifiable to one side. It looked like hoboes and tramps often used the place.

Andy moved forward, keeping in the shadow, trying to get closer to Hayley. She didn't see some junk on the floor and tripped, landing noisily.

The man swung around, gun in hand. He looked tense and dangerous.

"You won't need that," Andy said, sounding calmer than she felt. "I am not armed."

It was just as well he couldn't hear her heart thumping in her chest.

Andy pushed herself up and the man approached and quickly frisked her with his free hand then, satisfied that she had spoken the truth, poked the gun back in his belt.

"Who are you?" he snarled in a gravelly voice.

"Who do you think I am?" Andy countered.

"Cappell?"

"The family likeness is rather obvious!"

"Where is it? Where's the money?" the man snarled again, he was about fifty years old with a scarred weathered face. He looked very menacing as he approached and put his face very close to hers. His breath stank but Andy held her ground. She had learnt to bluff her brother; this man didn't know her.

"The bastard never actually told me," Andy admitted. "I am not convinced that anything is here. The police searched the place thoroughly."

A knife appeared in the man's hand as if conjured out of the air.

"That's not the answer that I want!" he growled, waving the knife for emphasis.

"No, it probably isn't," Andy said calmly. "I was going to say that if there was something here, it wouldn't be on the ground. See that little walkway, just near the roof?" Andy pointed with her good arm, there was just enough light to see what she meant.

"That's where I would start looking."

"You'd better not be having me on!" the man growled. He moved his head away and twisted to look up.

Andy continued to chat. "Martin thinks our father planted some money here. I refused to help him find it. Now, Martin hates heights. He must have been certain that he would find something worthwhile up there or he would never have climbed. He most certainly wouldn't have if he thought it was down here."

"Your brother owes me a lot of money" the man told Andy. "I want it or his life is worth nothing. He'll be dead!"

"That's almost tempting enough to leave right now."

Andy laughed easily.

The man gave her an appraising look.

"If it's up there, could you get it?"

"If our father left anything here, he left it for me not for Martin. I was his favourite. I could climb anywhere he could."

Andy made a show of examining the inside of the silo. The man didn't seem keen to climb either. There was no trace of any ladder on the inside, though Hayley had mentioned something. The only remaining way up was the ladder that had trapped Martin.

"Normally, I'd have no trouble going up to look," Andy boasted, and then indicated her shoulder. "I have an idea, but you probably won't like it."

"Either I get the money from you or your brother, I don't care which."

"Keep me out of your argument with my brother. He's no friend of mine and I know nothing about his business. If I find any money today, I will quite happily give you what Martin owes you and keep the rest, because it will annoy Martin no end. Also, I won't get him off my back until you're off his. If I find nothing today, you have my blessings to take the matter further with him. However, I have a score of my own to settle with him and I would like him to suffer a whole lot more."

"What's the deal?" the man asked suspiciously.

Andy relaxed a little; at least the man would listen.

"The RFDS plane will be arriving soon with people and rescue gear. I have no doubt that the local police will be with them. I can't see that ladder out there holding the weight of a solid adult, if it didn't hold Martin's weight. It will hold me, but with this sore shoulder, I won't climb it without a rope. I'll find an excuse to go to the top, say to anchor the rope for the others. I can look around, and if I find anything, lower it down inside. Though if you have a car nearby, you might want to move it, and then wait until they have taken the cop out before you return."

"I don't like it!"

"It's the best I can do," Andy told him. "That sounds like the plane now!"

The man listened and took off at a run.

Andy ran quickly back to Hayley, hoping that the delay hadn't been fatal. She never questioned the idea of helping him.

The wound was low down on the leg. It was bleeding a lot but it was dark blood from a vein, not an artery. She used the bandages that she had shoved in her pocket to make a pad and used more of it to bind the pad on the wound to control the bleeding.

It occurred to her to check his breathing, and as she did he became conscious, and seemed surprised to see her there.

"Lie still," Andy told him as she checked for other wounds. "The bloke has gone; he saw me and ran off."

"How did you get free?" Hayley rasped, not trying to move.

"I got myself free!" she said defiantly. "I didn't want you to bleed to death and I didn't think it right to stay out there when I had the ability to help you. Martin is another matter – I'd let him rot."

"It'll be in your favour if you help him!" Hayley said with difficulty.

"He won't appreciate it!" Andy pointed out. "Any way I think the doctors have arrived.

Andy left before Hayley could say more and ran out to meet the arrivals. The plane had landed on the road and taxied up to near Hayley's car. Jack looked up from his examination of his superior's car, saw her and strode to meet her with an angry expression on his face.

He must have seen the dangling handcuffs.

"The Inspector has been shot," Andy told him as he grabbed her firmly but carefully.

"He's inside the silo."

Jack decided that Andy was serious. He called to Tom Callaghan and increased his pace towards the door. Andy had to jog to keep up with him, but Jack didn't seem to notice her limping progress.

At the door, he halted to let his eyes adjust to the dim lighting.

"I saw the bloke go off," Andy told him trying to drag him into where Hayley lay.

When Jack was confident that they were alone, he allowed Andy to lead him to his superior, but he kept a grip on Andy whilst he squatted down to make his own assessment.

"Did you see your assailant?" Jack asked Hayley.

"No, he was in the shadows." Hayley managed to say.

"I can give you a description," Andy said bluntly.

Jack nodded as he moved away to let Tom and Kate attend to the injured man.

"What is going on here?" Jack asked her, as he walked her back outside.

"Apart from Martin being stuck halfway up the silo," she said with a complete lack of concern. Jack glared at her and she decided she had best co-operate.

She gave a very brief outline of the events that had occurred since her arrival.

"You saw this man well enough to describe?" Jack reminded her, taking out a red notebook and blue pen.

Her description of the man was concise.

"Anything else?"

"He had a gun, a knife and really foul smelling breath."

Jack looked at her sternly and Andy admitted talking to the man and most of what she had said to him.

"If you let me go up, I'll look around. I don't think he will have gone far – we might be able to lure him out of hiding."

"No!" Jack turned the idea down flatly. He walked her back to the police car and relocked the handcuffs. "Stay there!"

Andy waited. Hayley was brought out on a stretcher and loaded into the Nomad, Kate stayed with him. Tom Callaghan joined Jack and another man who carried climbing gear. It would be useless without somewhere firm to anchor it.

Jack kept casting glances in her direction, as he discussed options with the doctor and climber who were below where Martin was stuck.

Finally they decided to ask her.

"This won't help your shoulder," Tom told her.

"It'll hold me, Doc." Andy said eagerly. "I can climb anything – except horses. A ladder is simple."

She could tell they were reluctant to use her, but with her climbing skill and slight stature, she was a logical choice. Jack used his superior's keys to free her again. She removed the sling from her shoulder.

Andy was helped into a climbing harness and the man who had

brought the gear, adjusted it for her. He gave his name as David. A coil of light weight line was hooked onto the harness; it had a small grappling hook on one end.

David gave Andy instructions as to what he needed her to do and finally hooked a portable radio onto one belt of the harness.

The men boosted her onto their shoulders so that she could scramble onto the lowest rung of the ladder without having to pull herself up.

From the ground, they watched her climb with enviable ability. Tom Callaghan was paying close attention to her movements for any sign of trouble from her injuries.

Andy went quickly up past the weakened first section and it showed no sign of moving under her. She stopped when she reached her brother.

"Martin?" When there was no response she reached over and felt for a neck pulse.

He opened his eyes and closed them quickly. He was petrified of falling and obviously in great pain. Andy felt no sympathy for him.

"You aren't going to fall!" she told him callously. "If you were you would have by now."

Martin made no attempt to answer.

"Where do you hurt?"

"My legs," he managed to say through teeth clenched with pain.

Andy took in the matted blood on his trousers and said with deliberate malice, "Is that all? It looks to me as if you might have turned yourself into a girl too."

"Bitch," he muttered, opening his eyes to glare at her. He would not be able to see the people below.

"How badly do you want to get down?" Andy asked him with sickly sweetness.

Martin was not prepared to beg for help from her.

Andy shrugged and began to uncoil the line with the grappling hook. At the same time she deliberately jammed the transmitting button in the on position so the radio would transmit the conversation.

Ignoring her brother, she threw the hook up in an attempt to catch it on the next section of the ladder six feet up. She wasn't concerned that it missed. She hooked herself to the ladder so that she could lean out further to try again.

"What do you want," Martin asked, with difficulty.

"I want you to admit that you were trying to frame me, that's all." Andy casually coiled the line and flicked it up for another attempt. "No!"

"Go rot!" Andy told him callously. "I'll just be going on up to find the money, if it's there! Your foul breathed mate solved my immediate problem when he took out the Broken Hill copper. Now, he's done a runner, I'll have time to get away."

"Tench is here?" Martin seemed even more afraid. Andy hadn't thought it possible.

"Yes, Stenchbreath was all prepared to climb up here and put a knife in you, but I convinced him to let you suffer. He'll be back later."

Martin gulped visibly. He did not want to be indebted to his sister.

"Help me down and give me half the money," Martin told her slowly.

"And?"

"And I'll help you hide out and give the cops evidence of your innocence."

"Not good enough!" Andy said harshly. "Do you think I'd stand for some other poor sod getting blamed for crimes you and Merryl pulled? I know darn well you are as good with locks as I am."

"Take it or leave it," Martin tried to insist. He was not in a position of strength.

"I'll leave it thanks," Andy told him pitilessly. "I'll take my chances. The evidence against me is full of holes anyway. I don't know why you bothered in the first place."

"I wanted you out of the way. I wanted to know where you were."

"So kind of you to care!" Andy sneered. "If I help you down, we're quits. I will owe you nothing. You are no longer my guardian, you are no longer my brother, and you are nothing to me!"

"And half the money," Martin sounded desperate.

Andy thought for a moment, threw the hook again and felt it catch.

"You can have all the money I find here, if I could guarantee you will leave me alone in future."

"Deal." Martin agreed.

Andy nodded as if satisfied.

"So was it you or Merryl who did all of the jobs in Albury and Ballarat?"

"I did!" Martin bragged. "I'm better than you!"

"What about Broken Hill?"

"Merryl was helping me but when the cops came she freaked.'

"So why did you have stolen money in your bag?"

"I was going to plant it on you but you saved me the trouble."

"Thought so!" Andy said with a smug grin as she changed the position of the portable radio attached to the harness.

"RFDS portable to ground" she spoke softly into it and released the jammed transmit button.

"RFDS mobile one receiving."

"Did Jack get all that?" Andy asked, seeing the realisation dawning in Martin's eyes.

"Affirmative," was the reply in Jack's familiar voice.

Andy prepared to speak again.

"I'll get you, you bitch," Martin swore. "The deal is off!"

"You really aren't too bright, brother. If anything happens to me now, they will come straight to you. Half the outback probably heard what you just said."

Martin glowered.

Andy ignored him again and spoke into the radio.

"Tell the doctor he is jammed tightly. There has been some bleeding but as you can hear he is conscious and probably hurting a little. If you attach the other rope to the one dangling behind me, I'll pull it up. Then I will go up higher to anchor the other rope. This part of the ladder seems solid enough."

When the radio told her that the heavier line was attached, she pulled it up slowly, using her left arm more that her right.

She felt no discomfort from her shoulder but then she was on a high and the adrenalin was flowing through her.

As she climbed up the rope to the next section of the ladder, David started climbing the lower section, proceeding more slowly and with caution. He was carrying the extra rope that Andy would pull up when she reached the top.

She traversed the distance to the top very quickly. The ladder was in no better condition than the rest but easily held her weight. The railing around the top of the silo looked more solidly anchored.

Andy looked around before pulling up the rope. She had located a section of the railing in a position which was more sheltered from the elements and intended to secure the rope there.

Andy reported when she had fixed the rope and looked around further while waiting in case David needed her to pull on the rope.

Andy pushed broken glass from the frame of the nearest window and climbed into the walled catwalk. There was debris where generations of birds had nested undisturbed for years and years. Enough light came in through the broken and yellowed windows for her to search and to avoid the gaps in the floor.

In the end it was easy. Knowing how her father thought and being sure that the police had searched here, she ruled out the obvious places. The dark angle under the roof caught her eye and the odd sight of nests perched on a seemingly flat wall in the attitude of steps seemed like an arrow pointing to it. Breaking off the currently unoccupied nests revealed shallow niches that would have been as good as a ladder to Magpie Cappell, as they were to his daughter.

Andy freed the case from where it was jammed between the metal roof and a rafter and moved into a patch of light. The locked case was no barrier to her; she looked inside.

After a moment of shock, she laughed aloud and heard her laughter echo around inside the silo.

Andy looked down through the gap nearest her in the floor and saw the man Tench standing in a patch of light, looking up at her, gun in hand.

Andy moved out of the light and pulled the radio off the harness.

"RFDS portable to ground. Can I talk to Jack?"

"Jack here"

"That man is back inside the silo, with a gun. I found what Martin was looking for, and what that man wants. If you wait until Martin is free, I'll lower it down and that will keep his attention off you. Let him open the case, I want him to see what Martin was going to pay him with."

"Understood."

Then a different voice spoke on the radio.

"Andy, this is David, can you pull on that rope a little?"

"I'll try," Andy agreed, and climbed back out of the walkway. She had to pull most with her normally weaker left arm.

Andy obeyed David's instructions and finally heard that he had got Martin free. She knew that he had a special kind of stretcher in which to lower his patient to the ground. Although Andy couldn't see what he was doing with the stretcher, she could see that he abseiled down after it had reached the ground.

Andy went back into the catwalk and tied the light line to the case. She whispered briefly into the microphone to tell Jack that she was going to start. She suddenly thought to remove some of the contents of the case and having nothing to wrap it in, shoved it in her pocket.

Andy rubbed her hands on her clothes – picturing in her mind how she would tell her brother about the mess that rats or mice had made of a lot of money and savouring his reaction.

As she had predicted the man was so intent on the case slowly approaching the floor that Jack and the two policemen from Broken Hill approached him without his hearing them. They arrested him with only a minor scuffle.

"Open the case!" Andy called down. One of the Broken Hill sergeants did so and the prisoner fell to his knees and rummaged through the mixture of shredded currency and rodent droppings.

Andy could imagine what the man must be thinking but didn't wonder what he would do about it. She wanted to get down and was already pulling up the freed rope and coiling it.

For her, getting down was as easy as getting up. She untied the long rope and clipped it to her belt so it was still running around the support. When she reached the broken section, she used it to ease herself down to the spot where Martin had been. Then she unclipped it and allowed it to drop to the ground. The light line was still coiled and hooked to her harness. When she reached the lowest point of the ladder, willing hands eased her down to the ground.

David helped her out of the harness and told her to sit down. She could see no sign of Martin but the plane had taxied back down the road.

Suddenly the euphoria of the climb dissipated as the pain in her shoulder returned with a vengeance. Andy felt her vision going grey.

The next thing Andy knew was waking up in a moving car. The shoulder was throbbing and someone had put it back in a sling. David was driving the car.

"Where are we going?" Andy asked, feeling dopey.

"Back to the Crossing," David told her, glancing at her.

"Oh," Andy answered automatically, and then added. "Does Jack know you've got me?"

"He's following in his car," David said smiling slightly. "I'm taking his superiors car back for him."

"Thought it was too good to be true!" Andy said slowly as if forcing her mind to work.

"That was a skilful piece of climbing" David commented. "Have you ever tried rock climbing?"

"Never had the chance. Just trees, buildings, ladders and silos."

"Your brother probably owes his life to you."

"And hating the thought! Besides, I didn't do it to help him; I just wanted to climb the silo!"

David glanced sharply at his passenger, and charitably blamed the painkilling injection for her apparent lack of concern for her brother.

"How's Hayley, the cop?" Andy asked.

"Serious but stable. He is on his way to Broken Hill in the Nomad," David told her. "So is your brother, who has leg and groin injuries and some internal bleeding."

Andy snickered. "Did he turn himself into a girl?"

"No..." David said, refraining from further comment.

"Too bad!" Andy said quietly, as she dropped back into a doze.

Chapter 12

Andy didn't want the lecture Dr. Standish gave her about not climbing until her shoulder had healed. She was however relieved when he confirmed that it was no worse than before but was totally unimpressed when he arranged for her arm to be strapped to her side to ensure the shoulder was rested. He arranged for her to stay at the hospital overnight.

Jack Carruthers allowed her to promise not to leave the hospital and Andy was relieved to be on her own. She had no doubt that the hospital staff would be checking on her as often as their duties permitted. Nor did she doubt that as soon as more police arrived from Broken Hill that the situation would change too.

Andy was willing to lie down and relax for a while, but soon became bored and restless and paced the small ward she was in.

Tom Callaghan came to see her when he returned from Broken Hill that evening.

"How is the Inspector?" was Andy's question as soon as she saw him enter.

"The bullet was removed and he is recovering well. He gave me a message for you."

Tom saw Andy become tense.

"He said you should remember all you discussed in the car and suggested that you should make a statement to Jack about what happened from when he first saw you. He was lucid enough before the operation to arrange for a guard on your brother – ostensibly to protect him from friends of the man who shot Hayley but also so they can keep a watch on him and ask him some questions. He also said to tell you thank you and that he is proud of his Godchild."

"Godchild!" Andy echoed. "He was delirious, he had to be!"

Tom said nothing. Andy walked to the bed and sat down.

"How could a policeman become a god-parent to a thief's child? Why would he? Why tell me? He certainly isn't giving me any leeway because of it."

Tom shrugged.

"He couldn't have known what sort of person you were. Maybe he now feels he does," Tom suggested.

Andy fell silent, thinking furiously about what Tom Callaghan had just told her. She did not notice Tom stand up and leave the room.

Later, when Jack Carruthers arrived with a constable from Broken Hill, she had made some decisions.

Her first conclusion had been that her father must have though highly of the policeman Hayley, if he had asked him to be godfather to his child. In turn, Hayley must have had a certain respect for her father to have agreed.

The nebulous relationship hadn't affected his handling of the case. He wouldn't hesitate to send her to prison if she was guilty. It would explain why he had come in person to get her. He would be able to judge what the grown child was like.

Andy had come to respect Hayley in spite of his hard attitude and so she thought carefully about what he had said. She decided to trust him to be fair. She would answer any questions the police asked her, even if they were about her brother. He had forfeited any claim to her loyalty.

She was still deep in trouble, Andy accepted, but she had no friends or family to turn to. She would therefore trust in this newly discovered Godfather, use him as someone to emulate. If he was the instrument that put her in prison, so be it. It would be what she deserved.

The decision wasn't easy. She knew that she would have problems dealing with being locked away. Perhaps the police had doctors who could help her.

"Good evening, Miss Cappell. I'm Constable Dayton. I'll be driving you to Broken Hill tomorrow."

Andy looked up at the stranger with Jack Carruthers and managed to say, "Hello."

She suddenly realised that with Hayley injured, she was going to have to deal with policemen that didn't know her. Her resolution faltered.

"Sergeant, did you want me to make a statement about what

happened at the silo?" she asked meekly.

Jack gave her an appraising look.

"I would like a formal statement from you," Jack agreed. "That incident would be a suitable starting point."

It had probably been his intention because Dayton produced a notebook and pencil.

Jack Carruthers suggested that she tell things in her own way and did seem surprised at her lack of dissembling. Andy was aware of his scrutiny and how his lips grew thin when she mentioned picking the lock of the handcuffs to free herself. She just managed to catch the faint smile on the constable's face. She wondered what he had been told about her and by whom.

Andy continued to watch Jack's facial reactions as she spoke and felt she impressed him.

"Is there anything else that you can tell us about the man Tench," Jack asked intently.

"Only that Martin was obviously afraid of him and that is highly unusual."

"How well did your brother know him?" Dayton asked.

Andy shrugged. "Who is he anyway?"

Jack considered his words before answering.

"Corrie Tench is involved in organised crime. Police in both NSW and Victoria want him. It would be interesting to know what dealings your brother had with him."

"I'm not sure I want to know!" Andy said, feeling suddenly shaky.

That foulmouthed creature still wanted money from Martin and even in police custody may have contacts that might threaten Martin or her.

"Do you think he will send people after me?" Andy asked, glancing in turn at both men.

"There's more than a chance," Jack admitted seriously. "You would be a witness to the attack on CI Hayley."

Andy felt herself go cold and clammy. She hadn't thought of that.

"The Commissioner has insisted that you have a police guard," Jack saw Andy revert back to a scared teenager.

"I have typed up the notes of our conversation from when CI Hayley first arrived," Jack went on. "I'd like you to read them and see if you wish to add anything to them."

Andy reached out her left hand for them and hoped the men didn't notice how it trembled. Next they would be asking how she escaped.

"I can't think of anything," Andy said when she had finished reading the notes. "Do you want me to sign it?"

It seemed that she had anticipated Jack again. He handed her a pen and watched as she used her right hand, awkwardly, to sign her name.

"Now," Jack said carefully. "How did you get out of the cell?"

Andy was sure that Jack thought she had picked that lock too. Hayley couldn't have told him that he thought otherwise.

"The door was open ..."

Slowly, Andy told the story. The memory of the previous night threatened to shatter her resolve. It recalled to her mind, vividly, the panic when the door closed, the intense need to get out and the terror of meeting Martin at his angriest.

She tried to make them understand what was in her mind but felt her words were inadequate. However, both policemen also watched her unconscious body reactions and didn't doubt the truth of her story.

Jack finally understood the Inspector's veiled hints. He had obviously guessed the truth. Well, they now had something to hold against Martin Cappell.

Jack nodded to the constable who rose and walked from the room. Almost at once a woman constable replaced him.

"We will have your statement typed for you to sign," Jack told a visibly shaking Andy. He was not sure what to do for her.

Andy nodded, "O... Okay."

The constable sat down next to Andy and gave her a hug and began to talk softly to her.

"Leave her to me, Sir," the woman told Jack. "I have dealt with a lot of abuse cases. That's why I was told to come."

Jack nodded, relieved and went to find the doctors in case they decided they needed to do something.

Constable Kit Frawley had been briefed, albeit hastily, by Hayley as he was being prepared for surgery. He didn't have time to choose his words carefully. He had briefly summarised the case against her, which was serious indeed, and admitted his doubts about her guilt and her brother's innocence and his lack of proof.

He had implied that Andy was afraid to speak out against her brother and suggested that he was abusing her.

Frawley hadn't need to her more – she knew what to do.

"You are very strong to talk about your brother." Andy finally began listening to the soothing monotone. She tried to pull away from the policewoman, but Frawley didn't release her.

"You don't have to bear this alone, you know," Frawley said softly. "And nothing you say will go any further unless you want me to act on it."

Andy wanted to talk, needed to talk and her courage was at its lowest ebb.

"I don't owe Martin anything, I know that, but he won't forgive me for this or even for me helping to rescue him. He hates me."

"We can provide protection for you." Frawley told her.

Andy shook her head.

"That would be fine if Martin were my only problem. But it isn't. You can't be ignorant of the charges against me or the fact that more may be pending. Being beaten up by one's brother isn't a defence against criminal charges is it? I keep telling myself that I didn't break into anywhere, that it had to have been Martin but I really can't be sure. You see, I've been found in places that I don't remember getting to.

"Before I left Melbourne I was found on the safety railing of the West Gate Bridge. I don't remember getting there. They found stuff in my locker at work. I don't remember putting it there but I might have. I found money in my bag that was probably stolen from the Laundromat and I can't be sure I didn't take it. I did go there to use the machines and the locks would've been simple to open. I want to prove myself innocent but I am so afraid that I am not. I can almost hear the cell door lock behind me and I can't stand being shut in."

"I know things look bad for you," Frawley agreed. "I can't help but be impressed by your strength, because you could have run away and haven't …"

"Right now everything below my neck feels like jelly." Andy said

Frawley gave Andy a briefly tighter hug.

"You have taken the first steps to freeing yourself from your brother's influence. Now, listen to me…"

Frawley drew Andy's eyes to meet her own.

"Some good has come of this. Firstly, as a witness against that scumbag Corrie Tench, we can keep you in protective custody, not in prison or in remand but in a more comfortable setting. On the same excuse we can hold your brother while we continue to investigate him – perhaps in not so comfortable conditions."

Andy managed a faint grin.

"While you are in custody, we can bring in people to help deal with your problems, the phobia, the memory lapses and dealing with your brother. You also helped to save the life of a senior policeman and to catch a dangerous criminal; two not so little points in your favour. Finally, we as police do not set out to prosecute the innocent and you are innocent until proven guilty."

"I want to know I am innocent, I want to be proven innocent," Andy insisted softly.

"There's nothing wrong with that." Frawley agreed.

Chapter 13

Whilst Andy slept, Constable Dayton received orders to impound Andy's car. The instruction had come from C. I. Hayley who, once he came out from the anaesthetic, was too mentally active to sleep. He didn't explain his reasons, but he further instructed Dayton to have it transported on a tray truck to the police yard in Broken Hill and carefully searched.

Hayley also instructed his subordinates to have Andy flown back to Broken Hill rather than driven. He had received reports from his colleagues that indicated that associates of Corrie Tench would act to protect him.

"I thought we were going by car," Andy whispered to Constable Frawley as they walked through the small terminal at Coopers Crossing airport.

"Change of orders," was her brusque reply, which implied that was all she knew and that she was simply obeying the orders of her superiors.

"Oh," Andy answered, hiding her apprehension. She had never flown before and she was dreading reaching Broken Hill. She concentrated on the thought that she was not about to be confined in a cell, and tried to ignore the niggling little voice that said, "Yet."

The plane was a small six seater, but in addition to the pilot, the only passengers were Andy, Constable Frawley and the other constable, Warren.

A strong hand grasped Andy's as the plane taxied to take off. Frawley felt the tension in her charge and saw how she had her eyes tightly closed.

"Are you alright?" Frawley asked

"No," was the whispered reply.

"But you like being high up!"

Andy cautiously opened one eye and then the other. From the window she had a clear view down over the wing. She took a deep breath and began to relax. This was the ultimate high place that she had ever experienced. In her mind, 'high' always meant safe. For the remainder of the trip she kept her eyes on the ground far below.

It was a very short trip, though, and Andy's relief ended when the plane finished taxing to the terminal at Broken Hill. Her escorts, even out of uniform, were obviously authority. She was glad that they had accepted her promise to behave and not put handcuffs on her. Even so, Andy felt that the small crowd that were waiting for the plane from Sydney were looking at her. It was a relief when she sat in the back of the unmarked police car parked outside the building. With Frawley beside her and Warren in the front next to the driver, the car accelerated away.

Conversation during the short trip was non-existent and when they reached their destination – the police building in Broken Hill, Andy received terse orders which she obeyed with growing trepidation.

First she underwent the formalities of being charged with the two robberies. She was fingerprinted and searched but allowed to retain her own clothes. She then answered all sorts of questions aimed at confirming her identity. Finally she was taken to an interrogation room and only the presence of Frawley helped her maintain her inner calm.

Andy had no inclination to talk, but after a short while a young man entered and introduced himself as Jason Frost. He explained that he would represent her. He brushed aside her concerns about paying him as Frawley withdrew to allow them to talk confidentially.

Andy privately thought Frost was useless but accepted that he was better than nothing. She did her best to explain the major facets of her situation then listened to his advice. However she had already chosen her course of action.

When two policemen entered the room, Andy felt cornered. They gave their names but Andy only took in the fact that one was from Ballarat and the other from Albury. They seemed to look at her as if assured of her guilt.

"Please be seated, Miss Cappell," the first instructed her. He was the one from Albury.

Andy sat in the indicated chair on the opposite side of the table feeling trembly. The policeman who had spoken took out a notebook, pen and tape recorder.

Andy glanced briefly at Frost before agreeing to let them record the interview.

The questions began and if at first they were almost friendly, they soon became intense. Andy tried not to be trapped by the phrasing of their questions, which were worded as if she was guilty and the questioners gave her no chance to answer properly in her own words.

The two sergeants took turns asking her questions and made Andy switch from place to place. She quickly developed a dreadful headache which made answering even harder. Finally they seemed to tire of asking her for the same information countless times and one place a sheet of paper in front of her.

"What's this?" she asked dazedly, confused by the columns of figures.

"It is a statement from your bank account," she was told.

Andy tried to make sense of it but the amounts were absurd.

"It can't be," Andy objected. "I only had $1500 in my account and I withdrew most of that to get my car. And I certainly haven't had that much at any one time to deposit."

The sergeants looked at her as if she was stupid but Andy was too tired and tensed up to figure out why.

Finally the man from Albury pointed out dates and amounts and correlated them to the robberies they were investigating.

Andy turned to Frost in desperation. She was relieved when he firmly insisted that they continue the questioning at a later time. He cited that she was still recovering from a brutal assault. The arm in a sling supported the claim.

The detectives agreed, but as they left they looked no less hostile.

"Are you still convinced that your way is best?" Frost asked her. "They are certainly convinced of your guilt."

"I know they are!" Andy snapped, betraying her frustration and fear. "But I didn't commit any of those robberies, I'm sure I didn't. Any evidence they have has to be circumstantial."

"What about your bank account?"

Andy rested her head in her hands. "I don't understand where they got those figures. The only money that I have put in since I left Melbourne have been the small amounts that Mrs. Haddie in

Albury paid me. The other figures have to be bogus."

"I will look into it," Frost promised. "I'll be back to see you later."

Constable Frawley, still out of uniform, returned when Frost left, but made no attempt at conversation. Andy paced the room in furious frustration until her two other escorts arrived and told her to come with them.

"Where to?" Andy asked rudely.

"A safe house," Warren told her calmly.

That reminded Andy of the other part of her situation and she fell silent, obeying Warren's instructions with no further comment. In the car she shrunk into her seat and continued to say nothing.

When they reached the 'safe house' Andy was shown to her room.

"I hope you don't expect me to be sociable," Andy muttered, and added in a softer voice, "I thoroughly dislike policemen right now."

She closed the bedroom door in their faces, went over to the bed and buried her head under the pillow.

Frawley entered later with some food on a tray but Andy refused to talk to her.

"They had to ask questions," she reminded her charge.

"They didn't have to be so horrid," Andy's voice was muffled by the pillow. "I didn't rob those places. I didn't! I'm sure I didn't."

Frawley was not allowed to take sides on the issue of Andy's guilt or innocence of those crimes. She could however give her encouragement and sympathy in matters concerning her brother.

"The police surgeon will be visiting you tomorrow."

"Why?"

"To examine the bruising on your back and to discuss how you got it."

"I already told the police that!"

"He will make an official report," Frawley said calmly, ignoring Andy's rudeness. "Based on what he finds and what you tell him he can recommend charges be laid against your brother. You will need to be truthful and frank with him."

The defiance and anger drained out of Andy and she slumped onto the bed again, shaking. Now, Frawley could help her. She supported Andy into a sitting position.

"He can't hurt you here."

"He has a long memory. He will pay me back. He always does." Andy's voice shook.

After a while, Andy managed to eat a little of the meal Frawley had brought in but it was a long time before she slept and only then with the help of a sedative.

The interview with the police surgeon was even more harrowing than that with the detectives. First he examined her, and then he took photos of the bruising on her back and front. After she had re-dressed, he began asking questions, quite gently, about her brother and her relationship with him.

Andy found it hard to be frank and open about Martin. For so long he had insisted that she keep out of his business and tell nobody about him. It was hard to change. It was a tearful, worn out Andy who was finally left alone, but not for long.

Jason Frost arrived just before the detective from Albury returned to question her further.

When the questions returned to the matter of her bank account, she tried to tell them her opinion but he gave her no chance. Finally, Andy had had enough. She buried her head in her arms on the table and refused to say any more. Her stubbornness did not endear her to the detective.

"Refusing to cooperate won't help you," they told her sternly.

Andy looked up and said with barely restrained anger. "I have been trying to cooperate! You are assuming I am guilty – you aren't giving me a chance to tell you anything to help you prove that I am not. I will not tell you what you want to hear because it will be a lie. I did not do any of those robberies. I did not pay those large sums into my account. I think you should compare notes with your colleagues here in Broken Hill. Then I think that you might as well send someone around to shoot me and put me out of my misery because I don't intend to answer any more questions from anyone!"

Andy's voice had gradually being getting higher in pitch. The detective noticed the tension in her and thought she was on the verge of breaking, but she was fighting a different battle. Andy wanted, more than anything, to run and hide, but she couldn't go out of the house.

Her mind agreed with the logic but her instincts were not rational. She wanted to be alone before she lost control of herself.

The policeman left. Jason Frost tried to tell Andy about some information he had discovered but she wasn't listening.

"Go away!" she screamed at him.

Frost gave up and departed.

Frawley had heard the shouting and went into talk to Andy but she too was told to get out. She did and went to the telephone to make a report to her superior.

Frawley returned to Andy's room a short time later with one of the sedative tablets that had been prescribed for her. She was prepared for a fight to make her take it but there was only silence in the room.

"Andy?" she asked quietly. Her first thought was that she had fallen asleep.

The bed was unoccupied, and after putting the tablet and water on the bedside table, Frawley searched the room and the adjoining en-suite. Andy wasn't there and she had not come out through the door to the main part of the house. That left the supposedly deadlocked window, which wasn't.

Cursing in an unprofessional manner, she went and alerted her colleagues and they all went outside to look around.

The three of them, briefed about her tendency to run and climb, scanned the roof of the house and looked around for climbable trees. It was getting dark when they finally spotted her on the roof hidden between the upward slope of the roof and the blue plastic covered evaporative cooling unit. They did not want to call attention to themselves so Drayton volunteered to climb up and talk to Andy. Frawley went inside to call off the reinforcements they had summoned.

Andy seemed to be staring at something in the distance and unaware of Drayton's presence and attempts at conversation. Her state worried him, but at least she was no longer a screaming harridan.

"...anyone could come up here and hurt you." Dayton was beginning to think she would never answer.

"I knew it was you!" Andy said quietly.

"You would be a perfect target for a sniper up here," Dayton chided.

"It would be a difficult shot."

Dayton looked around and conceded her point.

"Are you going to come down now?"

"I guess so, since you asked me so nicely."

Andy walked with instinctive balance and climbed down where she had climbed up. Dayton returned to the ladder, stepping carefully on the tiles and envying Andy's casual skill.

Dayton hurried into the house through the back door and was relieved to see Andy entering the front door and walking into the house's lounge room. He heard unfamiliar voices coming from there and hurried after her.

Andy stopped two paces inside the door and looked to be pinned to the spot by the gaze of the man seated on the sofa. Dayton entered and came immediately to attention.

"Commissioner," he nodded rather than saluted as neither of them were in uniform.

"Constable," the Commissioner returned the greeting politely. "I see you found your charge.'

"Yes, Sir" he answered smartly, noticing Warren and Frawley standing not quite rigidly on opposite sides of the room. He deduced that they had been reprimanded for letting Andy get out and knew he could expect the same later.

"It is well that you decided to return, Miss Cappell."

The Commissioner's tone was severe. "I can recommend that you be kept somewhere less comfortable. It is our intention to keep you safe. If you insist on taking unacceptable risks, we will act. Is that clear?"

Andy managed an affirmative. Her imagination easily conjured up the alternatives.

"Furthermore, Corrie Tench's associates are actively looking for you. He will be taken to Sydney tomorrow and you will be following at a later time. Broken Hill is simply too small a place to hide you effectively, particularly if you repeat this evening's activity. We don't waste taxpayer's money on running a holiday camp for undisciplined teenagers."

The Commissioner glanced at Warren who was nearest the door and he understood he was to escort Andy back to her room. Andy turned to leave, glad that the lecture was over.

"You are as foolish as your brother, Miss Cappell."

Andy turned back to look at the Commissioner.

"He tried to leave the hospital but misjudged his stamina. Fortunately his guard were more alert and managed to get to him and push him to safety before the sniper took him out."

"They shouldn't have bothered," Andy commented as she turned again to leave. She hoped no one noticed that she was trembling like a blob of jelly.

Warren didn't follow her into her room, for which Andy was grateful. As the door shut, Andy's eyes went to the window. The curtains were open and she walked over to close them and noticed that the window was now screwed shut. She quickly closed the thick curtains.

Andy felt her earlier calm desert her, she no longer felt like screaming but the thought of being the target of an assassin scared her to her core. She wasn't taking the idea lightly and at the same time she was trying not to squirm at the memory of the police commissioner's cutting remarks.

Frawley found her pacing like a caged beast and without a word handed Andy the glass of water and tablet. Andy stopped and looked at the Constable and seemed to slump. She did not want to be drugged into sleep for the second night in a row but forced herself to admit she probably needed it. She took the water and swallowed the tablet before walking to the bed and sitting on the edge.

Andy seemed to become aware of something in Frawley's manner.

"I'm sorry I got you in trouble. I'm not sorry I went out, but I didn't think!" Andy apologised.

Frawley shrugged. "We'd been warned about you and I am glad you managed to calm down. Your timing however was appalling. We had no warning that he was coming, but when you disappeared we had to call in reinforcements – just in case. I assume that the Commissioner wanted to judge your character for himself."

"And I turned on a prime demonstration!" Andy said with a shiver, still embarrassed by the deserved reprimand.

"Yes," Frawley agreed without elaboration. "He did seem surprised that you had only climbed onto the roof."

"I wasn't running away, I just needed out!"

"Well, I can't stress how dangerous your actions were. You are an extremely important witness and the Commissioner doesn't want anything to happen to you. He has mentioned that he will be arranging a psychiatric assessment for you."

"And no doubt they will find that I can't help provoking dangerous people."

Andy suddenly changed subjects. "I never did get a chance to get my car looked at! I suppose it is still in Coopers Crossing."

She was surprised at the answer.

"Frank had it brought to Broken Hill. It's in the police compound."

"Frank?"

"Constable Dayton," Frawley amended. "C. I. Hayley wanted it here and checked over."

"Searched, you mean! Didn't Jack Carruthers already do that?"

"Yes, but I think he wanted it done again here."

"What about my money that Jack confiscated?"

"Still being held as evidence."

Andy pulled a face. She doubted that she would ever get it back.

"Are you going to eat something before you go to sleep?" Frawley nodded at the covered tray on the bedside table. "You haven't been eating much."

Andy lifted the lid and considered the chicken roll. Her mouth was dry but she made an intentional effort to eat. When she began to feel drowsy, Frawley took the roll from her and let her lie down.

Andy found Jason Frost at the house when she emerged for breakfast.

"Good morning Andy, How are you today?" he greeted her.

Andy took his meaning as 'are you going to listen to me today?'

"OK," she muttered, helping herself to toast and buttering it.

"I need to talk to you," Frost told her.

"Come through to the lounge," Andy suggested, taking the plate in the hand protruding from the sling and munching hungrily on the toast.

"I looked into the matter of your account," Frost began as soon as they were settled. He took a copy of the statement from his case.

"I have discovered some interesting points. Firstly, the woman in Albury was paying you weekly?"

Andy nodded.

"You always went to the same branch to deposit it?"

"Yeah, the closest one – I didn't really want to be seen around too much."

"Second thing then, all the large deposits were made in different ways each time. They alternated between ATM deposits, night safe deposits or deposits at various branches. The amounts deposited were approximately half of the total estimated cash stolen. I have a contact with the police, they have been showing your photo at the different banks and you have been identified at several. Large deposits tend to stick in people's minds."

"I swear they are wrong. I only ever deposited small amounts at one branch."

"I was told that the police are searching for any other accounts that you might have – do you have any others?"

"No! Why would I?"

Frost accepted her answer.

"Can you tell me how they could recognise you at three banks other than the one you claim to have used?"

"It had to Merryl!" Andy insisted and explained what she had seen in Broken Hill and about the false ID's she had found in her brother's case.

"Do you still have the driver's licence?" Frost asked intently.

"I think so," Andy said thoughtfully. "I don't think Jack found it when he searched my bags. Hayley knows that I used a false one, but he didn't ask me about it."

"I think that I should keep it for you, can you go and get it?"

Andy went to her bedroom and emptied her pack. She checked all the pockets in the pack and in her clothes but didn't find it. She returned and flopped back into the chair. "I can't find it!"

Frost was more concerned about the failure to find it than he let on. "How good was the likeness?"

"It would fool people who don't know me well," Andy said

thoughtfully. "The wig was permed into my normal style and she has similar height, build, complexion and facial shape to me."

"Last thing, did you give the police permission to check your accounts."

"Yes, I had nothing to hide!"

Frost shook his head at his client's naïveté. Well, he'd have to work around that situation.

He rose and closed his case, telling her he would be back later.

When Andy returned her plate to the kitchen she was told that she would be going to the hospital to have her shoulder checked and to see C. I. Hayley. She shrugged as if disinterested and went to put on her hooded jacket; knowing that her brother was at the hospital made her want to be less noticeable.

The unmarked police car dropped Andy and her two escorts at the ambulance entrance and the latter steered Andy via back passages to the office of the doctor she was to see.

Andy kept facing the way she had to go, but her eyes were flicking every way they could.

The doctors, nurses and other hospital staff blithely went about their business and did not seem to take particular notice of her. The jacket was hiding the white sling in which her arm rested.

The doctor was expecting her and he had her records from the small hospital at Cooper's Crossing. He briskly examined her shoulder and pronounced it improving. He wrote a prescription for an analgesic cream for her shoulder and another for a cream for her now peeling sunburn. He spoke quietly to Frawley and gave her the prescriptions.

On their way to Hayley's ward, Frawley stopped at the nursing station and asked them to arrange to have the prescription filled.

Andy was looking forward to seeing her newly discovered Godfather, but when she actually entered his private ward she found herself feeling very shy.

"How are you, Sir?" Frawley greeted Hayley formally but she was smiling. "You look much better today."

"I am, thank you. Miss Cappell, I wanted the chance to thank you for helping me."

Andy shrugged uncomfortably.

"How are you coping?" he asked her gently.

"Ok."

Hayley glanced at Frawley as if for a second opinion and noticed in passing that the nurse who was assigned to tend him had entered the room and was busy with some task on the far side of the room beyond the unoccupied second bed.

"I'm trying to do as you said, but the cops from Albury and Ballarat were being horrid. They act like they are sure I am guilty."

"I never said it would be easy, these things take time to work out."

"Frost, the lawyer, says I am stupid to tell the police everything," Andy said, almost sullenly.

"That's not surprising," Hayley commented. "It's his job to get you off, not to try and find the real culprits. Have you told them everything you can? You aren't hiding anything?"

"I answer their questions as best I can – but they don't seem to be really listening."

"Give them time, they can't rush their investigation and any court case will have to wait until Tench is convicted."

Andy made a rude noise and changed the subject.

"Is Martin really going to be charged with assault?"

"I haven't had the report from the doctor yet." Hayley told her. "Are you going to stop running away from situations you don't like?"

Andy looked away and noticed the male nurse leave the room.

"Well?"

"I'm trying..." Andy muttered.

It was apparent that the Chief Inspector had received a report of the previous night's episode.

Half an hour later, after the discussion had turned to matters unrelated to official ones, Andy was more relaxed and pleasant to be with. She was feeling less nervous when Dayton and Frawley walked her to the office of the visiting court appointed psychiatrist. Once again, she was wearing her hood up.

"About time you got here!" Martin Cappell snarled at the male nurse entering his room.

The man closed the door before replying. The two police guards had already checked the trolley of equipment that he had brought in. They accepted the assurance of the now familiar face of the nurse that the man they guarded was to have a blanket bath.

"Did you pass my message on?" Martin demanded.

"I spoke to Tench's lawyer, Pullman."

The nurse drew the curtains around the bed for extra privacy.

"He promised to pass it on, but Tench is proclaiming that you tricked him."

The nurse spoke quietly, telling Martin what had happened at the silo after his sister had arrived and before Tench was arrested. According to Tench, the case your sister lowered down was full of confetti and mouse shit."

Martin lost any trace of colour in his face. He did not believe for one minute that his sister was trying to help him and if he could have thought of a way that she could have substituted the case – she'd be dead. Trying to now wouldn't help – his mind was furiously trying to think of another solution to his problem; something that would take him off Tench's kill list.

Suddenly the colour returned to his face and a malicious grin appeared.

"Get Stafford up here!" Martin told the nurse, who was also one of his most trusted associates.

"I think there is a way to fix this but I need his advice on some legal aspects. It may be quite simple now that my bitch sister is eighteen!"

"She's here!"

"Who, Andy?" Martin deduced quickly.

"I saw her in Hayley's room. She has a police guard but she isn't cuffed. Hayley is treating her like a friendly witness."

"I don't like the sound of that!" Martin thought aloud. "The bastard should be out of the picture. Too bad Tench didn't finish the job. What was being said?"

The nurse gave an accurate account of what he had overheard.

"So, she's got him on her side!" Martin realised. That was definitely not in his plans.

"They may be coddling her because she is a witness against Tench. If we took her out, he'd be in our debt."

"Clem, that idea is almost too tempting to resist. Not only that, but the money in her trust account would be mine. The police would assume that Tench's people got her."

Martin kept thinking as the nurse gave him his bath.

"No, not just yet. I have a gut feeling that she may still know where some of Father's loot is. I will, however keep the idea in mind."

"One other thing," the nurse, Clem, mentioned. "I think they are considering charging you with assaulting your sister."

"The bitch! If she thinks she can talk about me just because the police are playing nursemaid..."

Clem was glad it wasn't him that had angered his boss.

"Get those overpriced lawyers of mine up here, today, and ..." Martin thought for a moment. "Can you get your hands on that Metracine/immox mixture?"

"No problem!" Clem assured his boss. His smile wasn't nice.

"Find a way to get a dose of it into my sister and find out where they have her stashed. Are you sure that it's not the detention centre?"

"Positive and it's not the low security centre either. They probably have her in some safe house."

"Andy needs to be reminded to keep her mouth shut! And I need to get out of here as soon as possible!"

Martin and Clem spoke together until Clem had finished his task. The latter assuring his boss that his wishes would be carried out.

The staff at the desk had been told by Clem that the police department had hired him. He was to help care for the Chief Inspector and the man under guard. Therefore he had the perfect excuse to be in and out of those rooms on a frequent basis.

When Clem returned to the nursing station he was give the prescription to have filled for Andy Cappell. It was quite permissible to query the patients name and was told that the woman was another "police guarded" patient. As it played right into his plan, he agreed to attend to it at once.

On his way to the pharmacy, he went into a store room where he had a few items stashed in a hidden corner. Amongst these were some of the standard hospital prescription forms and a vial of tiny blue and yellow capsules. The latter went deep into the pocket of his trousers and the forms were quickly modified to include Andy's name. One of the hospitals doctors had signed it already, albeit unknowingly. Then carrying a few innocuous items to restock his bath trolley Clem relocked the storeroom door behind him.

Clem knew that at this time of day the pharmacy was usually very busy so he simply asked for the prescriptions to be delivered to his duty station on the fourth floor. On his way back he stopped to make several phone calls to initiate Martin's orders.

Clem re-entered Hayley's room as usual, without knocking. He merely grinned at the instinctive reaction from the four policemen standing around the room. The conversation had stopped as he entered.

Clem went to Frawley.

"If the scrip isn't ready by the time you are ready to go, have me paged and I will chase them up. This time of day is quite busy and they may take a while to get to it."

"That's fine" Frawley assured him, "We'll be seeing Dr Morton at eleven."

Clem grinned and left the room. He knew that Morton had been the shrink that had examined Martin Cappell and it had been one of his signed prescription forms that he had used only a short time ago.

Andy lay back on the couch with her eyes closed, resting after an exhausting session with the psychiatrist. It wasn't that the man had been over bearing, rather it was because Andy's imagination had supplied her mind with a multitude of conclusions that the man could come to. She wondered if his report on her would only go to the police and if she could read it too.

One thing was sure – this wasn't going to be a one off session. He had told her that she would be seeing him on a regular basis. She shuddered at the thought, even though he had given her hope that her claustrophobia could be treated.

As for the memory lapses, he would be working on those too. She was also to see a specialist to have some tests done in case that problem was from a medical condition. In fact he had just gone off to see if this hospital had the means to do one such test.

Andy heard the door open and peeked to see if the psychiatrist had returned. It was only the male nurse who had been in Hayley's room. If her escorts, who had been told to wait outside had admitted him then she could ignore him. She went back to listening to the soothing music playing that had been playing softly in the background during her session.

The quick prick on her arm made her eyes open, but there was no one, not even the nurse in her line of sight. He idly rubbed her arm and decided that she had imagined it.

When the voice began whispering in her ear she opened her eyes again and found her vision blurring. When she tried to sit up she discovered that something was holding her head down and she was too weak to fight it. With her panic rising, the words began to make terrifying sense.

The voice wasn't Martin's and her mind could not even decide if the voice was male or female.

"You will not say anything about your brother! You will insist that no charges be laid against him. Your brother will be leaving here and he will find you. When he finds you he will give you a thrashing you will never forget. Then he will give you to his pack of thugs to use as they please. Then you had better hope that he is merciful and lets you die."

The voice brought back memories of every threat and every punishment that Martin had ever dealt her and her body went rigid with tension.

Andy dared not even move, even when she felt hands moving under her clothing towards her most private places.

Martin had never touched her like that – but she had no doubts that he knew people that would.

The voice continued, warning her to say nothing about these threats.

After enduring the groping hands and probing fingers for what seemed like a long time, the voice told her to stay as she was with her eyes closed. She dared not disobey.

The psychiatrist returned with her escorts but Andy was too befuddled to understand what was being said. She simply allowed Frawley to lead her back to the car.

During the short trip she didn't speak and back at the house she quickly sought the privacy of her assigned room.

Frawley had noticed that Andy was very tense but then she had been like that after speaking to the police surgeon too. It seemed to be her reaction to having to talk about her private thoughts.

As the afternoon progressed and Andy stayed in her room, Frawley began to worry. She made a point to check in on her at intervals, each time seeing her in the same position, staring at the roof.

Finally, Frawley decide to check closer and went and sat on the bed. Andy didn't seem to notice her but there were traces of tears on her face.

"Andy?" Frawley said quietly.

Andy began to tremble and didn't answer.

"What's wrong?"

"N – Nothing," Andy forced herself to say. "I – I'm just resting."

"Do you want to talk about anything?"

"No, No I don't."

It occurred to Frawley that Andy was terrified.

"You are quite safe here!" she said firmly to the younger woman.

"No! He's going to come after me!"

Andy hugged herself tightly.

No matter what Frawley said to her Andy simply repeated, "He's going to get me."

Frawley knew she was having no effect on her charge and debated whether to give her a sedative; one of the ones that zonked her or one of the new milder ones. This time at least, she knew that Andy wouldn't climb out the window.

As she considered her options, Frawley analysed Andy's behaviour and had the strong notion that something was seriously wrong. She mentioned her fears to Dayton who took them seriously enough to go outside to where Warren was watching from the garden.

Frawley decided to report her concerns to Hayley and her fingers dialled the direct number for Hayley's bedside.

As she reported her concerns and gave a report of the rest of their visit to the hospital she sensed that her superior was greatly concerned. When he heard that Andy had been left alone at one stage with the nurse his manner changed. He brusquely told her that he would call her back.

That if anything convinced Frawley that something was amiss.

Warren came in and spoke to her. "I have the car ready to go. I think the place is under observation."

They both instinctively checked they had their weapons.

"I'll throw Andy's things into her bag," Frawley commented.

Andy continued to stare at the roof the whole time the policewoman was in her room.

Frawley ran to the phone when it rang.

"Get out of there!" Hayley wasted no time on preliminaries. "Take all reasonable precautions to deceive possible observers. Go to the house. I will have reinforcements sent there. Don't give Andy anything! Go!"

Frawley issued orders to her colleagues.

"We have to leave. Frank, carry Andy. I'll get her stuff. We have to make it look as if only one of us is going out. We have to go to his house."

The three worked as a practiced team and they left lights on and their own stuff lying around.

Warren was to drive the car in which Andy was lying on the back seat and Frawley would be crouched on the floor behind the front passenger seat. Dayton remained, watching the house and the observers from the garden.

Warren watched his rear-vision mirror carefully but saw no sign of followers. It seemed that their ruse had worked. He went first to the police garage and transferred Andy into Frawley's car. He took three extra police back to the safe house.

Frawley drove to Hayley's house, a route she knew well and was met by the squad of officers who had received orders to check the house and gardens and patrol the grounds.

Frawley asked one of them to help her get Andy inside and settled her onto a couch. She was no more aware than before.

Half an hour later, her uncle, Chief Inspector Hayley entered the lounge room. He was dressed in a coat over his pyjamas and was hopping on crutches. The psychiatrist, Moore, was with him.

"What's going on?" She was able to drop the formality in her Uncle's house.

Moore had gone directly to Andy and checked her pulse and looked at her eyes. Then as he took from a case the equipment he needed to take a blood sample, Hayley answered.

"Neither I, nor the Commissioner organised a police nurse. The hospital authorities know nothing of him. He simply appeared and told the floor staff that we sent him. The other staff members agree that he is competent and have no complaints with his work. I sent Verger to check on Martin Cappell – he's gone and the two guards I had on him have critical head wounds. The hospital has no address for that nurse."

Doctor Moore walked over to where Hayley stood.

"Sir, you should be sitting down!" he reminded the policeman.

Hayley smiled ruefully and hopped to his favourite chair and settled into it awkwardly.

"She has definitely been drugged," Moore reported. "I can't tell you what it is, but it is muddling her mind, sight and hearing. If it was given to her before she left the hospital, it should be starting to wear off. I would also agree with your observation that she is terrified, barely coherent and nothing like she was when I saw her this morning. I have a blood sample that needs to be taken to the pathology lab. If there is a bed that I can settle her in, I will stay with her until I can get one of my nurses here."

Frawley took charge. "She can have the guest room. The bed is already made up."

Andy roused a little as they helped her to stand up. She was confused by the unfamiliar surroundings and did not seem to recognise those around her.

"Leave me alone! Let me go!" she began to struggle weakly.

"Andy, it's me Kit Frawley. You are safe! No one is going to hurt you."

"Your voice sounds funny! You look funny" Andy said, twisting around.

"How do I look?" Frawley asked neutrally.

"All blurry and your face is all mixed up!" Andy began to tremble, her face lost all trace of colour and she only just reached the bed before she fainted.

Andy woke up to be aware of a strange room but before she could panic, the calm voice of Doctor Moore spoke to her and reassured her.

His gentle questions kept her mind off things she feared and she really had no memory of how she was answering him. Moore realising this took the opportunity to ask some questions about her and her brother.

While he was talking with her he had a tape recorder going and was taking notes of her answers. He knew that he would have to ask these same questions again, when she wasn't affected by an unknown drug but the things he was learning now would help him approach the subject again. His instinct was that the answers she was giving him were true and not fantasy and he was learning things she had not told him at their earlier session.

Finally he let Andy drift back into sleep.

Chapter 14

"What did you give her?" Hayley demanded of his niece.

He had been awakened from sleep in the early hours of the morning by the commotion from his guest room.

"It was a mild sedative," Frawley said, pulling the bottle from her pocket.

"I asked the nurse at the hospital about it. I was told that it was a mild sedative and it should relax her without knocking her out."

"Which nurse?" Hayley asked quietly, realising that his niece was not very alert at that moment.

Doctor Moore took the bottle from Frawley and examined it.

"The nurse at the floor station. When I picked up the prescription it was with the salve and the sunburn cream. The doctor who saw her about her shoulder mentioned that stress wouldn't help her shoulder heal and it had been on one of his prescription forms."

"The capsules look like they should," Moore added thoughtfully. "Just a moment."

Moore strode from the room. They could hear him a short while later talking on the phone extension in the front hall. What he was saying was unclear – there was still too much screaming coming from the guest room.

Frawley looked haggard. She could picture Dr Moore's nurse and the two officers that had been summoned to assist her. When Hayley had ordered her from the room, they had been only barely restraining Andy.

Andy was struggling fiercely, recognizing no one, totally out of control and it seemed out of her mind. She had been bad enough before Moore had given her the okay for the mild sedative – nothing like she had become.

Frawley badly needed sleep – but forced herself to try and solve this new problem.

"Damn, Uncle," she swore suddenly. "That nurse, Clem, was organising the prescription."

Moore returned.

"Sorenson didn't prescribe them, but the pharmacy claim the signature was his. They know it well. To check my earlier comment, I described the capsules to them and they agree they should be what is on the label. However..."

Moore came over to the coffee table near where Hayley was seated. He squatted down, took one capsule out of the bottle and carefully separated the two opaque halves. Inside, instead of white powder was a smaller blue and yellow capsule.

Hayley looked thoughtful, Frawley appalled.

"I'll need those for evidence" the Chief Inspector remarked calmly. "Can the pathology lab at the hospital analyse one of them? Kit, I think the ambulance has arrived, let the paramedics in please."

Doctor Moore had also spotted the red and blue flashing lights through the window.

"I'll take this open one with me to the pathology lab and also have a word with the pharmacy to see if they know what they are. Will you be sending officers to guard the girl?"

"Already arranged, they will be waiting when you get there."

Frawley watched as a restrained but still struggling and screaming incoherently Andy was wheeled out to the ambulance, followed by Moore and his nurse. In her current state of near exhaustion she was glad she didn't have to deal with Andy but she still berated herself for thinking that way. She closed the door behind the nurse and walked slowly back to the lounge.

Hayley had stood up and came to meet her.

"Stay the night, Kit. Get some sleep; we'll talk in the morning."

Kit Frawley opened her mouth to object but said nothing. She was hardly in a fit state to drive anywhere and her Uncle's house was like a second home anyway. So she forced a brief smile and went off in the direction of the spare bedroom.

Hayley didn't take his own advice. Instead he sat back in his chair and waited for a report from the safe house and one on the nurse, Clem.

A subdued Kit Frawley sat at her uncle's kitchen table talking to his housekeeper.

Cheryl Moroney had been working for the Chief Inspector for years and knew his niece well. She was giving some tactful advice on how to handle Andy. The previous night's debacle had not been mentioned.

Hayley entered the kitchen some time later, properly dressed and looking as if he had slept all night instead of only half of it. If he noticed the lack of a normal greeting from his niece he made no comment.

Frawley was reluctant to initiate a conversation with her uncle because she was feeling very sensitive to the Senior Constable – Chief Inspector gap in rank.

After Hayley had started his breakfast and Cheryl had disappeared into another room he looked at his niece.

"The Commissioner has asked me to commend you for your perceptiveness last evening," he began, knowing that would get her attention.

Frawley looked up.

"Your timing – causing me to check on Cappell – probably saved the lives of Grey and Kingsley. We also discovered that Cappell was missing sooner than we might have."

"Hardly commendable!" Kit said sourly. "I should have acted sooner. Besides there is no official charge against Cappell."

"There is now!" Hayley said with grim satisfaction. "He is wanted for assaulting his sister and both he and that nurse are wanted for the attack on our officers. The alert has gone out state-wide."

"Did you tell the Commissioner that I fouled up again and tried to poison Andy?"

"I told him what had happened. He agreed that you had been as careful as possible. Now, Andy is in good hands and there was another useful outcome of your actions."

Frawley looked at her uncle and waited for him to continue.

"The extra men that went back to the house after you left it caught three intruders. Frank Dayton saw them go in and reported it and the team were ready to catch them when they came out. The men had silenced machine guns. None of them are talking, but two have been identified as Tench's men."

"That's amusing, Martin Cappell doing his sister a favour by drugging her!" Frawley said aloud. "How did they find us?"

"You must have been followed from the hospital," was Hayley's suggestion.

"Will she be safe back at the hospital?"

"For now, we haven't any choice – but as soon as she can travel, she is to be moved to Sydney. The Commissioner does not want to lose his most valuable witness against Tench."

"Doesn't that make you a target too?"

"I didn't see who shot me, not clearly anyway. At the moment, Tench is claiming to be innocent; that he had sent someone else, as yet nameless, to get the money from Cappell. That person ran off and Tench says he came later to finish getting the case. Andy is the only one who saw Tench both times."

"What about Martin Cappell? Didn't the recording of his conversation with Andy at the silo have him recognising Tench from her description? Would that make him a witness too?"

"Not a good one and certainly hostile. He owes Tench money but he didn't actually see Tench there."

"There's a lot I'd like to know about Martin Cappell" Frawley said thought fully.

"Yes, Moore learnt some unpleasant things about him from Andy, but when we first asked Melbourne to check on him they found nothing. If indeed he is a crook, he has so far hidden his tracks very well. However, the police in Melbourne are keeping on the case. His so far tenuous association with Tench is worth following up, because Tench has been the money controller for a large criminal organisation that we have been trying to break for years."

Frawley couldn't help commenting.

"For someone who is supposed to still be in hospital and certainly on sick leave, you are remarkably well informed."

Hayley chuckled.

"The Commissioner has been busy. He has put Ted Kline into my office to handle the day to day business and anything new that comes in. I have to concentrate on getting back to peak fitness but I am still to coordinate this case with Tench until he has been moved to Sydney and Andy has also been moved. Then it will be out of my jurisdiction. Tench is to be moved today."

Hayley's smile disappeared.

"Isn't it time you were reporting for duty?"

"Yes, but have you heard how Andy is this morning?"

"The report this morning is that she is resting quietly"

Hayley kept his voice carefully neutral and his niece seemed satisfied and went off to dress for work.

Hayley wasn't alone long before his housekeeper showed the Commissioner into his lounge room. He began to rise but the Commissioner waved him to remain seated and found a seat for himself.

Commissioner Kelly stared at his subordinate for a long moment.

"If one of your team received a serious wound, high-handedly discharged himself from hospital and was insisting on staying on the case – what would you do?"

"Order him off it, Sir," Hayley said formally.

"So why are you still on this case? Do you think your people can't handle it?"

"No, Sir."

"Do you want personal revenge on your assailant?"

"No, Sir."

"And why did you have to go, personally, to Coopers Crossing to question a smart mouthed, teenage criminal with no respect for authority and a proven intention to escape the consequences of her crimes?"

Hayley sighed softly and began to explain.

"Andrea Cappell and Martin Cappell are the children of Frank Joseph Cappell, the jewel thief nick named "The Magpie". I had a lot to do with him when he was active and I arrested him on several occasions. The first time, his wife had just had a baby girl and he asked me to be a sort of Godfather to her. I saw no harm in it. Nine years later, I arrested him again and he had his daughter with him. She was already skilled at his trade – I decided to give her some incentive not to continue with it..."

Hayley continued for some time – admitting that he had been convinced of the girl's guilt and curious too. Even after he had met her he had shared his superior's opinion of her but he had begun to have doubts and to change his opinion of Martin Cappell. He didn't have enough proof yet to drop the charges he had laid against her but he had come to respect her because she had not simply freed herself, taken his car and gone off. Instead she had helped him, helped also to trick Tench and to rescue her brother even though she hated him.

"Frank Cappell was a likeable rogue, but still a criminal," the Commissioner pointed out.

"I haven't forgotten that, Sir," Hayley said stiffly.

"So you have developed a soft spot for the girl."

There was no use denying it and Hayley didn't reply directly. Instead he reached for a folder and handed it to his Superior.

"The psychiatrist, Moore, examined her yesterday at your request. His transcript of the session is in here. Also in there are his notes from when he spoke to her here along with his evaluation of her condition when I had her brought here. The notes can't be used in court because she was under the influence of some illegally administered drug at the time."

Commissioner Kelly took the folder and read the contents carefully. The expression on his face changed when he read the answers Andy had given to the questions the previous night.

"Moore believes the answers are factual and to be used in court the session would have to be repeated under controlled circumstances."

"He also feels that if the nurse did actually threaten her on her brother's behalf, she may not want to cooperate with him if he asks her to allow him to question her under hypnosis," Hayley added.

"So what is your final evaluation of her situation?"

Hayley didn't miss his Superior's choice of words. "I think we should double and triple check the evidence against Andrea Cappell before we take it to court. I have found one point of discrepancy regarding the alleged robbery of Martin Cappell though I can't speak of the crimes in Albury and Ballarat. I am certain that Martin Cappell is not the guiltless character he'd like us to believe."

"And these memory lapses that the woman seems to have?"

"A complication," Hayley agreed. "One that Tench's lawyers may try to exploit."

"Do you consider Andrea Cappell to be stupid or unintelligent? I was not impressed with her escapade at the safe house."

"Nor was I Sir, but I would not call her stupid. Somewhat naïve and poorly educated perhaps. Her behaviour is sometimes compulsive. She connects being high up with being safe, she suffers from severe claustrophobia and tends to run from situations that she finds intolerable.

"In her favour, I believe that in Melbourne she ran away from her brother, not the court hearing. Since then she may have tried to avoid us but not actually run away from us. She has agreed to help us, even though what she has told us does not seem to agree with our evidence. She gave us permission to check her bank accounts, signed permission. I don't think she would have suggested it if she was banking stolen money."

"Ah, yes," Commissioner Kelly interrupted, taking a folded report from the pocket inside his jacket.

"The results of your enquiry into accounts in Miss Cappell's name."

It was Hayley's turn to read carefully.

Two other accounts had been found, one was a statement account opened two years before and from the attached statement containing what was likely to be the missing half of the money from the robberies in Albury and Broken Hill.

The second account was a trust account, opened ten years before and jointly in the names of Martin and Andrea Cappell. It had been added to twice and half the total had been removed five years before. An attached note indicated that the terms of the trust were that the shares could not be realised until the share holder was eighteen.

Andy's share was still there, untouched and the sole authorised signatory was Martin Cappell.

"I don't like this," Hayley said thinking quickly. "This trust account, Martin Cappell is desperate for money. That was his reason for going to the old silo, to find the proceeds of his father's last heist but that I've been told was shredded by mice. He is the sole signatory on the account, he's taken his share and there is nothing to stop him taking his sister's half now that she is eighteen. She might not even be aware of this account."

"Well, it means that she can't take it and run."

"I think that Martin Cappell would be more dangerous if he's got Tench off his back than not," Hayley proposed.

"All he's have to do is have his sister killed and the money would go to him anyway."

The Commissioner realised at once where that thought was leading. "Perhaps he's already tried with that drug business."

"Which came close to finishing Andy last night," Hayley reminded his Superior. "If that had failed the raid at the house might have got her. Cappell could have got the nurse to arrange for her to be followed and then tell Tench where she was to earn some favour with him."

"I'll get a court order to freeze Andrea Cappell's accounts, including that trust account. It is possible that the deposits were from the proceeds of crime," the Commissioner promised.

The Commissioner seemed to come to a decision. "I came here prepared to take you off this case. However, I think it would be better if you go with her when she is taken to Sydney. It will be to our advantage if she has come to trust you. I'm surprised that young lawyer the court appointed for her hasn't tried to stop her talking to you or tried to plea bargain."

"She has ignored his advice about talking to me and Kit tells me she wants us to prove her innocent."

"If she had sense she would ask for us to drop charges for the benefit of her testimony," the Commissioner said. "Then the question of her guilt or innocence would be moot."

"And her brother would still be walking around free," Hayley said.

"Have you had a report back from the forensic lab in Sydney about Martin Cappell's hire car or his sister's car?"

"Not yet Sir," Hayley reported. "I'll call them before I go to the hospital."

"How are you feeling?" the doctor asked Andy.

He could see that see still looked very pale, her skin almost waxen. "Shaky, throat hurts."

The doctor looked at her chart and then checked her pulse, blood pressure and breathing.

"Your vital signs are back to normal," he reassured her. "I think we can move you back to a normal ward. Do you remember what happened?"

Andy shook her head slightly because he neck also hurt. She remembered nightmares and screaming but not what caused it.

"Well I want you to keep resting," the doctor advised as he made notes on her chart.

Andy did not try to protest, she had no energy for anything and her mind was fuzzy. Sleep was the only thing she felt like doing.

Andy woke again sometime later and took a while to recall that the room appearance had changed. It was a few moments longer before she realised that a warm hand was gripping her own. She turned her head but said nothing. Her mind could not reconcile the gesture with her memory of the man, nor did she have the energy to pull her hand free. Instead a very faint blush coloured her cheeks and tears leaked from her eyes. She closed them again.

In spite of the gesture of support she felt a wave of depression sweep over her. Hopelessness and helplessness battled for supremacy as she recalled all she had endured in the past week. She didn't think that she could take any more of it.

"I'm told that you are probably feeling like a mountain was dropped on you," Hayley said gently. "A side effect of counteracting a rather nasty combination of drugs. You've been lucky!"

"I don't feel lucky," Andy croaked.

Hayley passed a glass of water with a sipper straw so that she could drink from it.

"No, I suppose you don't, but you are."

"Why?"

"Well, that male nurse injected you with something before you left Dr Moore's office. He threatened you too, didn't he? He reminded you not to talk about your brother...?"

Andy nodded, wondering how he knew. Her face betrayed her memory of that terror.

"My niece, Constable Frawley, decided that there was something wrong with you so I had you moved."

"Your place, we went to your place."

"Yes, quite right. Doctor Moore had taken me home, so he was there when you had a bad reaction to the mild sedative. It was probably due to a trace of the other drug still being present. That's why you were brought here to the hospital."

Hayley felt justified in glossing over the full details. Andy was in no state to deal with the fact that she had almost died.

"Coming here was lucky because if you had been well enough to return to the house you might have been killed. Tench's men launched an attack there but we caught them all."

Andy said dully. "I don't know why you are bothering with me. Martin will get me in the end. I can't hide forever. Even if he goes to jail, he'll get me when he gets out."

"With your help we can put him away for a very long time."

"Just for hurting me – it won't be long enough. And he has others he can send after me. Maybe I'll be better off drugged senseless in prison."

"I don't agree!" Hayley said firmly. He was rewarded with a flicker of a smile as Andy suddenly realised that her Godfather was trying to help.

"That wasn't a bad reaction to a sedative!" she surprised him by saying. "Martin was trying to punish me again."

"Again?"

Andy fought the fuzzy minded sensation of the tranquiliser she had been given.

"Martin didn't want me to have friends. He particularly didn't want me bringing any home or my visiting anyone. I pretended that I had to work after school. I had one friend, Lynn Wales. She was the only one who didn't try to ignore me.

"I was a lousy student. The teachers always picked on me for being late, inattentive, whatever. I was often away and I had a perfectly awful reputation – the details of which depended on who you spoke to."

Andy paused to get her thoughts back on track.

"Martin, somehow found out about her. He must have come home one day early, when I had slipped out to the shops. She must have rung me, and been invited over by Martin to wait for me. He would have been quite charming, but he must have slipped something into our drinks. I don't remember how we got back to the school grounds – but we were found there by the police and Lynn's parents. I had some pills in my pocket. She was screaming and trying to fight demons only she could see. I was just sitting, watching, they said. I couldn't do anything, but I knew what she was going through. I knew exactly what she was going through. It was luck she didn't die – but our friendship did."

Hayley nodded to himself, recalling the report he had received from Melbourne about her. The file recorded that she had been charged with possession of drugs and if the girl had died it would have been manslaughter. Instead, she had been put on probation. She had kept out of trouble until that was over.

"He had given it to you before?" Hayley asked.

"Yeah! I can't remember what I had done to him that time."

Andy's voice was blurring, her energy depleted.

Hayley let her doze off again and took out a notebook into which he recorded what he recalled of the conversation. He couldn't use the information in court, but it offered him avenues for investigation. He wondered if the hospital where the girl had been taken had identified the drug.

What Andy had described fitted her own behaviour of two nights ago. And this time it had been Andy who had survived by luck. Shortly after arriving at the hospital, she had gone into convulsions. The pathology lab had rushed through the testing of the drug in the yellow and blue capsule and the pharmacists had been able to suggest a counter agent. The convulsions had stopped, but Andy's vital signs had been erratic and they had kept her in intensive care. When the hourly blood samples gave undetectable levels of the drug, she had been sedated to allow her to sleep and her body to recover.

Hayley considered Andy's words dispassionately. She blamed the incident on her brother, but that earlier time she could have administered the drug to her friend. This time he was sure she hadn't done it to herself.

Andy woke again near noon, calm and alert. She seemed surprised to see Hayley.

"As soon as you are fit to travel, you will be going to Sydney," Hayley told her.

"Tench is on his way there now."

"What about Martin?" Andy wanted to know.

Seeing Hayley hesitate to answer the question, Andy guessed the truth.

"He got away, didn't he?"

Hayley nodded and Andy turned her face from Hayley.

"What happened to me – no, I remember what happened. Who drugged me – that male nurse?"

"We think so, he's no longer in the hospital. He threatened you, didn't he."

Andy nodded, turning back to Hayley.

"I heard a voice warning me about what Martin would do to me if I talked about him – and whoever it was, was groping me – so I could imagine exactly what he meant."

Andy shuddered in revulsion.

Then Hayley posed a question that took her mind right off that incident.

"Why didn't you tell us about your other bank accounts?"

"I only have one!" Andy said, astonished.

"Our investigations have found two more."

Hayley told her what they were and the amounts they contained. There was something uncompromising in the look he gave Andy.

Andy shrunk back into the pillows supporting her. She knew how things looked, and didn't know what to say. Then something occurred to her.

"That statement account, where do they send the reports?"

Hayley was startled by the question.

"A post office box in Altona," Hayley answered cautiously.

"What number?" Andy asked, not succeeding in hiding her interest.

"Don't you know it?" Hayley countered.

"No, I don't!" Andy snapped, showing a bit more life. "I only knew Martin had one, somewhere. He left his keys lying around once."

"Why do you want to know?"

"No reason really," Andy lied. She had the idea to send anonymous letters to him, detailing how slowly and painfully he deserved to die.

"Why!" Hayley asked sharply. His manner reminded Andy of her current status, so she sighed and admitted her moment of fantasy.

"Would you agree that provoking your brother is a dangerous game?"

Andy nodded and muttered, more to herself, "That hasn't stopped me yet."

Hayley took her chin gently and forced her to look at him.

"I am impressed by you. That comment shows me that in spite of everything your brother has done to you, he hasn't broken you. However, you – will not – undertake any unauthorised correspondence with him. Do you understand me?"

Andy nodded.

"Now, if you are willing to annoy him, wouldn't telling us all you know about him be more satisfying, more aggravating to him? Don't you want us to prove what he is really like?"

"I do," was Andy's soft reply. She considered the warning Martin had given her against the protection of the police, which had failed two days ago.

"I am usually careful what I do. I know how far I can push him – most times. Anonymous letters is one thing, talking about him is more akin to playing with dynamite. And I am not so brave when we are face to face."

Hayley considered that silently.

"We'll leave that for a minute. About these accounts..."

Andy was jolted back to the matter and thought of another question.

"If someone opened an account in my name, they would have had to go through that 100 points of ID nonsense. My account was opened before that came in, but two years ago ... Martin may have a copy of my birth certificate, and back then I was still a second name on his medicare card. I don't know what else he would have needed. Is that something you can find out?"

"Why do you want to know?" Hayley asked.

"What do you think! I didn't open that other account! I thought of opening one, but was told that I had insufficient ID. And if I didn't, Martin is the most obvious person who could have. Besides, I'm still wondering why Martin had all those fake ID's with my name and Merryl's face, in his bags."

"We only have your word for that."

"If Martin knew he was missing money from his bag, he probably realised that I had been there. He'd not keep them around, he's too careful for that."

"Why you? Why not an itinerant hotel thief?"

"I told you and Jack that I saw fake ID's in his case. I pinched the one that was a driver's licence! That's what I used to prove my age when I brought my car."

"Another point you omitted to mention!" Hayley said sharply. "Where is that item now?"

"Frost asked me that. I searched my stuff and couldn't find it. It might have dropped out in my car."

"It wasn't in your car," Hayleys tone was positive.

Andy had the sudden sinking feeling that something had been found in her car.

"What did you find in my car?"

"We didn't find a driver's licence."

Andy stared at the policeman, but he said no more on the subject

"Are you claiming you had no knowledge of the trust account?"

"I am." Andy slumped back onto her pillows again and sighed. "And if I have to be 18 to access it and Martin is the only signatory – I doubt that it will last more than five minutes there, once Martin remembers that I am 18 now."

"He knows you are 18," Hayley commented. "Why would he take your money?"

"Pick a reason! Because he can, greed, spite, to pay off Tench and prolong his miserable life, to stop me having it and running off ..." Andy shrugged.

Then another idea struck her.

"If I was dead, would it all go to him?"

"It may depend on the terms of the trust. Do you have a will?"

"What? What would I need a will for? Those are for old people – besides, I have nothing of value to pass on – oh!"

Andy realised what Hayley was getting at.

"So I should write a will, saying that if Martin kills me, he can't have it?"

"More like, if you should die, that money in that account should go to a person, organisation or charity of your choice."

Andy grinned maliciously. "That's assuming that it's still there."

Hayley chose not to mention that the account had been frozen by court order.

"How would I go about getting my signature on that account? Will I need ID?"

Hayley was saved from answering by the arrival of a female nurse and two policemen.

The nurse began packing clothes from a bedside dresser into Andy's pack. The policemen saluted Hayley and showed him their ID's as they introduced themselves.

Andy heard them say that transportation to Sydney had been arranged and Andy had been declared fit to travel.

Distracted by the sudden activity, Andy didn't think she could have heard right. The two solid looking policemen were from Sydney and part of a tactical response unit? Surely she wasn't that important?

The nurse laid out some clothes for Andy to wear. The jeans were not particularly clean, and she must have found her only clean underwear and t-shirt. Then she drew the curtain around the bed to allow Andy to change from the backless shapeless white gown.

Even standing for that short time had made Andy dizzy, so she was quite happy to let the nurse wheel her out into the corridor and along back passages to a side door where an armoured truck was waiting. Hayley had walked beside her all the way and the two policemen she had seen had been joined by two more.

To Andy, the truck looked like a fortress on wheels, where she could be solidly locked away.

"We'll be quite comfortable, and quite safe," Hayley assured her quietly.

Andy relaxed, realising that Hayley would be travelling with her to Sydney.

Hayley had been correct. The inside was comfortable. One wall had a bank of instruments along most of its length. The other a small fridge, table and sink. In the centre were six chairs, two facing the instruments, four around a second small table. All could swivel and be fixed in any direction, and even had seat belts attached. There were even two bunks that could be pulled down from under the instrument panel and the bench on the other side.

"Is this how all prisoners travel or just those that need a Chief Inspector for a nanny?"

Andy caught a smile on Hayley's face.

"Just the latter group," he said. "Tench had the standard model. The armoured prison van."

Andy's momentary amusement evaporated at that reminder of the alternative.

Andy was surprised when a short while later, Jack Carruthers entered the truck. She managed to greet him with a 'Hello' and then muttered, "Two baby sitters."

Hayley told her to strap herself in and two of the policemen did likewise.

Jack Caruthers passed Hayley a document wallet and he extracted a coloured booklet and passed it to Andy.

"Can't have you getting into mischief," Hayley said neutrally. "When you think you know everything, let me know."

"What is this?" Andy started to scowl, but changed it to a grin. A fleeting glance at Hayley caught his faint smile and she realised that she was being teased, but at the same time it was a subtle reminder of her blurted admission earlier.

Andy settled into her seat and began to read the NSW Road rules booklet that would help prepare her to get a learner's permit. Studying it would certainly help pass the time.

The truck stopped two hours down the road to let everyone have a break. The driver or the front seat passenger opened up the back door for them.

Andy noticed that Hayley was moving stiffly as he climbed down from the truck, but he sounded his normal self when he instructed one of the tactical squad officers to arrange some cool drinks for everyone.

Jack Carruthers told Andy that the little dust bowl of a town was Wilcannia, and it looked much better after rain. Andy stayed in the shade, looking around her. She missed seeing Jack move suddenly to support his superior, but turned on hearing, "Here, Sir. You've been doing too much! Sit down here on the step."

Andy turned and moved a bit closer, noticing blood on Hayley's trousers. Jack went and spoke to their driver and in a very short time a car from the local bush hospital had taken Hayley off with one of the tactical team. Everyone else was told to get back in the truck. The drinks would have to be consumed as they travelled.

Andy listened as the squad leader, who had been the driver for the first leg, reported directly to the Commissioner in Sydney via the radio in the truck. She understood that a plane would be dispatched to bring Hayley to Sydney and, for some reason, the truck had to keep to a schedule.

"Have you finished studying the book?" Jack asked after they had been travelling again for a while. He was noticing that Andy was yawning as if bored. He had agreed with Hayley that Andy would behave better if her mind was occupied and she did not have time to brood.

"Yeah, I've finished."

Jack had the opinion that Andy couldn't possibly know all the answers already.

He began to quiz her and Andy replied in a tone that suggested that she found the information was so old as to be boring. She didn't seem to be thinking about the answers but every one was correct, almost to the same wording.

"You seem to know it. How about doing the permit test as we go along?"

Andy swivelled her chair around in surprise.

"Ok."

Jack set out a paper and pencil in front of her, and watched as she went through the multi-choice questions without hesitation, ticking boxes one after the other.

Wordlessly, she handed the paper back and watched as Jack checked the answers.

"Congratulations, you passed. I'll write you up a learner's permit when we get to Sydney."

Andy smiled to herself as she turned around again to watch the video monitor that was showing the scenery ahead.

Just over an hour later, Andy awoke from a doze as the truck pulled to a stop.

"There's an accident ahead," the driver's voice came over the intercom. "We are just going to check it out."

Andy unbelted herself and tried to see more detail by going closer to the screen.

A campervan, originally a bus, had turned over.

After a short time, one of the tactical team ran back to the truck and opened the back door. Jack and the other tactical team member were motioned out.

"Stay here, Miss Cappell," Andy was told, but she stepped out just enough to watch as the police tried to free the trapped people. The truck driver was already calling for assistance for the camper's occupants.

After five more minutes, unsuccessfully trying to open the driver's side door, the police moved to the back window of the bus.

Without thinking her intentions through, Andy went back into the truck, found some useful tools and ran over to the bus. The police, busy at the back did not see her climb up onto the upper side of the bus. In moments, Andy had the jammed door unlocked and partly opened. She was not expecting the door to suddenly spring fully open or to have her ankle grabbed and twisted with enough force to make her unbalanced and almost fall. An involuntary squawk escaped from her.

"Put the knife down and release the woman."

A hard voice beside her ear caused Andy to glance around. The tactical squad leader had a gun aimed at the man holding her ankle. The hand released her and Andy moved away from the door.

"Get down, Miss Cappell."

Andy began to climb door the undercarriage of the bus, and was grabbed by another member of the tactical squad.

"Slippery thing, aren't you!" the man muttered angrily. He carried her unceremoniously back to the truck. "With the brains of a jack-in-a-box. Get in! Stay in!"

The truck door closed behind her.

Andy was angry with the reprimand and with herself. She kicked at one of the chairs.

"When are you going to start thinking? They will be convinced you are an imbecile. Some impression you've made!"

She continued to fume in silence until her police escorts returned. That was about an hour later, after the flying doctor plane had taken the elderly couple who owned the bus off for treatment and the police from Cobar had the two male hijackers in custody.

Andy sat back quietly in her seat, glad when nothing else was said to her. She listened as the incident was reported to Sydney and their new ETA estimated.

They stopped to buy food in Dubbo, but by then it was 9:30 pm and they were lucky to find a fast food outlet open. They needed to make up time, so again they ate as they travelled. Andy was only allowed out to go to the ladies room and she was escorted to the door and back.

Jack gave her a dose of sedative after her tea. It relaxed her enough for her to fall asleep.

They arrived at their destination at two o'clock in the morning. By then Andy was so tired that she didn't care where she was as long as it had a bed.

A strange voice, followed by a clanging noise, woke Andy early next morning. She had scarcely taken in the fact that she was in some kind of cell, when the owner of the voice, a solid woman of middle age and dressed in a brown uniform, told her to get up.

The woman stood over Andy until she stood, then spun her around and handcuffed her wrists together behind her back.

"You are wanted upstairs."

"Where are we?" Andy asked in a small voice.

"The remand cells below the court house," the woman told her as if she should have known. "They will be convening a special court session for you shortly."

With that, Andy was hustled along a corridor to some stairs and up two flights, then along a short corridor to a small room with a table, several chairs, a phone and a large screen.

Two more brown clad security officers were in the room. Andy was pushed, not too roughly, into a seat and the hand cuffs were removed. The woman departed and moments later Jason Frost entered.

"Where have they had you?" Frost asked her.

"Down in the cells."

"I heard that you were a little idiot again yesterday," Frost told her.

"Not a little one!" Andy agreed. She was suddenly certain that the night in the cells was to drive home the Commissioner's lecture of the other day.

Frost returned to business.

"They are going to convene a teleconference with Melbourne to deal with the matter of the misdemeanour hearing you skipped out on. We'll be here, the judge and the witnesses will be in Melbourne. I have received a summary of the situation – can you quickly tell me about it?"

"Ok," Andy agreed, grateful for his presence. She stuck to the main points and tried to explain her reasons.

"This shouldn't be a problem," he reassured her and then sat in the chair beside her to wait for the conference to start.

Andy wasn't aware that the conference included Hayley, now installed in a private nursing home, not too far away. She only saw the judge.

Andy finished telling her story to the judge. She had to take oath first and stand as she spoke.

The judge questioned her gently, finally touching on her relation with her brother. Though a teleconference was not the same as seeing the defendant in person, the judge used his experience to read her body language.

Finally, he finished asking questions and told her to stay where she was.

When the face on the screen had blanked out, Andy sat down and buried her head on her crossed arms, trying not to cry.

"Have you had breakfast?" Frost asked Andy, to distract her.

"No," was the muffled answer.

"I'll arrange some. I just have to go next door."

The food arrived while Andy was still waiting. She roused enough to start nibbling on a sandwich. Her eyes were red rimmed.

Frost had adjourned to the adjacent room to attend the proceedings as the judge spoke to the witnesses. Andy would 'attend' again when the decision was announced.

Frost returned and nudged Andy into a standing position. The screen became active again.

"There's nothing to worry about," Frost assured her and she stood a little straighter.

Andy had not disputed being on the Westgate Bridge, and the judge, speaking for the official record, explained that a fine was the normal penalty, however due to Andy being in no position to pay a fine, a period of twenty days community service would be imposed.

Andy breathed a sigh of relief.

The incident would go on record but as Andy had already a number of similar incidents on her record, she was to receive psychiatric evaluation and treatment or counselling to seek the cause of her memory lapses and to ensure the incidents did not recur.

The judge then indicated that he wished to speak to the defendant 'in camera'.

Andy whispered to Frost, "What does that mean?"

"He wants to speak confidentially. To say something that he doesn't want made part of the public record. As far as everyone is concerned the case is over."

On the screen, the view was of everyone leaving the courtroom, in Melbourne. When the judge rose, the connection was terminated. A few minutes later, the view was of the judge in his chambers.

"Explain all that to me again," Andy asked Frost, after the conference had finally ended.

"You won't have to do the 20 days community service because the police here have told him, in confidence, that you will be a witness in Tench's trial and receiving counselling."

"Why didn't he just say that?" Andy said sarcastically, very relieved to have at least that matter resolved. "What am I to do now?"

Frost shrugged. "You will have to be placed in protective custody.

At the moment there are no other cases being tried in this building. The first case is due to start in an hour. You will be moved before then. I expect you will be going to an evaluation centre."

Andy was soon to find out. The woman warder returned, replaced the handcuffs on her, this time at the front, and led her to a small room where they waited until a man in civilian clothes arrived with orders to drive Andy to a place called Willowmort.

He took Andy by the arm and led her out to a black car in the garage beneath the building and helped her into the back seat and secured her seat belt. The first thing Andy noticed was the grill between her and the driver and then she realised that there was no way of opening the rear doors from inside.

The car moved smoothly from the basement garage and out into the morning traffic. Andy watched the scenery for a while, trying to ignore the handcuffs. The driver had mentioned they were routine, but Andy suspected that orders had come from the Commissioner. Out of boredom, Andy asked the driver where they were going. He was quite happy to talk to her, and from him she learnt that her destination was north west of Sydney, about two hours drive away, in a sparsely populated area and even the security section was "comfortable".

In the centre coordinators office, Andy stood waiting patiently whilst the man read the file that had accompanied her. Her chauffer had already left, after relieving her off the hand cuffs. He had to return to his normal duties of being driver to the Police Commissioner.

Andy saw the coordinator frown momentarily, but when he spoke, his face was carefully neutral.

"You are a rather peculiar case, Miss Cappell," he told her thoughtfully. "In that you are to be housed in the visitor's section. However, you will be expected to conform to a similar routine to those in the security section and you will not be afforded any special privileges. I will also inform you that the security around the visitors section is as stringent as around the security section and the lands around the compound are monitored for a mile around."

"I expected something like that, Sir," Andy managed to say calmly. "I have no intention of straying from here. At the moment, the big wide world outside isn't very safe for me."

The Coordinator frowned slightly as if he had expected her to be difficult.

He quickly outlined meal times (which she would have in her room), exercise periods (she would use the gardens) and a short list of rules she was expected to obey.

Appointments would be made with the people who would evaluate her.

Finally, a female warder came to take her to her assigned room. There was a set of shapeless grey brown clothing waiting for her and even though they reminded Andy of prison garb, she was happy to change out of her own clothes that desperately needed washing.

Andy asked about having her clothes washed and was told she would be allowed to wash them before they were stored.

Then Andy asked about access to newspapers or some kind of reading matter. If she was well behaved, she was told, she would be allowed to spend time in the common room with the TV, library and newspapers.

The woman withdrew and locked the door, taking Andy's clothes with her. Andy crossed to the window and looked out onto the gardens. She was up on the second level.

Andy took a deep breath and let it out, with the window and the view; she could keep the claustrophobia at bay. The routine would be no worse than being at school. It didn't seem to be aimed specifically at her – but to be followed by all 'guests'.

It occurred to Andy that the strict rules were a test of obedience and they wouldn't be hard to tolerate. She hoped however, to be able to find some activity to fill her spare time or her mind would become her worst enemy.

In between visits from Dr. Moore, (three in the first week) and sessions with centre staff, Andy had visits from Frost, her lawyer, who was her only source of information as to what was happening in the outside world.

The psychiatrist, Moore, had even obtained copies of her school records. He was discussing them with her, and Andy was not surprised that they painted her in a very bad light. At least the doctor would listen to her reasons for her behaviour.

Two weeks after arriving at Willowmort, the coordinator gathered reports from his staff to discuss with those who requested the evaluations. Andy was a model 'guest'. She was pleasant, cooperative, uncomplaining and followed all instructions. Since gaining certain privileges, she had spent a lot of time in the library, reading whatever she could find.

If she were aware of the close surveillance, she showed no sign. Not once had she been caught acting oddly.

Dr Moore felt he had a good understanding of why she acted as she did, but only had hints of her relationship with her brother.

"She had bad reports from her school, but if you removed the influence of her brother, I believe she would have been a good student. She was expelled from the school because of a drug related incident – for which she blames her brother. Even under hypnosis, she believes that. I learnt more about how her brother treated her under hypnosis than she would tell me voluntarily," Moore summarised. "I believe that her 'memory lapses' are her response to feeling threatened and not being able to control her environment. Andy recalls times that she has climbed places and not recalled getting there – but even under hypnosis she hasn't revealed any hint of robbing places. All suggestions that she has broken into somewhere, without remembering, have come from her brother."

"So," Hayley thought aloud. "Would you agree that she's been behaving well here because she feels safe and not personally threatened?"

"I would agree with that, but I would also take it a step further," Moore stated. "I feel that there are two situations where her lapses are likely. As I mentioned in a situation of threat. The other situation is related to her claustrophobia – when the threat or fact of being locked up is very strong. Her brother has dominated her for years. He knows how to make her think – victim, helpless. She still fights that idea when she is not actually in his presence."

"So much comes back to Martin Cappell," Hayley summarised.

Chapter 15

This can't be happening, Andy thought to herself, as she was dragged along by the skeletally thin, grey clad escapee. The man looked like a cartoon character that had just been zapped by electricity. His thin brown hair stood up from his head, even though it was only an inch long, and he kept running his hand through it in a nervous gesture.

Slight he might be, but his grip was steely strong, more than a match for the struggle Andy was giving him.

If Andy could have, she would be yelling, but the man had first gagged her with torn cloth and tied her hands together. He had warned her to obey him, with the threat of being cut by the wicked looking weapon he'd somehow contrived.

It had not been pleasant, waking up to such a helpless situation.

Andy could not understand where the guards that should be guarding her were, nor how, even in the middle of the night, the man had not been found missing or an alarm raised.

She was half convinced that this was a test to see how she would react. Why else would the man risk capture to take her with him – let alone even know she was in the visitor's wing?

Her certainty was shattered as her captor dragged her past one of the guards, grey uniform shirt drenched in blood.

Andy wanted to be sick.

The grey clad man seemed to know exactly where he needed to go to get out. It wasn't until they were almost at the door that the alarms began. The man hurried faster and Andy had to run to keep her feet on the ground.

Lights came on and the man ducked into the garden and used the trees for cover. He slashed at the material binding her wrists and shoved her towards the wall."

"Climb up there! Take the rope with you."

His voice was savage, and when Andy tried to argue, he drew a gun and held it inches from her face.

"Tie the rope round your waist."

Andy complied, eying the gun as she fumbled the rope. Then she turned and began finding finger and toe holds.

"Martin said you were good!"

Andy sat on the fence and held steady as the man used the rope to help him climb. She was thankful that there were no sharp things embedded in this section of wall.

"Down fast."

Again the gun was in her face. She swung her other leg over and jumped, landing heavily.

Hands gripped her clothes, turning her over. Brilliant lights blinded her. All she could see was the gun barrel in her face.

"Stand up slowly. Keep your hands where we can see them."

Andy complied. It seemed like the creep had a friend. She tried to block out some of the glare with her arm, then realised that her mouth wasn't bound.

"Go away, leave me alone," she tried to yell, but it came out in a whisper.

Her arms were forced down behind her and she felt handcuffs tighten on her wrists. Only then was the gun lowered, and its wielder came close enough to block some of the glare.

The man she saw now wore the blue uniform of the warders.

No wonder the escapee got as far as he had – he had had inside help.

"Take her back inside," the warder ordered the ones holding her. Inside? But...

Andy struggled to look around. If this guy wasn't the accomplice of the escapee – where was the man who had abducted her?

If these were real warders, she was safe.

Andy found she was breathing more easily as she was marched back through the main gate. She was feeling weak with relief, but the relief was short lived. She was taken into a section of the building she hadn't seen before and to a white painted room that contained only a bunk. Two women warders replaced the men and a man carrying a first aid case followed them.

Andy was released from the handcuffs, after the door had been locked. The women began undressing her, making no comments and allowing no protests.

Only then did Andy notice that her clothes were torn and bloodstained and her body began to hurt.

Later, left alone with clean clothing over numerous treated cuts and scrapes on bottom, thighs and hands, Andy felt too depressed to even think. She stayed lying on her front with her face to the wall where no one would see her tears. Even when she heard the door open, she stayed as she was.

The mattress on the bunk depressed on side as the newcomer perched there.

"Andy?"

It was Hayley's voice, but Andy didn't turn around.

"Andy, talk to me. Why did you try to run away?"

The voice was gentle, even if the tone was official.

"I didn't think I was running away," Andy's voice was muffled.

"Then why did you climb over the fence?"

"Did any of the confined guests escape tonight?" Andy asked, still turned towards the wall.

"No." Hayley assured her. He wondered at the question. "The alarms were triggered by you going outside. The security cameras show you leaving your room and running for the door."

"Alone?"

"Yes."

"I dreamt it all then." Andy finally turned over, carefully. "Until now, I was convinced that I was being abducted..."

"A very vivid dream," Hayley commented when Andy finished telling him what she remembered.

"What do you think triggered the dream?"

"I don't know. But I remember hearing a voice, either TV or radio, mentioning Tench's hearing tomorrow, I mean today. I went to sleep feeling very glad I was here. In spite of the insane rules and routine, I don't want to leave here, just to go back to my room."

"No one but the coordinator knew about the trial. Certainly not the news media."

Andy said nothing, she had heard what she had heard and it

seemed the information was fact.

"I believe you," Hayley told her, making a mental note to check for a media leak and a leak from the coordinator's office.

Andy began to relax.

"Get some sleep, if you can. There are still a few hours before we have to leave for the hearing."

We! I won't be going alone, Andy thought after Hayley left. Surprisingly, she slept.

There seemed to be no obvious security around the Court building, at least that Andy could see. It surprised her and did nothing for her state of nervous tension.

"We're early. The prosecutor wants to talk to you first," Hayley explained. "We also switched the location for the preliminary hearing."

Andy just nodded. She felt like a piece of a game, being moved from square to square. Her head and the bandaged parts of her were still throbbing from the helicopter ride.

The office of the prosecutor seemed to be crowded. However she found the familiar face of Jason Frost amongst the group. He approached her with an older man following him.

"Hello, Andy. Glad you made it here safely. I'd like to introduce my father, Reg Frost. He's here on a watching brief."

Andy smiled briefly at the older man then turned her attention back to Jason.

"All you need to say today is what happened after the Chief inspector went into the silo, until after Tench was arrested. Why you were there is irrelevant to the matter today. You are here to identify Tench as the one who shot the Chief Inspector. Today's proceedings will be recorded. I insisted on that. Everything will be done so that you shouldn't have to appear again. I won't say that you won't have to."

Andy nodded and was led over to meet the Prosecutor, who was introduced as Thomas Blyth-Britton. The man had 'presence', and scrutinised his prize witness as he shook Andy's hand.

Andy was glad then, that the cuts on her hand had almost transparent stick film over small absorbent pads, instead of great white bandages. She was even more thankful for the thoughtfulness of Hayley, who had returned to the centre with some neatly pressed, preloved clothes. Her own, had she worn them, would have made her look like the teenage runaway that she really was. The borrowed clothes made her seem more honest and reliable.

Blyth-Britton took her aside and talked her through her testimony and tried to prepare her for any cross-examination. He stressed her need to be assertive and positive, as if these were qualities he felt she lacked.

Finally, Hayley took her to a small waiting room, where they were joined a short while later by Jack Carruthers and Kit Frawley.

Jack greeted his superior formally and Andy with a slight smile.

"I have something for you, Andy," Jack took something from the inside pocket of his formal uniform jacket.

Andy took the small laminated card and examined it in delight. Her photo was on the learner driver's permit. It seemed like the most precious thing she had ever owned. It didn't even matter that her photo looked suspiciously like a mugshot with the height line blanked out.

"Thank you, oh, thank you," she smiled at Jack Carruthers.

He smiled back and turned to talk to Hayley. Andy went over to Frawley and sat down.

"Did the police find something in my car?" Andy asked her, catching Frawley unawares with the question.

Her face betrayed a moment of surprise.

"I've heard no official report," she answered immediately.

"Unofficially, then!" Andy insisted, now that she finally had a chance to find out. "You said it was being looked at again."

"Yes, it was, but if anything important had been found, you would have been questioned about it. I did hear that your brother's car – the one he hired – contained traces of blood in the boot."

That distracted Andy from asking about her own car.

"Did he get questioned about it?"

"No, Uncle only got the report after he had escaped."

"You obviously haven't caught him again."

"Obviously!"

Frawley knew things, revealed in confidence by her uncle, which she wasn't going to tell Andy. Martin Cappell had not been seen back in Melbourne and there had been unconfirmed sightings in Sydney.

Kit Frawley and Andy were in the middle of a discussion about clothes when Hayley was summoned to the courtroom. The usher returned a short time later requesting Jack Carruthers. After a further interval, it was Andy's turn. Frawley walked with her to the door of the courtroom, and then took a seat with the audience. From there she watched Andy walking carefully to the witness box to seat herself in the chair.

Andy spoke quietly, but firmly, stating her name when requested and repeating the oath to tell the truth. She found it difficult to be the focus of so many eyes, particularly Tench and his lawyers, so she turned to watch the deliberate movements of Blythe-Britton as he approached her.

Andy gave her testimony, managing to keep her voice even and limiting the scope of her testimony as she had been directed. She turned to Tench only when she had to positively identify him.

Then it was the turn of Tench's lawyers to question her. When the questions were obviously intended to discredit her, she parried them with the phrases that had been suggested to her.

"My lawyer has advised me not to discuss those matters. Or, I was told that...'

Such phrases usually prompted an objection and the question was rephrased or dropped.

Finally, she was allowed to go back to the waiting room with Frawley. This time she was aware of patrolling tactical squad officers.

"You did well," Frawley commended, as Andy collapsed back into one of the chairs.

"I feel like I have stepped up to the edge of a hole and the ground has started to crumble. The way Tench looked at me... was frightening. But if I ever have to testify against Martin, He'd just have to look at me and I'll go to pieces."

"Let us catch him first, and then worry about that," Frawley suggested. "I have orders to go to Willowmort when you return. Uncle has recovered sufficiently that he doesn't need me to make him behave. I might start showing you some self-defence moves."

"I'll be glad to have you there," Andy admitted shyly.

Frawley smiled back, choosing to forget for a time that Andy still wasn't cleared of the robbery charges. That was something that Senior Constable Frawley, would have to deal with when a decision was made on the matter."

Andy had wanted to hear if the Tench hearing had made the news, but she was not allowed radio or TV privileges on her return to the evaluation centre. With a suppressed sigh, she obeyed the coordinator's directive to go and remain in her room. She knew it was the result of her activities of the previous night.

She didn't like the situation but had to admit to herself, that the rules of her stay had been clearly spelt out to her, and the enforcement of the rules was a matter of procedure, not personal malice. If it came to that, it was better than the rules back at school, the warders here enforced the rules quite impersonally. Her teachers had always thought that a demeaning lecture was also necessary.

It was Hayley, the following day, who told Andy what she wanted to know. She and Kit Frawley met with him in the visitor's lounge and as he was not in his official uniform, he seemed less formidable.

"Tench has been bound over for trial on the attempted murder charge," Hayley told her with satisfaction. "It means that he will be kept in a secure remand centre until his trial. In the meantime, if we can find any evidence of his other crimes we will be able to charge him with those too."

"How long will I be kept here?" Andy asked then.

"A couple of weeks more," Hayley answered.

"Then?"

"We'll see," was all the answer she got, but Hayley's face took on an official blankness that decided Andy to drop further questions.

Instead, Andy told him how Kit was teaching her some self-defence. Kit reported that Andy was an apt pupil.

Andy soon regained her 'privileges' and in addition to being able to watch the news, Kit kept her supplied with books to read and often discussed them with her. She still had regular sessions with

Doctor Moore, and had started seeing a counsellor to help her deal with matters relating to her brother. She did not discuss these sessions with Frawley.

Kit Frawley had begun to notice a gradual change in Andy, from frightened teenager to an adult starting to take control of her life.

Further evidence of her improvement came when she went to a combined session with Dr. Moore and her counsellor, Sherri.

She walked in and saw the headmaster from her high school with them. They had shared too many confrontations for her to be in any way happy to see him.

From his first words to her, it was obvious he had no knowledge of her current situation.

"You seem to have ended up where I predicted you would!" he said with a trace of smugness.

"Not quite, Mr Strathfield," Andy said in a controlled voice. "I seem to recall several occasions when you said I would end up in hell. Instead, I'm a guest here."

"In a criminal evaluation centre, charged with robbery."

"That is not the reason that I'm a visitor here. Visitor, not internee."

"And the charges?"

"Have not been proved," Andy interrupted. "Any more than most of the things that you accused me of were ever proved."

"Your brother told me a great deal about you."

"Then you are a greater fool than I thought for believing him! You don't know me at all! You never gave me a chance to be anything other than a troublemaker and recalcitrant brat. If I tried to defend myself I was punished, given detention. The best thing you did was to expel me so I didn't have to put up with you."

"You will show me some respect young woman!"

"You? You no longer have any power over me. I owe you nothing more than ordinary civility. I don't need to cower in your presence, but you should find out the facts about me before you start preaching to me based on faulty observations and preconceived ideas."

The teacher no longer looked smug, and his gaze showed a little more respect. He settled back in his chair and refrained from further comment.

Andy went to the remaining free chair and perched on the edge and leant away from the teacher.

Throughout the confrontation, Dr. Moore had sat quietly and observed, but he spoke quickly once Andy had been seated.

"I asked George Strathfield here for a number of reasons. I wanted him here to talk further about your time at high school, and I also asked him to bring up some prepared tests in English and English Expression. I know you have been reading the books you need."

"I haven't been studying," Andy protested. "Why do you want me to do the silly tests anyway?"

"I'll discuss that another time!" Moore said firmly. He ignored the expression on Strathfield's face.

The teacher was thinking that Andy had not changed.

"I am aware that you do not have fond memories of school, Andy," Moore went on. "However, I want to know how you viewed school and how the school viewed you. To start off, I want you to tell me what you thought of your headmaster, other teachers, fellow students, the work you did, whatever you want to. Then, I want you to listen to what George says – without interrupting. Then we will discuss any issues."

Andy nodded, she felt sick, but that was normal for these sessions with Moore, particularly when he was getting her to face things she would rather forget.

She sat back in the chair, without looking at George Strathfield, and thought for a moment.

"I thought you were a pompous, arrogant bastard," Andy began and she continued to tell him what she thought of him back then. It actually felt good to be able to express it, knowing that she would not be punished for doing it.

"You had me pegged as a delinquent. You couldn't see me as anything else," she said finally.

"George," Moore prompted.

Strathfield had no need to organise his thoughts.

"I found you to be rude, argumentative and often disruptive in class. Other times you were totally inattentive. I still believe you were using drugs and I have never forgiven you for almost being responsible for my niece's death."

"Lynn was your niece?" Andy looked at Strathfield. "She never told me that. She was the only friend I ever had ..."

Andy tried to brush away the moisture from her eyes. That memory still hurt.

"Sir, I swear – I wasn't responsible for that. I never gave her anything. I have never, voluntarily, taken illegal drugs."

There was something in Andy's voice that begged the teacher to believe her.

"I really can't believe that," Strathfield admitted. "You were showing symptoms of drug use. Neither the teachers nor your brother could actually prove anything. Your behaviour swings, frequent absences, absent mindedness, seemed to point that way."

Andy shook her head in denial. "What did my brother say?" she asked with a quiver in her voice.

"He said he was having trouble with you, and that you frequently ran off and couldn't be found. He said that you had some totally unsuitable friends and he was trying to keep you away from them."

Andy swallowed an angry comment.

"I shouldn't have called you a fool," Andy said, looking at her feet. "I didn't realise that Martin had been telling you lies about me. I know he comes over very believable and respectable – but he is a two-faced bastard."

Strathfield had a hard disbelieving look on his face.

Moore intervened.

"Andy, why don't you explain what things were like for you at home," he suggested quietly.

Moore knew things about her past from Hayley and from the hypnosis sessions. This would be the first time, Andy voluntarily talked about her brother. He glanced with approval at the counsellor, who was sitting quietly at the back of the room.

Andy glanced at Sherri as if for moral support. Sherri smiled back with approval.

Once again, Andy looked away from the others in the room. It was easier to talk if she pretended she was alone.

"The nicest thing I can say about Martin is that we are not friends. He was my guardian. I had no option but to stay with him. I tried to run away twice. Both times I was dragged back by the police. Human services gave me a hard time because to them, Martin was a perfectly satisfactory guardian. They checked him out. There was never a breath of unsuitability about him. He had a responsible job. He didn't smoke, drink or gamble. The neighbours never heard anything to make them suspicious. My complaints were treated as sour grapes – and he was probably telling them the same lies he told you. I was given to believe that my only options were to stay with Martin or be put in a juvenile centre. I didn't want that.

"Anyway, I stayed, but I had to do all the housework and cooking, in addition to trying to study. I wasn't allowed to visit friends or have any over. More often than not, Martin ensured that I had no time to study. I had a 10 pm curfew, and my light didn't work after that."

Andy went on to reveal the ways her brother had to punish her, control her and make her do as he insisted.

"My God!" Strathfield exclaimed. "I never saw any signs of that!"

"No," Andy agreed. "I didn't come to school when I hurt too much, and he made sure the bruises wouldn't show."

"And Human services never had you examined?"

"They were before I started high school and before Martin started that."

"I really find it hard to believe."

It was Moore who answered. "There is currently a warrant out for Martin Cappell, relating to an assault on Andy."

Strathfield seemed stunned. This session was full of unpleasant revelations. Andy seemed at first, exactly as he remembered, but he had never expected her to apologise to him nor to hear about the abuse she had endured and he had never suspected. And the police believed her…

"What happened that day with Lynn?"

"You know!"

"I mean, what do you think happened – you swore you never gave her the drug."

Andy told him the same story that she had told Hayley. Moore nodded and Strathfield noticed his recognition of the story.

"You might have been right too," Andy allowed. "I might have been on drugs too, but not known it."

"I have certainly had my eyes opened today. You have my sincere apologies for not hearing your plea for help.”

Andy finally looked at Strathfield, but didn't know what to say.

“Sometimes I was just so angry with everyone that I was deliberately obnoxious.”

That admission brought a wry smile to Strathfield's face.

“Thank you for sharing your story with me. I intend to be more alert from now on. I don't want any more of my students to be hiding such abuse.”

Andy just nodded, in recognition of that promise.

Moore asked then for some confidential time with his patient and Strathfield went out of the room and waited in the visitor's lounge.

Andy emerged some time later with Sherri. She went over to Strathfield.

“I have been told to try those tests you brought. But you will have to come back to my assigned room. I'm under movement restrictions at the moment.”

“I am impressed by your new maturity,” Strathfield remarked.

“Huh!”

“Yes, you are calmly accepting movement restrictions. Why would a visitor be restricted?”

“I'm kind of an unusual case,” Andy muttered uncomfortably. Her earlier elation at changing this man's mind about her was wearing off.

“Because?”

“Because, you still don't know everything about me!” Andy snapped.

“You still can't keep out of trouble.” Strathfield deduced.

“Bingo!” Andy said very softly, as she stalked off towards the stairway to the second level. Sherri kept with the teacher to show him the way.

Andy did not like being watched by Strathfield, but she was making a concentrated effort to ignore him and answer the questions before her on the paper. The whole exercise was too reminiscent of being at school. Of having detention, in particular.

The hardest part wasn't the paper – the questions were very easy. No, what was difficult was that her former headmaster and English teacher was watching her with his dissecting gaze as if once more he was waiting for her to make a mistake.

Well, she really didn't care how well she answered the questions – there was no report card involved.

In just over half the time she was allowed, Andy gathered up her papers and walked over to Strathfield, and wordlessly dropped them on the little table beside his chair.

With equal detachment, Strathfield passed her the page of questions based on the books she'd been reading. Andy realised that this had been planned for a while – since Kit had been supplying the books to her.

Strathfield noticed the return of the sullen look he recalled as being characteristic of Andy Cappell. The main difference was in her degree of control. The Andy of three years ago had not been able to concentrate this long. By now she would have been doing something to distract her classmates, knowing she would be sent from the room. Or simply walking out because she didn't want to do the exam. He watched her for a while. She seemed to be writing the first thing that came into her head. He really doubted that her answer would be of any passable standard. One of the books had been used the year he had her as a student, she may have recalled some of the discussions. As far as he knew, the other books had been unfamiliar to her. Trying to keep an open mind, he decided to look at the other test.

He was expecting most answers to be wrong, but that wasn't the truth. The answers were mostly right; the grammar mistakes minor at worst. If he hadn't been watching her, and if he didn't know there was no possible way for her to have known about the test before hand – he would have been convinced that she had cheated.

When Andy brought the second test over to him, she handed it to him.

"Was there another?"

"There is. Do you want a break?"

Andy shook her head.

"This is better than sitting here doing nothing," Andy admitted, back to a more pleasant frame of mind.

Strathfield passed over the third and last test; again questions about books that she had read, but set at a higher standard than she had been taught.

This time he noticed signs of greater signs of her concentration wandering, but she still kept on with her questions. This time, the test took her the full length of time that he'd allowed her.

"You are going to have to leave now," Andy told Strathfield when she gave him her papers. "I have an exercise period in a few minutes."

"Aren't you curious about how you did?"

"Not really," was the answer that surprised him.

"There is no prize for right answers. Dr Moore is simply making me face up to things I don't want to remember. He's working me up to facing down Martin. You and your tests are just a practice run."

At that moment the door opened and one of the warders told him it was time to leave. Andy went with the warder without protest.

Strathfield put all of the papers in his case and allowed himself to be escorted back to the visitors lounge. His mind was on his former student.

Her comment had been very intuitive, since Moore had told him she had no idea he would be here today. And the answers he had read for the book questions had also been very intuitive. Moore had wanted the tests as a guide to her level of knowledge. He had not said why, but that didn't matter. He had tonight to consider the tests before seeing Moore again in his Sydney office tomorrow.

That led him to wonder why a psychiatrist of Moore's eminent reputation was treating a teenage thief who was a 'visitor' not an 'internee' at an evaluation centre.

Chapter 16

Andy was feeling very strange. For so long, she had not had more than a dozen people around her at a time. Now, walking with Kit Frawley through Sydney's Macquarie Centre, she felt totally exposed. Her eyes flitted everywhere, but no one seemed to be paying her any particular attention. It just felt like they were.

Frawley had sought permission to take Andy out, and with all the attention on the court in the city where Tench was on trial, this unexpected outing was deemed an acceptable risk.

Andy was beginning to enjoy herself, because Kit Frawley was helping her to choose a new outfit. New! Not second hand. The sort of clothes that were not expensive, but still not affordable on the pittance her brother had allowed her. Even when she had started work, her pay had been partly appropriated by Martin for her 'board' and the little left over was being saved for her escape.

For a little while, Andy was able to forget the trial; though every time she heard a mobile phone ring, she jumped. Tench's trial was in its final days, and today the defence was putting on its final rebuttal. Frawley was to be advised by phone, a departmental mobile, if Andy was required. The defence lawyers had accepted her testimony from the preliminary hearing, but had insisted on the right to call her in for cross questioning. For the past three weeks, she had been kept in readiness for a summons and a helicopter had been standing by to collect her from the evaluation centre. Today they had been driven to Sydney, leaving very early in the morning.

"That really suits you," Kit remarked as Andy tried on a mauve turtle necked sweater.

Andy luxuriated in the feel of the soft wool.

"Does it cost too much?" Andy asked wistfully.

"No. I still have enough to pay for it." Frawley had her reward in the delight in Andy's expression.

Andy took the jumper off long enough to have its barcode scanned and to remove the labels. It completed the new outfit of jeans, t-shirt, socks, shoes and jumper. She felt a whole new confidence in herself.

"Let's go somewhere for coffee," Kit suggested and led the way to her favourite spot in the centre.

Frawley left Andy minding two chairs at a small table that was still in her line of sight as she purchased two coffees and a snack. Andy glanced around as she waited and enjoyed the feeling of freedom.

A tall man in a long overcoat sat down at the next table. He had longish black hair that needed combing and probably washing. For a moment, his gaze returned Andy's glance. She averted her eyes as his regard made her feel uncomfortable. When Kit returned, Andy's quick sideways glance showed her that the man was staring at some other table with single women.

"Here you are. Coffee and doughnuts."

"You are spoiling me, Kit," Andy warned. "I can't ever remember anyone buying me morning tea."

"You have been doing so well; I thought you deserved a treat."

"The condemned ate a hearty meal," Andy said with a smile, but she hadn't forgotten that when Tench was sentenced, her period of grace would be over.

"Have faith in the system," Kit urged.

"It isn't easy! If I can't prove I'm innocent, how can you? You know how I had that session with the Albury boys last week? Well, they put me in a line up and I'm sure several of them picked me."

"I shouldn't be telling you this, but the result was inconclusive."

"How?"

"Most of them said that the woman looked like you, but they couldn't be sure you were the one."

"Hardly comforting. If you put a black wig on Merryl, she'd pass for my sister. Too bad you can't find her."

"We are looking," Kit admitted. "We know she hasn't returned to her usual haunts in Melbourne. We haven't even got a good picture of her."

"I wish I hadn't lost that ID I pinched from Martin..." Andy suddenly put her hand over her mouth. Kit gently put it back down. It had my name, but Merryl's face."

"Where do you think you may have lost it?"

Andy shrugged.

"I used it to get my car. And I didn't look for it until at the house in Broken Hill. I thought I had it shoved into the pocket of my pack. And Jack went through my stuff while I was fetching my car and I am sure he didn't find it. Your Uncle said it wasn't in my car. It must have fallen out somewhere between Broken Hill and Cooper's Crossing."

At Andy's words a well-dressed woman passing by, turned around. Andy recognised Julia Cullen, but the woman's gaze lit on Kit Frawley.

"Kit! Is it really you?" Julia exclaimed in delight.

Kit stood up and hugged Julia.

"Jules, what are you doing here?"

"We've just come from visiting my specialist," Julia claimed. Then she seemed to notice Andy.

"Andy?"

"Hello, Julia," Andy acknowledged.

"You look well. Did you end up getting your car to town?"

"Yeah, I met a bloke at the pub. Luke Mitchell. He came out and helped me start it."

"Luke's a sweetie. I hadn't realised he was in town then. You know, that trip back we saw three cars broken down. Yours and two more about half a mile back. The others looked deserted, so we didn't bother with them."

"Well, I'm still very glad you stopped for me. I was told I was well on the way to being dehydrated."

Andy noticed Julia's husband, glancing idly around. He had stopped when his wife did but hadn't joined the conversation. He seemed just as taciturn as he had in the car. Andy decided he must be like that with all people he didn't know.

"When are you heading back to Murrawindi?" Kit asked.

"Not for another week," Julia prattled. "We're staying at the Hyatt. Friday I have to go back to the doctor to get my test results."

"Nothing serious, I hope," Kit asked.

Julia shook her head, "No things are looking very promising. Give me a call, and we'll chat over old times. Are you based out here now?"

"No, still in Broken Hill. This is temporary."

Julia flicked a glance at Andy and smiled at her and Kit.

"We've got to keep moving, and if I'm not mistaken, I can see your Uncle bearing down on us. Give him my love will you."

Julia and her husband moved on and Andy twisted to see where she'd been looking. The man who had given her the jitters suddenly stood up and walked off. Hayley drew up the newly vacated chair so he could sit at their table and talk softly.

"What's up?" Kit asked quietly.

Hayley glanced at the retreating couple. Frawley understood the unspoken question.

"Julia Masterton, my old friend from school. Married Jim Cullen of Murrawindi."

Hayley dismissed them as unimportant.

"Andy, you are wanted in court. The judge issued a recess. We have just over half an hour to get you there."

Andy felt herself turn pale. This was what she had been dreading. Tench's trial was a media Mecca. All the reporters would be watching as the defence tried to discredit her.

"Is there time for me to go places first?" Andy asked, feeling a sudden need.

"I need to go too," Frawley added quickly, exchanging a glance with her Uncle.

Andy didn't miss it. They were afraid she was going to run.

"Five minutes," he warned as they stood up.

Frawley led Andy to the nearest ladies room. They way led through double doors into a bland grey painted brick passage.

Hayley waited outside the door, automatically scanning the crowd. His eyes alit on a man in a long coat who went into the passage, then passed to the cleaner wheeling a trolley into the passage, then setting up a 'closed for cleaning' sign.

Some instinct roused in Hayley as the five minutes passed and then two more. Acting decisively, he pushed his way through the doors. The passage was empty; he strode along it, pushing open the door of the family room, glancing into the baby feeding room. Proceeding more cautiously, he drew his gun. He approached the ladies toilet, quietly. No sounds came from in there. He continued to the door of the men's toilet and heard voices coming from inside.

Two men had been waiting when Andy and Kit emerged from their respective cubicles. Andy didn't even see the man coming. She was grabbed from behind as she washed her hands and a hand was put over her mouth. In the mirror she could see a second man, with a gun. That one, as well as her attacker wore masks. She tried to make a noise, but she was lifted off her feet and carried out into the passage and then into the men's toilet.

Frawley managed a short struggle, but she wasn't given a chance to draw her weapon.

The whispered, "Drop it or you're dead", influenced her to obey.

"What do you want?" she asked in a voice of normal volume.

"You. Silent or dead."

The gun stayed aimed at her waist.

"Walk."

Kit found herself walked into the men's toilet too.

"Get real, Martin!" Andy was saying defiantly, as a man in a long coat held her against the wall and kept a gun in her face.

"I didn't know about those accounts until the police threw the information in my face. They may be in my name, but you know darn well my signature won't do anything!"

"How did you stop me accessing those accounts?" The gun was being held higher so the butt was hovering near Andy's face.

"The police froze the accounts," Frawley said to draw the attention away from Andy.

"They have no right..." Martin snarled at her over his shoulder.

"We have reason to believe that the deposits were stolen money," Kit went on, ready to turn the table on the attackers.

Andy did something that Martin never expected. She suddenly drew up one knee and used it to jab Martin in the groin. Then she used both hands to grab the one still holding her and twist it. Martin collapsed into a writhing heap.

The moment's distraction was all she needed to disarm her assailant and break free.

A whistle from out in the passage made both men suddenly alert and prepared to forget their injuries. They climbed to their feet, pushed Kit aside and stumbled out the door.

Andy returned a hard smile to her brother's venomous look.

Hayley heard the whistle and looked around. Two men had come up silently behind him.

"Stop there, Cop. Drop your weapon and raise both hands."

Hayley began to obey, twisting around slowly as he did so. One of the men was reaching for his gun. Hayley dived under the outstretched arm, twisted his body and took the man's legs out from under him.

The second man, seeing his two mates stumbling out of the men's room covered their retreat, backing after them, not prepared to shoot unless Hayley followed. Hayley placed handcuffs on his prisoner and used a small portable radio to call for assistance.

"Let them go for now," Kit advised, seeing Andy turn white with the after reaction. "Well done! You've just proved that he isn't so tough after all."

Andy smirked and stood up straighter.

"No, he's not. Is he?"

Frawley approached the door cautiously, having heard sounds of a scuffle outside. After peering through a gap in the doorway, she beckoned to Andy that it was safe. While Andy waited with Hayley, Kit went to recover her gun from the floor of the ladies toilets.

Two uniformed police ran into the passage.

"Keep this prisoner safe until I've had a chance to question him," Hayley instructed.

"Two men ran out of here a moment ago," Frawley added.

"Three," Hayley corrected.

"One was tall, dark haired, wearing a long coat. The dark hair is probably a wig. His name is Martin Cappell," Frawley told the uniformed policemen.

Hayley understood Andy's smirk. He used his radio to summon his driver to the nearest exit – the one the men had fled through.

"What did your brother want?" Hayley asked as they walked

briskly to the exit.

"He'd found out that you had frozen my bank accounts. Why did you do that?"

"Later! We've got very little time to get back to court."

Hayley hurried them out the door.

"I think that it was pure chance, running into him," Andy said as she hurried. "I didn't recognise him at first in that get up."

"We'll find him," Hayley assured her as they stopped at the loading bay.

"Why did you come, Uncle?" Frawley asked then. "Why didn't they call me?"

"We did, we were getting no answer."

Frawley checked that the phone was on and noted that there were no missed calls.

"Odd, there's meant to be a repeater in this building. I will mention it to Superintendent Lynch when I return it. He can have it checked out. Good thing you came though."

"There's still some life left in me yet."

The police car approached along the laneway to the loading bay and braked sharply.

"What is the great rush?" Frawley asked.

Hayley opened the back door for Andy and his niece then got in the front.

"The defence have been angling for another overnight adjournment. The prosecutor wants it finished today. I think putting Andy on the stand is a last ditch attempt to get the jury on his side and to delay."

Andy needed the confidence of having new clothes to bolster her courage as she followed the court usher to the witness box. The second time around, her voice was steady as she repeated the oath.

She had arrived with only moments to spare before the court reconvened and barely had time to catch her breath.

The defence lawyer had thought of some questions that he could ask and have answered, that did not impinge on her status as an accused criminal.

Why had she run into danger at the silo? How long had she delayed? Why that long? What had she observed when she entered.

How good was the light? Had she known the man? Did she know he was associated with her brother? Did the man give his name?

Andy wasn't allowed to mention what Tench had told her or that he had guessed who she was.

How good was the light later? Where was she when she next saw the man? How could she be sure it was the same man?

"Because I could see him clearly. Because he knew what I was lowering down, I'd told him before. And he was so engrossed in what he was expecting to get, that he was an easy capture for the police!" Andy said finally.

The defence wasn't looking happy, Andy thought, as they fired similar questions, phrased differently, in a constant succession. It seemed obvious to Andy that they were trying to get her to contradict herself, as if he believed her to be stupid.

Finally the judge put an end to the repetition and Andy was allowed to step down. As she was walked back to the side chambers, she heard the defence beginning to sum up their case.

Andy was taken to a room with a security guard outside. As she entered, she glanced at him and wondered at his presence. The room itself was empty of all but a few chairs. Andy was disappointed that Kit Frawley wasn't there to talk to, but she remembered her shopping trip with a smile.

The chairs were hard and there was nothing in the room to occupy her mind. So she pulled a chair over to the window so she could at least look outside by standing on it."

The view was restricted to the backs of other buildings. She could just see one anyway, and the only traffic on it consisted of police cars and armed guards patrolling on foot.

A glimpse of movement on the roof opposite caught her attention. She moved her head for a better line of vision, but the glass was in the way. If only she could lean out the window.

Andy didn't stop to think what the guard would think. She just had to get a better view of the person – who had dark hair and a coat just like Martin had been wearing.

The person had gone from her view. She pushed open the now unlocked window and poked her head out. The person was crouched down behind an ornamental parapet, watching the lane below.

"Step down from the window, Miss Cappell," an uncompromising voice spoke from behind her.

Andy visibly jumped, but obeyed, putting her feet back down onto the chair before turning around. The Commissioner stood there in his formal uniform, and the security guard had his weapon aimed at her.

"There's someone on the roof over there. I think it's my brother," Andy said defiantly.

"Step down from the chair."

Andy stepped down and didn't move as the security guard holstered his weapon then walked behind her and handcuffed her wrists. He did however, step up on the chair and glance outside.

"No sign of anyone, Sir."

"Take Miss Cappell out to the car," Commissioner Kelly instructed neutrally.

Andy was hustled out, by a firm grip on her arm. She squashed her annoyance.

Commissioner Kelly spoke briefly to the guard in the corridor, and then increased his pace to keep up with her. Ahead was a huddle of guards, a brief gap in the shields enabled her to spot Tench. That group passed outside.

"Down!" came a sudden loud command.

The guards around Tench pushed him down as the report of a single gunshot echoed between the buildings.

 Andy was dragged further back inside the court house as the crowd of guards flowed back inside. Commissioner Kelly, as senior officer on site, began issuing orders.

Tench was pushed past Andy, and he spat at her as he passed. His guards jerked him harder. She moved further back towards the wall.

When the crowd had thinned, a smaller one remained around a prone guard on the floor.

Instructions to get an ambulance were issued, but Andy, looking at the amount of blood, thought the guard was a goner.

Andy felt sick and weak as she was pulled in turn towards the front of the courthouse. It wasn't the blood that sickened her but the thought that it might have been her brother that had shot the guard – even if he had intended to get Tench.

With the confusion caused by the shooting, the reporters didn't notice a relatively insignificant female prisoner, so the terse "Keep your tongue still!" wasn't needed.

The Commissioner must have delegated matters at the courthouse, because Andy had been alone in the questioning room at Police Head Quarters for no more than ten minutes, before he entered the room.

"Sit down!" Commissioner Kelly instructed, waiting until she had seated herself before sitting down on the opposite side of the table. Andy didn't believe it was a matter of courtesy.

The constable who had entered behind the Commissioner, sat at a third chair and prepared to take notes.

"Did you catch the gunman?" Andy blurted. She had placed her now free hands on the table in front of her.

Kelly answered her questions with a steely glare.

"That is of no concern of yours. What needs to concern you, is explaining to me why you were halfway out the window when I came to talk to you."

"What's the big deal? I agreed to stick around and testify against Tench. I did. What's the big deal about opening a window? I wasn't going anywhere. I told you, I was only trying for a better view. I thought I saw Martin."

"May I remind you, that you are still under remand for two crimes in Broken Hill? You did not go into voluntary custody whilst free on bail. Your action can be considered as trying to escape."

"That's not fair!"

Kelly stared at her until she looked away first.

"How did you open the locked window? Witnesses are not meant to be able to open them."

"May I remind you that you aren't meant to be questioning me without my lawyer present?"

If Andy thought that shelved the matter she was wrong. She did not want to answer that question. She had not really thought about what she was doing at the window, any more than she had thought about picking up some loose hairpins of the floor of one of the change rooms at the Macquarie Centre. Collecting odd items that had dual uses was an unconscious habit.

Kelly caught the attention of the guarding officer.

"Have a female officer come in here please, constable."

Andy moved back on her chair and wriggled uncomfortably.

"One of my men did catch a glimpse of a dark haired man, just before the shooting," Kelly commented, watching Andy closely. "I recall that Martin Cappell is described as having short blond hair. What made you think it might have been your brother?"

Kelly was counting on Andy to not think.

"I had a run in with him this morning," Andy said sullenly.

"Really? When was this?"

Andy realised that he can't have had a report on the incident yet.

"I was visiting the Macquarie Centre this morning with Constable Frawley," Andy told him, not meeting his eyes. "She cleared it with Superintendent Lynch."

When Andy looked up, Kelly seemed to be waiting for her to say more. He betrayed nothing of his thoughts.

Andy belatedly realised that she had better shut up, at least until Frost was around.

At that moment the female constable arrived, following the messenger.

"How did you open the lock?" Kelly asked sharply, but Andy remained silent.

Kelly gave the female constable a glance as he pushed himself up from his seat at the table.

"Constable Samnos, I need you to check Miss Cappell's clothing for items that could be used to open locks. Constable Peters, would you let Chief Inspector Hayley know that I wish to see him and have Constable Frawley recalled from wherever she is and have her report to me. I'll be with Superintendent Lynch."

"Empty your pockets please, Miss Cappell," Constable Samnos asked firmly.

Andy stared back at the Constable, but reluctantly produced several paperclips and some scraps of firm plastic from shirt boxes.

"Take the clips from your hair," Andy was further instructed. Five hairpins and two hairclips joined the little pile on the table.

The Constable then frisked Andy, quickly and expertly. She found the stretched out paperclip and pushed wide hairpin that had been at her waist. Still the search continued, with Andy flushing red with embarrassment. She was instructed to remove her shoes, socks and jumper and had to submit to having the seams of all her other clothing items checked. Kelly returned, just as a final piece of wire was removed from the folded up cuff of her jeans.

"Not very original, Miss Cappell," was Kelly's comment. Then to the constable he added, "Take the items to my office and tag them."

Samnos produced a zip top plastic bag from her pocket and transferred all the items to it, then left the room.

"Miss Cappell, there are others waiting to talk to you. Please cooperate fully. Where you will go after here will be decided by your attitude. Do you understand?"

Andy forced out a surly acknowledgement.

Chapter 17

"The PO Box address on the bank statement was followed up. The address for the business was for a vacant block of land, and the business name and number are not officially recorded. The post office staff don't recall very much mail ever going in there. The Melbourne boys will try to find out if Cappell has any other boxes anywhere else."

Hayley paused in his report and checked his notes.

"I spoke to the Altona Council, they have no complaints about his work as County Sheriff and by-laws officer. His boss mentioned he had applied for three months leave of absence to deal with family matters.

"The court permitted us to search his house. There is no sign that it has been occupied since about the time Andy left. A neighbour is removing the local papers and junk mail, but the chap says no letters are delivered there. There are signs inside that Martin's girlfriend had moved in with him. Talking to Merryl Street's girlfriends confirm that they haven't heard from her for a couple of months. Last they heard was she had got engaged.

"The search of the house gave us no clues. There isn't a lot of furniture inside, all of it is old and there is a thick layer of dust everywhere. We found no sign of any covert hiding places. In fact, nothing to suggest that he is not the upright citizen he claims to be. We found no photos of Martin Cappell, his girlfriend or his sister."

"And nothing to confirm Miss Cappell's claims," Commissioner Kelly summarised. "I agree that they seem to hate each other, but we have no proof."

"What about the psychiatrists report?" Hayley suggested.

Kelly brushed that aside. "It still isn't proof."

Hayley didn't disagree.

"Now, about Miss Cappell. Did you suggest this little shopping jaunt this morning?"

"Yes, Sir," Hayley admitted, showing no signs of doubt about his decision.

"Explain your logic to me."

Hayley gave his reasons in concise point form.

"Well, I agree that she presented well and answered the questions well," Kelly conceded. He reached for the plastic bag of oddments.

"However, this is the result of that little reward for good behaviour. All of those items came from Miss Cappell's clothing, a short time ago. I found her half way out the window of the witness room at the courthouse."

Hayley's expression hardened. "Did she give a reason?"

"She claimed to have seen someone on the roof and was trying to get a better look."

"That was probably the truth," Hayley defended Andy. "She gave you enough warning to save Tench."

"The tactical squad didn't need to be warned," Kelly demurred. "She should have mentioned it to the duty guard. And I don't consider that collection of potential lock picking tool as 'acting in good faith'. I see it as she was preparing to run. How do you see it, Hayley?"

"She gave her word to cooperate with us. So far she has done her best."

"I find her best, far from good enough and I don't agree with your assessment of her honesty."

Kelly passed a copy of a report to Hayley.

"From the Albury boys."

When he finished reading it, Hayley let the page fall back onto the table and stared out the window.

The police in Albury, acting on an anonymous tip, had searched the premises of Mrs Haddie, the woman Andy had stayed with. They had found a bag containing most of the non-cash items stolen in the robberies linked to Andy – in a hole beneath a loose tile on the roof of the bungalow. The hole was only accessible to someone on the roof.

"Do you agree with me that your judgement on this case may be compromise?" Hayley was asked.

"Yes, Sir," Hayley had to admit.

"Very good. I am putting Superintendent Lynch on the case. You will take two months leave before returning to Broken Hill. As from now, you are officially off the case. I advise you not to interfere."

"Does that include investigating Martin Cappell?" Hayley asked calmly.

The Commissioner considered his answer.

"I'll permit that. I would like to know more of his involvement with Tench. If Miss Cappell is correct, he might have shot at Tench, so we need to find him. If you chose to spend your leave time, liaising with the police in Melbourne, I'll ratify the appointment. You will report any findings to me and to the Melbourne boys. Anything leading to Tench and his bosses will be passed to the Special squad."

"And anything that supports Miss Cappell's position?"

"Will be passed to Lynch," Kelly agreed.

"Will Miss Cappell be going back to Willowmort?" Hayley asked impassively.

"I'll make that decision after I've had a report on her current interview with the boys from Albury."

Hayley had a fair idea what that decision would be and his expression must have betrayed that.

"It's time we stopped coddling the woman, Chief Inspector. We no longer need her to testify against Tench. She passed up the opportunity to do a deal in exchange for her testimony. Therefore, she will be subject to standard procedures."

"Has the jury presented its verdict yet?" Hayley asked carefully keeping his voice neutral.

"Not yet."

"Shouldn't we continue to maintain protection until the verdict is announced and sentence passed?"

Again Kelly considered his decision.

"Very well, she will remain in protected custody until the verdict is made public, though I have had an unofficial communication that Tench's lawyers have proposed some sort of plea bargain. They seem to think that the verdict will come back guilty and that Tench believes that his bosses are behind the attack today."

"Have you considered what may happen if it was actually Martin Cappell who shot Tench?"

"I will allow for that possibility," Kelly promised.

Hayley had to be satisfied with that, but at the risk of endangering his position, he asked another question.

"Will I be allowed contact with Miss Cappell."

"Only as a private citizen," Kelly warned.

"What about bail?"

Kelly kept his features neutral.

"I won't oppose bail," he agreed.

Hayley nodded.

"Was that all, Sir?"

"You may go."

"Constable Frawley has gone home, Sir," one of the officers at the reception desk told him.

"She came in, gave a report to the Commissioner and left soon after."

"Thank you, Sergeant."

Hayley permitted himself a frown and a sigh. He could imagine what his superior had said to his niece. He could do nothing about Andy, but right now, Kit was more important. He walked to collect his car and then drove to the unit he was renting during his stay in Sydney. He had no doubt that he would find his niece there.

When he entered he saw his prediction was correct. Kit was pacing up and down his lounge area. He greeted her in a carefully neutral voice. He knew her to well to miss the subtle signs that she was upset.

"Her father was a likable old cuss too," Hayley said after he had made two cups of strong coffee and insisted that Kit sit down. "Tell me about it."

"I was given a very succinct lecture on professional objectivity," Frawley admitted. "I was advised that my actions endangered a key witness – he didn't say 'again' but it was obvious that he meant it. Then I was told that as the trial is over except for the verdict and sentencing, Andy no longer needed a chaperone and would be dealt with by the system. I have been ordered to take two weeks leave and report back to duty in Broken Hill. But I do not agree with his assumption that Andy is safe now."

"Nor do I, but I have been taken off the case and told not

to interfere. He considers the idea that Martin Cappell might have been the sniper as unlikely. He prefers to think that because Tench is trying to make a deal with the judge that his bosses wanted him dead."

"But Martin Cappell owed Tench money," Frawley argued.

"Well, I convinced the Commissioner to keep her protected for a while longer and I confirmed that she would be allowed bail. I can help Andy, but only as a private citizen."

"If you help her to get bail, and she runs..." Frawley considered.

"I'll be hearing about it!"

Superintendent Lynch sat in on the interview between the detectives from Albury and Andy Cappell. He was a big man with dark blond hair and grey eyes that sometime looked pale blue. He'd heard of the Cappell girl, but this was the first time he'd seen her, other than in court. She struck him as being a typical over-cocky teenager, so sure of herself, and just as typically stubborn in the face of overwhelming evidence. Even her lawyer couldn't make her see sense. Did she think the police were stupid?

Well, if she wanted to make things difficult for herself, that's how it would be. A night in the cells worked wonders on her type. The crimes she was charged with were hardly petty, but if she cooperated, her sentence would be lighter.

"I didn't do them, you idiot," Lynch heard Andy tell her lawyer in an undertone. "You are meant to believe me."

His reply was inaudible. She wasn't so cocky when she was charged with the fifteen Albury robberies. In fact she looked stunned.

But she still had the nerve to argue. "I'm meant to be going back to Willowmort."

"You are no longer required as a witness, Miss Cappell," Lynch found himself saying to her. "You will spend the night in the holding cells and appear in court in the morning. Is there anyone you wish to contact?"

"No, she snapped.

Andy slunk back into the corner of the cell for the third time. She knew without a doubt, that special orders had come regarding her.

Each time the guards came past the cell, she was ordered to show herself. It wasn't made easier by the fact that she refused to try and sleep on the fold down bed. Doing something that felt like rebellion was keeping her mind off being closed in. Hiding in the corner – gave her a means to cry without comments from the guards.

Some of the younger ones were full of themselves. These weren't police officers, but worked for a security firm associated with the prison warders union. The uniform was slightly different.

Their manner implied that those in the cells deserved to be there and if they didn't like it – too bad. They also knew what everyone was charged with and they referred to her as 'fifteen burglaries'.

This was another reason why she tried to remain inconspicuous. Two cells further down contained one of her brother's mates – the 'Macquarie cop mugger' and further down again was the 'Mafia Banker'; the reason why the security had been doubled. Tench was there, although she'd heard that he was going to be moved.

Andy was still awake when the guard shift changed. Two of the new guards, walked down the passage, this time flashing their torches on each cells occupant. Naturally they aimed it at the bed first, so she had time to curl up and hide her head as if asleep in the corner. This time she wasn't told to get up and show herself.

She peeped when the torch light moved off her. The nearer guard strutted like Martin did when he was feeling superior and particularly clever. He was blond like Martin too.

When Andy started to hear whispered voices close by, she rose very quietly and crept near the bars. The blond guard was talking to the 'Macquarie cop mugger' and he was opening the door.

Andy ran back to her corner and sat down, trying to decide if she wanted to interfere or not.

Not, she decided. If Martin didn't know she was here, her life would be healthier. She huddled and made no sound as the three men walked back along the passage.

Probably fifteen minutes later, (it was hard to keep track of time without her watch), the same two guards walked back. This time they didn't use their torches. This time, the bigger guard was nearest her and there was something familiar about him too. Something glittered in his hand.

Andy felt her body flinch in terror. Every detail fell in to place.

Martin, Clem with a needle, Martin's mate freed, and Tench down further.

They were going for Tench!

She didn't want him to murder Tench. Even if Tench was scum and Martin would be wanted for murder.

She could only think of one option – scream, cause a commotion, get the other guards running – or she would be next after Tench.

More guards came running as she intended; one prisoner was yelling "Someone shut up that bitch!"

The big guard, Clem, met the others outside Andy's cell.

"I'll solve this problem," he promised.

No one stopped him as he unlocked the cell and strode in and dragged Andy to her feet.

Her screams changed in pitch and she struggled. Clem wasn't giving her a chance to use the defensive tactics she had learnt. With demeaning ease he shoved her head in the toilet bowl and flushed.

Andy hadn't been quick enough to hold her breath. Her nose and mouth filled with water.

When Clem let her collapse to the floor, she had no fight left in her. All she could do was cough until she brought up all the water she swallowed.

The crowd of amused guards had moved on when Martin strode back along the passage, looking neither left nor right.

Only a short time later, four policemen walked past Andy's cell and returned with Tench walking between them.

"Hey!" Andy called out. "Hey, wait a minute! Tench! Tench, did Martin jab you? It'll be poison, tell them."

She'd scrambled to the bars to yell at the departing backs. The police ignored her; Tench twisted his head and spat over his shoulder.

A guard that she didn't recognise the face of, spoke to her after the police had gone.

"Keep it down or we'll give you another dowsing."

Andy stared back at him before turning her back on him and walking to the bed. She lay down facing the wall.

Andy woke by being shaken.

"You are out of here," the guard who had warned her before was now telling her. "Bail has been posted for you."

"What?" Andy asked, still dazed from sleep.

"You're free to go. Come and get your stuff."

Andy recalled vaguely that she was to appear in court in the morning.

"Who posted bail?" she asked.

"Bail bondsman said it was organised by a bloke called Hayley."

"Oh!" Andy relaxed. It must be alright. She began to walk faster.

The bondsman was a stranger, but quite professional. He explained the terms of the bail, waited whilst her belongings were returned to her and the paperwork completed. He then told her that he would take her to Hayley.

Andy woke from a doze as the car pulled up at the back of a block of flats.

"We want Unit 3," the man told her. "These lower units are on short term lease.

The man knew exactly where he was going and Andy simply trudged up the steps after him.

Hayley was woken by the loud ringing of the phone. That wasn't unusual, but here he had to get out of bed and walk to the hall to answer it. At home he had an extension by his bed.

"Hayley," he answered.

"Lynch," came the voice on the line. "I'm told you pulled rank and got the Cappell woman out on bail. Do you have her with you?"

"No, I haven't. I expected her to go back to Willowmort. I certainly haven't bailed her. What has happened?"

Hayley listened, not betraying his concern.

"She would know, Sir. Cappell has drugged her before. If you contact my office in Broken Hill – they can find the report on the drugs he gave his sister. The lab can check them against what's in Tench. The counter agent was also in the report."

When Hayley put the phone down, he saw his niece watching him.

"What's happened?"

"They went to move Tench from the holding cells. Andy was also down there. She tried to warn Tench of something but was ignored. Now Tench has collapsed and is in a critical state and Andy is missing. Someone bailed her out, claiming to be acting for me."

"Uncle Chris, why was Andy down there anyway?" Kit asked.

"The Albury detectives found a bag of stolen items in the roof of the bungalow where Andy was living there. The hiding place was only accessible from the roof. She has been charged with fifteen robberies."

"Her brother could have got someone to put the stuff there," Frawley commented. "Or have we been played for fools?"

"I'm withholding judgement," Hayley said softly. "Nothing about Andy is simple and straightforward. She promised me she would cooperate and she has. Though I admit she will keep things to herself at times. I intend to keep at Martin Cappell. I am allowed to do that much."

"What can I do?" Kit asked.

"Keep your eyes and ears open," was all Hayley could offer. "Don't risk your career over Andy. Lynch is a good officer. He may not know Andy as we do but he is fair and thorough."

Frawley was thoughtful.

"I have one idea," she said slowly. "About that false ID Andy used to get her car."

Hayley nodded, and listened as Kit told him of the conversation between Andy and herself over coffee. His eyes took on an intent expression as he heard her suggestion.

"Yes, that is certainly worth checking. You've got two weeks, Julia Cullen is an old friend and she's met Andy. It's a long shot, but worth following up. She might have lost it in Broken Hill, but if she had it in Coopers Crossing, Jack Carruthers would have found it."

"I know where Julia is staying; I'll organise a visit. But I don't like the fact that Andy is missing. If you didn't bail her out, who did?"

Andy woke slowly, and realised that she was lying on a concrete floor. Her clothes were disarranged, with her jumper and skivvy pulled up above her breasts as was her bra. Her jeans were unzipped but not pulled down. She sat up, embarrassed, and fixed up her clothes. That's when she took in the cage like structure she was in.

It was like several others that were full or sporting equipment and stuff for water games.

A door opened nearby and Andy turned around. Martin strutted in, smirking.

"What? Still in there? You must be hoping that Clem will come back and keep you company again. He enjoyed your body last night."

"Clem's a fairy. He didn't do more than feel. Now I know what you see in him!" Andy snapped.

The smirk changed to a scowl. "You won't be so cocky when I have finished with you!" Martin promised.

"You and what army?"

"I've never needed an army to deal with you!"

"Why don't you come in here and prove it?" Andy dared him.

Martin was, no doubt, recalling their encounter at the Macquarie Centre. That and the fact Andy wasn't acting quivering and scared. He controlled his temper.

"You'll keep!" he promised.

"You'll rot!" Andy retorted, and when Martin had gone, she went back to examining her cage.

Martin returned upstairs to the plush office of the health club. It was Sunday and the centre was still closed, but that hadn't bothered him. He had silenced the alarms and entered with ease. His mates were planted throughout the building, waiting.

It was unlikely that anyone would notice his presence, and his guests, when they arrived would not arouse suspicions because they were the club's owners.

The owners would be surprised to see him already there and that would give him the advantage in addition to the very lucrative deal they had offered him.

Martin had begun to think past his current trouble. This deal would give him enough money to pay off Tench's goons. He may not even need to bother finishing Tench off. The spectre of Tench's bosses would be banished. He would be able to expand his operations and his sister would become expendable. He might just have to forget about finding their father's cache of jewels.

Yes, indeed. His sister could be made to have an unfortunate accident in prison. Then her trust account would be his. The police probably froze the account to stop her getting money to escape.

Now Tench was next best thing to dead, the creep would not be able to talk about him. His sister was being hunted by the police – her credibility ought to be non-existent now. Maybe it was time to nudge the police towards the next little time bomb of evidence.

Evidence. Damn! That driver's licence that Andy stole and lost! He'd have to follow that up quickly before the police thought to search that woman's car.

Martin pulled out his mobile phone and dialled. He'd organise Clem to get someone to go out to that place, Murrawindi, Mirrabinidi, whatever it was.

The phone rang without being answered. Martin felt a stirring of alarm. He stood up from behind the desk just as the door opened. A big man in a fawn overcoat entered the room, followed by two younger men in suits. Martin's smile returned in full.

"Welcome Mr..."

"Smith!" the man said curtly.

"Smith," Martin finished. "Please have a seat."

He began to sit back behind the desk.

"You are in my seat, Cappell." Smith stared at Martin.

"Not today!" Martin replied with equal steel.

The two men in suits drew out silenced pistols from under their jackets. Martin stood up again, slowly. His smile was still in place, but it was forced now.

"If you prefer, Smith," he managed to sound genial.

The big man sat down where Martin had been and Martin feigned a relaxed posture in the other chair and stared back into the pale blue eyes.

"To business," Smith said, staring back at Martin.

"By all means," Martin invited. "Please proceed."

"Some preliminary matters need to be clarified," Smith said obliquely.

"Firstly," Martin prompted.

"Firstly – tell me the nature of the deal you had with my accountant, Corrie Tench?"

Martin felt the blood rush from his face. Smith leant forward like a predator.

"You might be aware that your little deal was not sanctioned by me."

"He leant me $150K to tide me over until the sale of one of my assets. I was to repay him $200K. The deal goes through in just over a week. I have been negotiating with his associates about the delivery of the payment."

The lie flowed confidently from his lips.

Smith stared back at Martin.

"Tench told me that he would be repaid over a month ago. Where is the money?"

"Tench brought forward the due date. I had arranged to get a payment to him, but I became incapacitated and he was caught."

"I think you are a liar, Cappell," Smith accused in an even tone. "Tench was double crossing me. Using my money to invest and putting the profits in his own pockets. I caught him at it. He told me about you. So once again, where is the money?"

"I have already explained…"

Smith glanced at one of the suited men and the man left the room.

"Let me make myself clear, Cappell. Any deal you had with Tench or his associates are now void. You will now deal with me. If you do not have the cash, tell me where it is tied up."

Martin licked his lips; a nervous gesture that Smith didn't miss.

"I gained possession of a building. Its owner owed me a lot of money. The building was valued at well over the $150K I paid him for it. I had the papers assigned to me and found a buyer."

Martin did not mention that the building had mysteriously burnt down the very day the papers were signed and it was the previous owner who had walked away with the insurance money – leaving him with a gutted ruin.

Smith considered what he had been told.

"I will return to that matter later," Smith said neutrally. "Second point."

"Why did you try to kill Tench? Was it because you have been telling me lies and have no way to pay back the money?"

"No, of course not! Tench was threatening me with spilling details of my operation to the police," Martin lied, trying to plant an idea in Smith's mind.

Smith again seemed to consider the matter.

"Surely he told you he was double crossing me. Did you think you were immune to double crossing yourself? What had you offered him to ensure his loyalty to you?"

"You are quite mistaken, Smith. I dealt with Tench in good faith. He loaned me money. I had a set time to pay him back in with interest. He changed the conditions, not me."

"I see," Smith said thoughtfully. He nodded to the other suited man, who also left the room.

Martin breathed easier, but only for a moment.

One of the two underlings returned. Martin swung his chair around. The man was no longer perfectly presented. The left sleeve of his jacket was torn half off and his hair was mussed. He was trying to slick it back into place.

"The building is secure, Sir," the man announced. "There are five men waiting in the equipment locker and we have a woman who was caught half way out the back door."

Martin realised that he was in a perilous position. He had underestimated the people he was dealing with. At least his men were okay and had put up a good fight and Andy, his insurance policy had not escaped. He squashed any idea of how close that had been. His men should have been watching her."

"Bring the woman in."

Andy was forced to walk into the room. A man, almost as big as Smith, had her in a firm grip. He had an assault rifle over one shoulder.

Andy maintained a defiant look, until she took in the scene in the room. As Martin was clearly in a subordinate position, she began calculating her chances afresh.

"Why don't you introduce me to your friend, Cappell," Smith said genially, rising from his chair and coming to have a closer look at Andy.

It was Martin's turn to consider his answer. "This is my sister, Andy."

"Andy." Smith studied her with a smile. She was eyeing him, trying to figure out who he reminded her of. She wasn't smiling. She had seen looks like he was giving her, on Martin's face. Instinctively, she knew that this big man was an even bigger predator than Martin. Her best defence would be silence until she had an idea of what she had been dragged into.

"What value do you place on your sister, Cappell?"

Smith sat down. His tone was so business like, she might have been a piece of negotiable property.

Andy saw Martin's calculating look.

"About $250K," Martin said calmly, thinking of all the money in her bank accounts.

"If you are thinking of killing me for my money, Martin," Andy found herself saying, "You might like to consider the fact that if I die, it all goes to three select charities that help deal with homeless and abused children."

Smith grinned broadly at the fleeting look of anger on Martin Cappell's face.

"No, actually I was considering the $500K I will get if you have an unfortunate accident."

Martin deliberately made eye contact with his sister. Andy smirked, she'd just learnt something she hadn't known.

"I think we have a basis for negotiations."

Smith turned his full attention to Martin and ignored Andy.

"Do you play squash?" Smith asked unexpectedly.

"Yes," Martin confirmed.

"Let's adjourn to the squash court," Smith suggested, indicating that Martin should lead the way.

Andy was forced to follow after Smith and she wasn't surprised to see two more 'muscle types' fall in behind Martin. She'd seen them outside the door when she had gone in.

The torn-suit man glared at Andy as she went past him. He followed behind with his neat 'twin'.

Smith spoke softly in Andy's ear.

"This is men's business, my dear, not suited to a lady's delicate sensibilities. I must ask you to keep your eyes facing the wall. This is your only warning."

He removed his coat and folded it over a chair that was out of place on the court. Andy shivered. She was pushed onto the chair, straddling it so she faced the wall. When the sounds of fists hitting flesh began, she hugged the back of the chair and tried not to hear.

She didn't take Smith's words for anything but a warning. If she looked, she'd share her brother's punishment. If she wasn't so scared, she'd be enjoying her brother being hurt.

Finally the sound's stopped. Was that her brother whimpering like a baby? She still dared not move.

"Now you know, we mean business," Smith said, he wasn't even breathless.

"If you want your sister delivered back to you, you will finish the job you started, killing Tench."

"I'd've finshed it if my bish sister didn't scream." Martin said awkwardly.

"Trust a weak effeminate... like you, to blame a woman for his failure."

"You have one month from today, to pay me $500K" Smith said implacably. "Or today will seem like a gentle massage."

"What if I can't raise that mush? Cam I do a deal with you?"

"What kind of deal?"

'You can be named beneficiary for the insurance policy, if Andy is dead."

"Messy," Smith stated. "More."

"I'll sign over all my businesses to you," Martin promised. It was his last offer.

"Deal," Smith agreed. He indicated for neat suit and torn suit to come over.

"Take Mr Cappell upstairs and make a list of his business assets," Smith indicated. "Then draw up a contract for him to sign. Have my lawyers check the details. If anything goes wrong, I'll keep his sister."

Andy was pulled to her feet and allowed to turn around.

"Let this be a warning to you, my dear," Smith said gently, cupping Andy's face then dropping his hand.

"You've got to help me, Sis," Martin pleaded. His face was already bruising and he had blood dripping from a cut lip onto his torn shirt.

"Why?" Andy shot the words at him.

"He'll kill me, ruin me." Martin's voice was shrill.

"Suffer, Bro," Andy said ruthlessly. "Now you know how I feel."

"You help me and I will get you off all the charges," Martin said with a trace of calculation.

"You've been telling me for years how stupid I am," Andy said coldly. "But you are wrong! As I told you before, I'll take my chances with the police."

"I'll have you when I've killed Tench!" Martin threatened, sounding more like himself.

Andy shrugged and turned her back on him.

When the footsteps of Martin and his two escorts had moved away, Smith recovered his coat and put out his arm to Andy.

"Come, my dear," Smith took her arm, but she tried to pull away.

"What are you going to do with me?" Andy demanded, inwardly quivering.

"Why, my dear, you will be my guest for a few days," Smith said pleasantly.

Smith ignored Andy's sceptical look, but as she couldn't twist free, she allowed Smith to lead her out the back door to a waiting limousine. He helped her into the back seat.

Andy scuttled across the wide seat and tried to open the far door. Smith settled himself, apparently unaware of her attempt to escape. Soon after the door had been closed by the driver, the car accelerated almost soundlessly from the Health Club.

Andy saw the windows darken and her view of the outside vanishing. The air in the car seemed to become hot and stuffy and she began to find it hard to breathe.

Smith gently forced a glass into her hand. He didn't seem worried by her symptoms.

"Have a little brandy, my dear, it will help you relax."

Andy heard him as if from a long way off. She held the glass but made no attempt to drink until she felt the glass touch her lips. She drank then without conscious thought; without tasting the tartness. A short time later she dropped obliviously into sleep.

Chapter 18

Andy awoke in a bed so soft that she felt she was floating. Aware of the strangeness of her surroundings, she sat up suddenly – only to realise that she was completely naked under the sheets. She snatched at the sheet to hide herself, just as the door to the room opened and a woman dressed as a maid, came in.

The woman had a pile of neatly pressed and folded clothes in her arms.

"The master instructed us to wash your clothes, Mam. He also wishes you to know that you are welcome to wear anything from the closet, if you prefer."

Andy merely nodded.

"Do you need help dressing, Mam?"

"No," Andy answered.

"When you are ready to go down to dinner, Mam, just ring the bell for me."

"Alright!"

Andy hoped the woman would hurry up and leave so she could get dressed.

The first thing she did after getting dressed was to examine the room thoroughly. Then she tried opening the window, but there wasn't any way to do it, short of breaking the window.

Andy felt a faint breeze and found the air-conditioning vent, but that was too small to get into. Finally she tried the door, and to her amazement, it opened and there were no guards outside.

She went out and ran along the passage, peeping in all the extra bedrooms as she did. Then she crept silently down the stairs, deducing correctly that the servant area was to her right. She had never even seen a house like this before and before she could find a back entrance, the maid found her.

"The dining room is through to your left, Mam," she directed without rebuke. "The master is waiting for you."

So was a tantalising smell. Andy's stomach rumbled and she decided to eat before prospecting further. She might find out what Smith was about.

The delicious meal and the conversation that contained no personal references, was still an ordeal. Andy had no delusions that she was still in a prison, even though it was a very luxurious one. She didn't plan to be seduced by it – if that was Smith's intention. She wasn't used to luxury and this was not a lifestyle she aspired to. And she still didn't know what Smith, the big predator, intended to use her for.

He watched her all the time, whenever she had glanced in his direction; those pale blue eyes were on her. The apparent lack of guards about him was probably an illusion too. The man was either high up in, or in charge of an organised crime ring – had to be if Tench was his accountant. He would not be a fool and he would be sure he was well protected.

Andy wondered how far she would be allowed to get if she tried to leave. That thought was quickly followed by the question of what he would do to her if she tried. He had warned her, by letting her be aware of what he did to Martin. It was a hundred times worse than what Martin had ever done to her.

At the end of the meal, Smith again took her arm, this time to lead her through to a small room lined with low bookshelves and expensive paintings. There were two chairs set at an angle but very close together, and facing a painted fire guard.

Smith sat Andy in the left hand one and when he sat in the other, his right hand still rested on Andy's arm.

"Time for business," Smith said, his smile had gone and his hand gripped her wrist loosely.

"First, some preliminaries," Smith went on, and he would have felt Andy tremble.

"I know who you are! You are the one who tricked my associate. Why did you do that?" the voice was carefully neutral.

Andy didn't answer for a moment and she felt the grip on her arm slowly increasing.

"He was a scumbag who Martin owed money to. He'd shot the cop, so I knew he was dangerous. I did what I did to get him off Martin's case, so Martin would get off mine. I didn't know who he was and I didn't care."

Smith nodded, considering the information.

"Why didn't you run away when you had the chance? Take the cop's car. Why did you help your brother?"

"My brother was convinced that there was money at that old silo," Andy smirked. "I stayed, even after I met Tench, because I wanted to climb up the silo and find the money. Martin was trapped half way up, he couldn't stop me. And I wanted to gloat!"

"Did you find the money?"

"I found a case," Andy chuckled. "I told Tench he could have what Martin owed him and I would have the rest to escape with. I wasn't going to let Martin have any of it."

"What happened to that money?"

Andy chuckled harder. "It was all mouse shit and confetti!" She saw a faint amused smile on Smith's face.

"Do you know why you are still alive now," Smith suddenly changed the subject.

Andy shook her head, suddenly sober. "Because you couldn't find me?"

"Not at all, my dear," Smith smiled. "I had you marked for attention; because you helped the police catch Tench. It was when I checked closely and discovered his double dealing that I had you put on hold."

Andy shivered, she was following the polite euphemisms and her mind was translating their true meaning.

"Then you wilfully interfered with your brother's attempt to kill Tench. I don't like interference."

Smith paused to let his meaning sink in.

"Why did you interfere?"

"I don't agree with murder. I didn't want Martin to kill him," Andy muttered.

"Such filial concern."

"Bull! I just didn't want him to succeed. Why didn't you kill me and be done with it?"

"Let us say, you currently have more value to me alive. Your brother wants you back, so my having you is incentive for him to do what I ask. And I have made a deal with him. If I simply killed you now, that would make things too easy for him. I don't do favours for f..."

At first Andy was shocked by the crude description of her brother's supposed sexual preferences. She couldn't help blushing.

"You know he can't pay you $500K," Andy accused Smith. "If you give me to him, I'll be dead in a week."

"That's business, my dear. Profit is the bottom line."

Smith let her consider his words before adding, "Unless of course you can propose a more lucrative offer?"

Andy was only thinking in terms of money, which she couldn't hope to get.

"Probably not," she told him, slumping back in her chair. It wasn't pleasant contemplating being murdered.

"You are a woman ..." Smith began rubbing his hand suggestively on Andy's arm.

Andy shuddered, guessing exactly what he meant.

"...of many talents," he went on, sensing her reactions. "What would you do if the only way to save your life was to help save your brother's life?"

"Nothing!" Andy answered instantly. She felt Smith's hand tense for a moment. Her answer had surprised him.

"Not a profitable option," Smith summarised.

Andy shrugged.

"So, you feel you have nothing to lose," Smith surprised Andy by saying. "If I could give you something of value to you, would you consider doing something of value for me?"

Andy looked around at the expensive pictures and tried to think of anything she would really want.

"What use is any of this to me? I have no use for valuable things, nor is that profit for you."

"Let me decide that. What would you want? Even if you think that it is impossible?"

Andy knew what she wanted right now, to be a very long way away from this man, his men and his house. Definitely impossible.

She wondered if it would hurt to tell this man more about herself. He already seemed to know too much.

What the heck...

"I want my brother jailed for all the crimes he committed and ensured that I have been accused of, and I want to be proved innocent. Then I want to be able to live my own life without his interference."

"What if I arranged your brother's death?" Smith was quite serious.

"No!" Andy pulled her arm free in revulsion.

"That wouldn't clear my name. That would be too easy for him. I want him ruined, yes, and I want him to suffer in prison."

Smith nodded thoughtfully, and calmly returned Andy's arm to the armrest where he again rested his hand on it. "Tell me about these crimes. Why do the police think it was you and what do you think is the truth?"

Andy told him what she could.

"What about alarms?" Smith asked.

"I don't know the first thing about them. The police have never believed me when I told them that."

Andy had the feeling that Smith had a definite goal in mind.

"At the moment, you belong to me," Smith stated baldly. "Which means, you don't go anywhere without my permission. If you try, you won't succeed and I will punish you. I don't make idle threats.

"You had better hope that your brother continues to fail. If he finishes the job he started, before Tench talks, I will give him his reward – you."

"If he doesn't..." Andy interrupted.

"You will have a chance to ransom yourself. You do a job for me tomorrow – successfully, and if your brother succeeds, I will let you go with a chance to evade him. If your brother fails in that time to finish Tench – I will provide protection for you for the following three weeks. By that time, your brother will have paid me or I will have everything of his businesses."

"And what if I fail..."

Andy was trying to pretend that she was discussing someone else.

"You will be out on your own."

"If I don't fail – what happens after the three weeks?"

"That will depend whether we can come to an agreement that pleases me, personally."

"Like what?"

"You will let me make what might be your last week of life enjoyable," Smith said blandly. "If you please me, and I haven't returned you to your brother, I will make sure his whereabouts are made known to the police. I understand that he has been charged with assaulting you."

"Yes," Andy agreed, seeing possibilities. "He'll be in custody. He won't be able to pay you. You'll have all his businesses..."

"He will be ruined. However, if you have pleased me for those three weeks, I will ensure that enough evidence remains after I take over his operations to put him in jail for a long time."

"Maybe that will put enough doubt in the right minds as to my guilt," Andy hoped.

"Are you willing to deal?"

"Can I think about it over night?"

"You have ten minutes."

Chapter 19

Kit Frawley left for Broken Hill after a hectic morning of shopping with her school friend, Julia Cullen. They had tried to catch up on ten years of gossip, and this had helped Kit push aside the worry about where Andy Cappell had gone. By the time they had parted company, Kit had successfully wrangled an invitation to visit Murrawindi, though without mentioning the real reason for wanting to.

There were still a few days before the Cullen's were due to return home and Kit planned to drive from Broken Hill to Coopers Crossing and speak to Jack Carruthers.

Before she left Broken Hill, she checked all the places that Andy said she had been, but no driver licences had been handed in at any of them. Finally she had called in at the police station and told the desk sergeant that she would be back at work in a week and a half.

Frank Dayton spotted her as he was going off duty and invited her for coffee.

They sat at a table inside the café – it hadn't started to get busy yet.

"So you've finished babysitting the Cappell girl then," Dayton remarked. "Did you hear they found a piece of jewellery in her car – from the heist here?"

"Yes, but it's odd. Jack Carruthers at Coopers searched the car thoroughly soon after she first arrived. He found nothing in it and he also searched her bags. So when did it get there?"

Frank shrugged.

"One piece, out of a dozen, with blond hairs attached, or so uncle said. Andy is dark haired. If she took it, it wasn't to wear. The brother is the blond one and his girlfriend."

"Well, it's up to the judge now."

"True," Kit agreed. "Anyway, I'm to keep away from the case."

"What are you planning for your time off?"

"My enforced break," Kit said wryly. "I'm visiting with an old school friend I met up with in Sydney."

The two police officers finished their coffee and went on their way.

There had been a little rain in the past two weeks, so the dry dusty red country was wearing a gauzy layer of green. It made beautiful country, truly spectacular.

The wreck she passed, which was 100m off the road, was the only blot on the scenery. The noise of her car scared off a small gathering of crows that must have been after a rabbit or something that had crawled into the wreck to die.

Kit Frawley continued driving to Cooper's Crossing and pulled up outside the police station. She was pleased to see the sergeant's car parked out front – it meant he was there.

Kit Frawley sat back in the chair in Jack Carruther's inner office and thought about what she had read. Most of the details she had known already but the report of Andy's talk with Jack after returning to the crossing with her car was new to her. Jack also had a copy of his report of his search of Andy's car and her pack. It was detailed; if that licence had been there it would have been found. If the jewellery had been there it would have been found. Jack had even got the mechanic, someone called Emma Patterson to look at it – and check for hiding places on the chassis. It seemed unlikely that the licence had been in there and stolen.

Jack returned and perched on the corner of his desk.

"Any new ideas?"

"No," Kit said glumly. "Did you ever identify that guy seen going into the pub?"

"No, without a photo of Martin Cappell, we could only go on the description and that could have fit a lot of people."

Kit scowled. "That is frustrating. Anyway, I'll be visiting the Cullen's in a couple of days. I'll ask about checking in their car. Actually, speaking of cars – how long has that burnt out wreck been out off the road?"

Jack looked thoughtful. "It probably turned up a week or two before Andy came through, only it wasn't burnt out or stripped then. It was reported stripped some days later and torched sometime after you went back to Broken Hill. Why?"

"I saw the wreck as I drove in. It had a lot of crows around it. I notice Andy didn't mention seeing it, but she may not have thought it important. However, when I met Julia Cullen in Sydney, Andy was with me and Julia remembered seeing two cars parked about half a mile back from where they picked up Andy. I wondered if one was the dumped car and the other Martin Cappell's. But Julia also said they both looked empty."

Jack thought for a while and then dialled a number. He might have been psychic; because he asked the person he spoke to if Luke Mitchell was around. Kit wanted to talk to that man too.

"Luke will come shortly. I'll get a tracker to come too. I think we need to look at that car. Isn't Cappell's fiancée missing?"

Kit nodded, as she assembled several pieces of information. If the second car, mentioned by Julia, had been Martin Cappell's he could have put a body in the wreck. His car had contained traces of blood. She would have to see if Julia remembered the type of car the other had been. It didn't mean that Andy hadn't stopped there too, after all the piece of jewellery had been found in her car.

An hour later, Kit drove her car after Jack Carruthers, who had Luke Mitchell and an aboriginal tracker called Dougie in the police four wheel drive.

Dougie had met Andy and volunteered that she was a 'good kid'. Luke knew exactly where Andy's car had been and they went there first.

Dougie looked around, and found nothing of value, but still claimed to see the hoof marks from Luke's horses.

Leaving that site, Jack drove to the position of the wreck and again Dougie looked around. Their arrival had scared off the half dozen crows, who now squawked from up in the air, before settling to the ground some distance away. At this spot there were no trees.

Dougie reported that at least four different vehicles had stopped near the car. He also said there was something bad about it. He was watching the crows as he said it.

As the group drew closer, they saw that it wasn't only the crows that were interested in the wreck. Ants and flies were also around in large numbers.

Jack examined the lock on the car's boot – the only section of the car that wasn't stripped. It was fused into a blob of metal, and in his opinion, not by the fire that had gutted the wreck. The line around the boot cover was jammed with burnt stuff of some kind. Fortunately, the fuel tank had not exploded.

"I don't like the look of this," Kit admitted aloud.

Jack nodded his agreement. He went to the back door of the wreck and wrenched it open. He stuck his head in and tried to see into the boot. The seats had been removed and there were holes in the chassis, but he could see nothing. There was also a foul smell, faint but putrid.

The noise of buzzing flies indicated that the creatures had found a way into the boot.

Jack made a decision. He strode back to the car and called the flying doctor base and they put through a radio telephone call to Broken Hill.

"I've requested a homicide team. Do you want to wait around?"

"How long?"

"Within two hours, they'll fly in."

"I'll wait in town and drive them back here," Kit volunteered. Jack nodded approval.

"Luke, do you or Dougie want a lift back?"

Both men declined.

Kit stayed back, leaning on her car. Luke Mitchell and Dougie squatted on their heels nearby. Acting Inspector Kline, who was filling in for her Uncle, had flown in with a team of four officers, including her friend Frank Dayton.

They were still trying to open the trunk. Dayton had taken preliminary photographs and was waiting for the boot to be opened.

Finally, they freed the trunk lid and lifted it. A swarm of flies and a powerfully fetid smell emerged from the compartment. Kit covered her nose, it was bad enough where she was, how much worse would it be for her colleagues? Frank took more photographs, somehow managing to deal with the smell and what they had found without retching.

"Good call, Frawley," Kline commended after the decomposing body had been transferred to a body bag and was in an ambulance en route to Broken Hill and a tow truck had come to tow the wreck there.

Kit nodded, glad of the compliment and that she had not been involved in the delicate task of moving the body.

"How long do you think it will take to ID the body?" Frawley asked.

"Hard to say, I'm going to suggest they check it against Cappell's girlfriend like Carruthers suggested. You might as well be on your way, Frawley, since you are on leave."

"Thank you, Sir."

Chapter 20

It was a roundabout way to get into the house, but Smith knew the type of alarms that Tench had in this secret office of his. Andy saw a weakness at once and asked if the man hole had an alarm. No, was the answer, but it had a steel plate and was bolted into a steel frame.

"What if we just put a hole into the ceiling of the room we want" Andy persisted. "No doors or windows to enter by."

"There is still an alarm sensor in that room, a monitored alarm."

"Don't you know what the code is? He was your accountant."

"I can't be sure that it hasn't been changed," Smith cautioned her.

"Well, didn't you say you had an alarm specialist to go with me?" Andy reminded her present minder. Smith smiled faintly and pressed a buzzer.

One of the two suited junior executive types entered the room. Andy thought she understood the smile. She too tried to picture the man climbing onto the roof in a suit.

Smith questioned his assistant who did seem to know about alarms. Andy didn't mind Smith suggesting entering via the roof. Was it her imagination or did the man turn paler?

"Many of those systems do have a component in the roof," the assistant agreed. "How would we get into it? The office is on the top floor, three stories up."

"There would be a fire escape, and after that, Andy will climb onto the roof and make an entry for you."

Andy tried to look unenthusiastic. The man staring at her was the man she'd tossed when trying to escape from the health club.

"I think it can work. How do we get through the ceiling? The steel cross beams have too little space between them for me to get through?"

"I should be able to squeeze through," Andy suggested meekly. "I can make a hole, drop down and unbolt the manhole for you."

The plan was agreed upon and Andy waited with Smith while his assistant, Call him Jack, returned dressed more appropriately. She had Smith's quietly stressed warning running through her mind, "Don't run off." He hadn't had to add, "or else."

Andy really didn't want to do this, but there was a benefit to her that was hard to ignore. In spite of Smith's words the day before, she had no way to be sure he'd keep them. Plus, she could sense, Call him Jack's animosity.

The other assistant drove them to a quiet street near to their destination. Andy had no idea where they were because they had blindfolded her before they left the house.

Acting like they had every right to be where they were, they walked to the block of flats where Tench had his office. It was in the middle of the day so few people would be around.

Andy slipped up the fire escape as if she had no care in the world, and hardly made a sound.

Call him Jack, to his credit, was just as quiet. He was watching her and keeping an eye on the ground below.

Andy didn't wait for him to give the go ahead, she climbed onto the roof, removed a few tiles and was inside the dusty roof space in a matter of moments. Her minder followed soon after, finally putting his gym work to use.

He crawled around and used his small flashlight to locate the backup battery for the alarm and the cable that led downstairs to a power point. Moments later, the alarm was disconnected and he was making a hole in the roof.

"We don't have much time. The alarm company will send out a man to check it," Andy was warned. She nodded and allowed herself to drop through the hole. She had already located the man hole from above and so had no trouble finding it on the rooms below. She was glad the alarm was indeed off. The bolts had no lock and she used a chair to stand on to pull them across.

"You open the safe, take everything out, put it in the case and relock the safe."

As Andy worked, making use of the gloves that Smith had provided, she was aware that her accomplice was purposefully attacking Tench's computer.

Her job was simple, the safe opened easily and she began removing folders of documents from it. Under them were two bundles of discs held together by rubber bands. She glanced at them and decided they were back up discs, in duplicate.

She hid her actions from Call him Jack as she put the discs in the case. The second bundle was put under the chair beside her and pushed to the centre. It had valances to hide legs and the discs wouldn't be seen. She then moved further from the chair as she finished placing the last items in a satchel and relocking the safe.

Call him Jack finished about the same time; he placed two parts of the computer in his case along with all the discs he could find.

"Let's go," he instructed after glancing around. "By the door."

Once in the passage, Andy removed her gloves and pocketed them, whist keeping up with Call him Jack. They saw no one as they proceeded down stairs, walking confidently. They did see a woman working in a small garden plot, outside, but they ignored her.

Back inside the car, Andy was ordered to hand over her stuff and she was in no way reluctant to comply. Before they moved, the blindfold went back on, which blocked other distractions and gave her too much time to analyse how she felt.

She was glad it was over, but at the same time, Andy had to admit she was on a high. Was this how her father had felt when he broke into houses? Was this why he continued to do so, even after being caught and jailed – to feel this elation?

Then she sobered very quickly. Martin might succeed yet and she would be given to him. And even if the contents of Tench's safe and computer memory was worth more than half a million dollars to Smith – he'd hand her over to Martin without regret, even if he had enjoyed last night as much as she had.

Even the memory made her blush. Smith had been gentle but persistent, and had so thoroughly roused her body that her mind wanted him to continue. She had been relieved though, to wake up alone.

Chief Inspector Chris Hayley put the phone down thoughtfully. His niece had just finished telling him of the body in the burnt car that might be that of Merryl Street.

It was late, but he decided to go out again, back to the flat that Merryl had shared with another girl until moving in with Martin.

He had already tried to find a way of obtaining any hairs that might belong to Merryl at the friend's flat. Now he thought he should ask about the girl's dentist and doctor. It would be useful for trying to identify the body.

The former flat mate, Justine, was dressed to go out when Hayley returned and not at all pleased to see him again. She returned, very resentfully, back into the lounge room.

Hayley asked about Merryl's doctor and dentist, but the girl was quick to guess the reason for the request.

"You think she's dead! Did you know about it when you were here before?"

"No, I only just had the report. We're not even sure it is her."

Justine's annoyance became shock. Then in a burst of emotion she said, "Look, when you were here before, I didn't want to get Merryl in trouble. I packed her stuff up in a box so I could rent out her room. You can look at it. She didn't want it anymore. It was all cheap stuff and she said the boss'd give her better stuff. I really don't know what she saw in him. A couple of the girls reckon he's gay. I didn't think he acted it."

"The boss? That would be Martin ..."

"Yeah, Martin Caldwell" the girl interrupted. "Look, I've got to get to work or I'll be in trouble. If she had a doctor or dentist it would be in her phone book – it's got a green cover."

Justine opened a cupboard and dragged out a box.

"Can you make sure the door's locked when you leave?"

Hayley assured her that he would and began to carefully remove bagged under clothes, no dresses he noticed, deciding that Justine was probably using those.

At the bottom was a plastic brush and comb set, from which Hayley removed several long blonde hairs, which he wrapped in a sheet of paper from his note book. He recorded the names of the three perfumes he found, as well as the talc and the lipstick. Finally he came across the address book and more interestingly a diary.

He glanced through the diary, it was more a record of income and expenses and cryptic appointment messages. The last entry was simple – moving in with Martin.

He copied down the names and numbers in the address book then repacked the box and carefully returned it to the cupboard before leaving and locking the door.

Hayley reported to Superintendent Gladstone, and arranged to have the hairs flown to the Sydney Police lab. He mentioned the numbers he had copied and was given permission to contact the local record division to run the name of Martin Caldwell through the computer.

Chapter 21

Andy got no further than two steps outside the door before being challenged by a tall, solid man with an automatic rifle slung over his shoulder. Ranging beside him were two large Alsatian dogs that were watching her as unwaveringly as the man.

"Proceed no further," was the man's warning to her.

The dogs began to growl softly as if to emphasise his command. Andy froze, not sure if she should turn around.

"Return inside."

The urge that had caused Andy to go outside was now replaced by an equally imperative urge to go back inside. She backed the two steps before turning around.

At first she didn't realise that the man was following her. When he caught hold of her arm, she jumped, and as he caused her to walk further into the house, she grew alarmed.

In the past hour, Andy had looked in every room in the house and found no one; not Smith, not his junior executives nor the servants.

Smith's office was unlocked and she had shamelessly searched the desk drawers – all were empty. She had tried the phone; there wasn't even a dial tone. The pictures and books were still there. In the kitchen, the cupboards and refrigerator were all empty.

The guard walked her back to her room.

"You are to remain here for another hour," he said in a flat tone. "Then you may leave. You may take whatever you want from this room."

"But I thought Smith..." Andy began to protest but stopped herself. The man was probably only hired muscle.

The man ignored her anyway by walking out the door and shutting it.

"Damn! Smith said I could stay here another week! And I don't know if Martin is in custody or not. I wish I knew what was going on," Andy said aloud.

Andy had no illusions that her affaire with Smith was anything more than an opportune fancy for him. No doubt something more lucrative had required his attention.

If it came to that, she had no regrets about his departure. As much as she had enjoyed his attention, she was glad he had gone. As for taking what she wanted from here – there wasn't much she was interested in.

The wardrobe was full of exquisite gowns that she had no use for, most were too long for her anyhow. There were a few more casual type clothes that might be useful.

Pushed into the back of the wardrobe was a kind of duffle bag. Andy pulled it out, curious as to its contents. In fact, it was empty but behind it was a small black handbag with a shoulder strap.

The hand bag was full of 'woman's stuff'. Andy ignored the makeup, keys, tissues, pens and the little note book but took out the purse. In there were credit cards, drivers licence and other plastic cards and about two hundred dollars in notes and coins.

Her fingers itched to take the money. She needed money.

The photograph on the driver's licence caught her eye. The face was vaguely familiar and her mind was suggesting that the woman was someone she had seen in a newspaper picture. It must have been a month ago, before the final day of Tench's trial. Before her brother had sprung her from jail, before Smith.

Andy sat down on the bed with a thump.

For three weeks, or at least the last two, she had given no thought to that incident. She still didn't know if she was officially bailed or not. Either way, she had missed another court appearance.

"Oh damn!"

She didn't need to be involved in any more trouble. Her conscience told her to give the handbag to the police – to give herself in to them. Not knowing what was happening with Martin frightened her. Could she trust Smith to be doing as he planned? Had he got Martin picked up?

Before she went near the police, she needed to catch up on the news of the last three weeks. A library would be the best place for that.

The hour was nearly up – perhaps she should stay here tonight and leave in the morning?

Perhaps be damned – she wanted out, now!

Andy rummaged for clothes she could use and pushed them into the duffle bag on top of the handbag.

Why did she have to wait anyway? Had Smith needed more time to get away? But the house had been deserted. Everything indicated that everyone was long gone. How long had it taken for him to remove everything? She couldn't have dozed for more than an hour or two. Or had she? Maybe Smith had doped her drink at dinner.

Andy walked out of the house, and saw no one. She followed the driveway to the gate and went out into the street. It was very dark and over cast so she couldn't see her surroundings very well. She had to assume she was leaving the estate of someone well off. The house had been huge and set well back off the street.

The gates at the entrance were metal and had no fancy work on them. The brick pillars had no name plate or street number. The street light just down from the gate only showed the pale coloured fence receding down the street.

Andy had no idea which way she needed to go to reach a shopping precinct, but at this time of the night little would be open anyway. All she could do was walk and pretend she had somewhere to go and if she were lucky she would find somewhere sheltered to spend the rest of the night.

The obviously affluent neighbourhood was very quiet. The street was more of a boulevard; it weaved around and seemed more like deserted parkland at this time of night. When Andy came to a patch of open parkland, she turned into it and hoped to find the sheltered place she sought.

There were little oases of light in the darkness – mainly around barbecue areas – and the rest was dark. Andy skirted the shadows around the lights until she saw, vaguely, a tree she could climb and wasted no time settling into it.

Andy woke to the damp chill of a foggy morning. She could hear from some distance away, the rumble of heavy traffic and the swish of cars. Her guess was that the freeway was close by – but which freeway was it? More importantly, where could she get some food in her grumbling belly?

There was nothing for it but to keep walking and try to find out where she was.

Eventually she came to a street used by buses and at one stop she ventured to ask a girl about her age, how to get to the shops.

The girl was happy to help her. The shops were, not too far away, further along the street. Andy's conscience was losing way to hunger. It was now telling her to use a small amount of the money in the hand bag to buy herself some food and a hot drink.

As she walked purposefully towards the shops, Andy saw a police car cruise past and it gave her a fright. The car didn't slow or stop and eventually her breathing returned to normal.

The shops finally came into sight and Andy was relieved to see it was a large centre and it already seemed to be busy. It gave her confidence to be in the middle of a crowd as she sought something to eat.

There were tables and chairs near the bakery shop and after buying a sweet bun, she went to another shop and bought a hot chocolate. The seats were welcome, and Andy carefully placed her purchases on the table before dropping her pack to the floor.

The bun was delicious, and it took a lot of willpower to eat it at a civilised speed. She had to linger over the still hot drink and that gave her time to look around and focus on the newspaper headlines in a nearby newsagency.

Not unexpectedly, they referred to things she knew nothing of. A man at an adjacent table rolled up the paper he was reading and returned it to the drink stall. Andy took the opportunity to go over to the stall again and ask to be allowed to borrow it. She received it without comment and settled bag on her chair to scan the headlines.

On page five she saw the headline 'Escapees caught'.

She read that two of the escapees from a Sydney remand centre had been recaptured but the third man, Martin Cappell was still at large. While it answered one question, it raised others. The article did not mention what he was charged with, but perhaps it meant that Smith had kept his word. Andy also wanted to know if Tench was still alive or not.

When her legs had recovered from her early morning walk, Andy stood up, collected her bag from the floor and returned the newspaper. She strolled to where she had noticed an information booth and picked up a guide to the shopping centre. That proved to be very useful as she caught the word 'library' and used the map to find the place which had just opened.

No one disturbed Andy as she systematically read through back issues of the Sydney Morning Herald, starting from the day Tench's trail finished and working forward.

The day after the trial, the details of the attempt on Tench's life and the disappearance of the state's witness were the main stories. They weren't calling it an escape, Andy saw with relief, but the public were asked to look out for her. That made her feel shaky, but hopefully, most people would have forgotten her face by now. She quickly closed that paper and opened the next.

The next useful article was three days later. The headline was ambiguous.

"Tench provides police with information."

It seemed that even though Tench's condition was listed as critical, he had been able to give the police information about his bosses. Andy grinned, considering how that would have affected Martin. Two days later, another attempt had been made to kill Tench.

Finally, eight days after the end of the trial, the papers reported Tench's death. There was no further mention of foul play. The following day, Martin made the front page, when he was arrested for the attempts on Tench's life, attempted murder of two police officers and other assault charges.

Andy grinned fiercely as she read and reread the details. Police acting on a tip off from a member of the public had moved in on a unit in Epping and arrested him. He was going to appear in a special out of sessions court. A short postscript revealed that he would be held in remand with bail refused.

A librarian passing by Andy saw the grin, idly glanced at the article on the page and wondered at her reaction. The woman walked back to the reading area and looked a picture in that day's paper then glanced back at the girl.

Andy was oblivious to the conference that took place at the main desk between the four librarians and the glances that were directed at her.

Andy looked up from the latest paper and saw two men at the desk glance in her direction. A shiver raced along her spine. She left the papers, grabbed her pack and ducked behind the nearest shelves. With them screening her, she moved to where she saw an exit sign.

The door was locked and alarmed, but the toilet doors right next to her were not. In a flash, she forced the exit door, starting the alarm and dived into the gent's toilet and locked the door. Luck was with her, the facility was deserted so she hid in the cubicle and crouched on the closed toilet seat lid.

Andy stayed very still and heard the men stop by the door and report by radio that she had run off into the shopping area. They must have checked the female toilet, for they tried the door of the men's and found it locked.

It wasn't a very good hiding place, Andy knew, and she looked around and found there was a small window. Without thinking further, she stood up and found the window would open.

It was awkward, clinging to a pipe and dragging her pack out of the window, but she didn't want to have nothing with her. The bag dragged on her arm and upset her balance as she climbed to the roof of the shopping centre. To make things worse, the roof and everything on it was damp and slippery but Andy kept walking carefully until she found a spot where she couldn't be seen from the ground. Once there, she curled up into a ball and tried not to think. After a while, she dozed off.

The thump-thump of a helicopter hovering woke her sometime later, but she didn't move from her crouched position. She had nowhere to go, so she stayed where she was.

The helicopter moved off after a while and began circling the shopping centre.

Andy didn't think she was important enough to warrant that sort of attention. She wasn't a violent criminal; she really wasn't a criminal. Breaking into Tench's flat had been her debut.

The helicopter moved further out as if the police assumed that she had run far away. Andy relaxed, but only a little. She began to try and analyse her reactions as Moore the psychiatrist had taught her.

Firstly, she had climbed up here deliberately. She remembered doing it. It had been pure fear that had made her run. Why was she afraid?

The two men had been strangers, though she had been convinced they were police. She had run from them. Was it because her brother had got away from the police? Did she no longer feel safe enough to trust them?

An image of Hayley came into her mind and she remembered her promise to him – to trust the system, co-operate with the police. She should go and turn herself in, voluntarily, and not wait to be dragged in like – well, like a thief. But there were still things she wanted to know first.

The police activity eventually slowed and died. The helicopter disappeared and the sun had come out and burnt off the fog. Andy stopped shivering and began to feel warm. She started to think about her next move.

"I can't go back to Melbourne," she whispered, just to hear a voice. Martin must be there, trying to save his little empire. She could go to Broken Hill but how would she get there?

She pushed aside the vision of the money in the purse. Useless thoughts kept occurring to her. An intense feeling of hopelessness replaced all other thoughts and when it began to rain, hopelessness became depression.

Andy was sheltered from the worst of the late afternoon torrent, but where she was sitting, collected water from higher up. Before long, she was soaked and shivering again.

Finally, Andy had to move. She was cramped from sitting for long hours in one position and it was finally getting dark again. The rain hadn't let up and a dying sense of self-preservation forced her to realise that if she was going to get down in the current conditions, she had better do it before full dark.

Andy couldn't walk yet so she crawled to the edge of the roof and looked down and glanced from side to side. There were too many people on the side with the main entrance, so she moved to the back. Sensation was finally returning to her legs in the form of painful pins and needles tingling.

Andy came to an access ladder and decided to use it to get down. She hardly cared if anyone saw her. On the last step of the ladder, she slipped and fell, twisting her ankle. She had no strength to do anything else but cry.

The dog found her, growled at her, but she ignored it. The police handler came up moments later, found the sobbing heap and called for his back up to bring the car.

"Andy?"

Andy was past caring, past hearing. She was shivering so hard her teeth were knocking together.

"Help me get her into the car," Hayley instructed the dog handler. He hesitated.

"She isn't dangerous," Hayley insisted. This time the dog handler obeyed.

Andy didn't resist. She couldn't. She was only slightly aware of being put in the front of the car. Hayley still had the engine running and he turned the heater up to full.

"Go and get her a hot drink," Hayley told the officer. "Units two and three will be here soon."

The younger policeman was seeing a young woman who looked like a lost, sick child and obeyed the request of his superior. This time though, he had an option. "Guard!" he instructed his dog.

Hayley reported to the control room, telling them that he had the suspect he had been seeking, in custody.

"Where've you been Andy?" he asked softly.

"I was on the roof," she said after a while.

"Before that? Where have you been for the last three weeks?"

"I...I don't know," Andy answered. She truly had no idea where the house was from the shops.

Hayley rethought his next question, aware that Andy was only barely coherent and he had very little time to talk privately to her.

"Who bailed you out?" he asked.

"I thought ...you. But he took me to Martin."

Andy began to shiver harder. Hayley's face grew hard.

"We arrested Martin a week after you disappeared. Where were you then?"

"With Smith."

"Who is Smith?" Hayley could see one of the other dog teams approaching.

'Tench's boss."

"And he let you go?"

"He'd gone already."

"I'm surprised he isn't worried about you talking to us," Hayley said thoughtfully.

"He said he'd relocated his business after Tench was caught."

Hayley mentally filed that information.

"No, I mean, Smith has had lots of women friends or escorts. Many of them have ended up with a fatal case of separation."

If it was possible, Andy would have paled further.

"We had a deal..." Andy tried to explain, but Hayley interrupted her.

"Andy..."

"Wha..."

"I have to take you in."

"I ...was on bail" Andy said faintly.

"The papers were false. You were meant to be in court the following day."

"I couldn't..."

The door beside Hayley opened and a covered cup with a sipper top was passed into him. Hayley pressed it into Andy's hands. She made no move to drink it.

"One of you collect her stuff and bring it to the local station and warn them to have a doctor brought in, the other follow me in." Hayley spoke to the other officers then he closed his door.

"You'll have a lot of questions to answer, Andy."

"What about?"

Hayley didn't answer her question.

"I'm off your case Andy. I'm not allowed to interfere."

"It doesn't matter," Andy said dully. "No one will believe me, nobody cares."

Hayley wanted to give her a reason to hope but if he said any more about the things he'd discovered, he would be disciplined severely.

"It's not all bad," he said softly, but Andy didn't seem to hear.

With dry clothes, food in her belly and her twisted ankle securely bound, Andy should have felt better, but she didn't.

The police had found the handbag in her pack, discovered it wasn't hers and couldn't accept that she had in turn found it. Nor would they accept her claims that she could not describe the house where she found it nor its location. They pushed her for more explicit details of her walk that morning. She was finding it hard to think, she had a really bad headache and the pain from her ankle was not helping.

When she had answered their questions twice and they started on the third round, she simply stayed mute. Finally, they gave her a warning about co-operating and gave up.

Hayley had contacted Andy's lawyer, Jason Frost and assured her he was on his way, but Andy waived her right to have him present; though it was more a case of being unable to keep her mouth shut under the pressure of new accusations. Frost would not be impressed, Andy finally realised.

When he finally arrived, Frost told Andy in very definite terms, that he would not be able to defend her successfully if she didn't think before she spoke. Andy stuck stubbornly to her insistence of innocence and wanting to help the police find the real culprits. That was about all they had time to talk about at the Epping police station, because Andy was to be moved to police HQ in Sydney.

Hayley stayed in the background while Commissioner Kelly questioned Andy. It would have been Superintendent Lynch's task to question her but he had been called to Melbourne on urgent personal business.

Andy was pale and subdued, and her answers were given in a dull monotone. She seemed to be expecting the worst and didn't care anymore. She sat at the table with her hands in front of her and kept her eyes off Kelly.

"Who helped you escape?" Kelly demanded.

"I didn't escape. I was told I was being freed on bail."

"You were meant to be in court the following day. You should have known something was wrong."

"Should I," Andy glared at him. "I didn't know how the bailing system worked. And I was so glad to be getting out of there I didn't care to argue."

Kelly let that go for a moment.

"You were creating a disturbance earlier. Why?"

"I saw my brother and his mate Clem in warder uniform. I heard and saw them releasing the bloke Hayley caught at the Macquarie centre. I stayed quiet, because I didn't want them to see me there. But later, when they came back again, Clem had a needle and I panicked. I knew they were going for Tench, but I thought I would be next."

That resulted in a lot of questions asking why she was so concerned about Tench.

Finally, they moved on to where she had been after leaving the remand centre.

"I thought Hayley had bailed me. The bail bloke said he was taking me to him."

"Where did you go?"

Andy described what she could recall of the bloke of units. It wasn't very helpful as it had been dark at the back of the building.

Then she told them where she had been when she woke up, though she couldn't describe that building either.

"If you are so good with locks, why didn't you get out?"

"Martin came gloating just after I woke up and then when I did get out, Smith's men caught me before I could get outside and dragged me upstairs to the office."

"Smith? Who is Smith?"

"Tench's boss. He knew Martin had a deal with Tench and hadn't paid the money back. He was calling in his money."

"What did your brother say to that?"

"He was going to use the money he stashed in an account he had in my name and money from my trust account, to pay him off. I told him he couldn't. Then he claimed to have a $500K insurance policy out on me."

"Then what?"

Andy tried to explain how she was being held by Smith at a house, whilst her brother was to finish off Tench before he talked. If he'd done it in a week, she was to be given back to her brother and he'd have a month to pay what he owed.

"How was your brother going to get that much money?"

"He would have had me killed."

Kelly stood up so he towered over Andy.

"Really Miss Cappell, you can make up a better story than that! Tench died without talking; from the drug he'd been given."

"The newspaper said..."Andy began to protest. The first spark of her normal self.

"Said what, Miss Cappell?" Kelly invited her to continue.

"That he had," Andy insisted. "I assumed that was why Smith kept me at the house – to spite Martin. So Martin wouldn't have an easy way to get the money he owed and would have to give Smith all his businesses. He was going to ruin Martin."

"He was going to ruin your brother – for you?" Kelly insinuated.

"He may have put it like that," Andy retorted, "But I don't for one instant think he was doing it for me. He would be doing it for his own reasons – top of the list because he doesn't like f...He had Martin bashed to teach him not to try double crossing him. Promised me that the same would happen to me if I didn't do as he said."

Hayley watched, feeling sympathy for Andy but hiding it behind a façade of practised detachment. He knew that animosity between Andy and Kelly. She hadn't given him a good first impression, nor subsequent ones. He was prepared to assume the worst about her.

In fact, Kelly was making Andy answer variations of the same questions, trying to get her to betray herself. The questions implied she was lying.

Finally, something in Andy snapped and she screamed at Kelly.

"I've answered your questions three times already! What the hell do you want me to tell you?"

"The truth."

"You've got that!"

"The real truth!"

"It is!" Andy screamed at him again.

"Let's try this over again," Kelly spoke firmly. "If you saw or heard no news while you were with Smith – how did you know about Tench talking?"

"I went to a library to read the old newspapers," Andy said in a modified tone. "I only read a week to two weeks after the trial ended."

"Did you read that your brother's fiancée had been found?" Kelly asked her unexpectedly.

"No," Andy looked at Kelly now. "Where was she? Where is she? Did you ask her...?"

"She was dead, Miss Cappell."

"Wh... Where was she found?" Andy sensed that she didn't want to know the answer.

"In an abandoned car on the Coopers Crossing Road."

Kelly watched Andy closely and saw her face go blank as if she was thinking back.

"We also found a hairclip with blond hairs attached, in the boot of your car."

"That's impossible!" Andy snapped and she couldn't help her eyes straying towards where Hayley sat.

"The hair clip was an item stolen from the jewellery store in Broken Hill," Kelly went on ruthlessly.

Andy put her hands on the table and looked about to stand up.

"I don't like what you are implying Commissioner Kelly," Andy told him her mind clear. "I did not rob the jewellery store. I never saw any jewellery from it. If it was in my car, it was planted. If it had her hairs attached, Martin put it there. I did not see her after that evening in Broken Hill when she was following me. Martin told me that she had left him after I had phoned in a tip to the police about him. If I had stolen that clip, I would not have given it to her. So what are you implying?"

Andy stared at Kelly with not quite defiance. In fact, Hayley decide she had finally decided to stand up for herself. The attitude seemed to give Kelly pause.

"I think that you and your brother have been working together, but had a falling out."

The answer stunned Andy speechless. The very idea was repugnant, nauseating.

Andy looked helplessly at Frost, wishing he'd say something. When he didn't Andy continued to stare up at Kelly until something occurred to her.

"When my brother was stuck up the silo, he admitted that he and Merryl had robbed the places in Albury and Broken Hill," Andy told Kelly. "Jack Carruthers heard him."

"The conversation was held under duress. It can't be used as evidence," Kelly told her.

Andy collapsed back into her chair and closed her eyes. She wished this session would end.

A buzzer sounded, and the door to the room was opened and closed.

Through her partly raised eyebrows, Andy peeped and saw Kelly was talking to a uniformed constable and now had a folder in his hands.

"Miss Cappell," Kelly's voice sounded sceptical. "Why should I believe anything you have said today? What proof can you offer of your good intentions?"

Andy's eyes flew open.

"Because I am telling you the truth!" she insisted.

"Not good enough," Kelly said coldly. "Perhaps you could explain to me why your fingerprints were on the bolt of the manhole in Tench's office? And why a woman from one of the flats in the block gave us a description of you leaving there, shortly before the security firm rep arrived."

"Did you only just find that out?" Andy asked quietly, staring at the table.

"I have had the information for a while. We learnt about the place. Why were you there?"

"I wasn't lying about what Smith threatened if I didn't do as he said," Andy shivered at the thought. "But he offered me a chance to ransom myself. If I did a job for him, and Martin finished Tench before he talked, he said he's let me go with a chance to avoid Martin. Otherwise, I'd be handed over to Martin, tied up like a parcel. I told you what Martin would have done then."

"What did you do there?"

Andy described what she had done, getting both herself and Call him Jack, into the apartment and emptying the safe.

"A very practised job," Kelly said in a hard voice.

"Thank you," Andy said sarcastically. "It was my debut into theft!"

Kelly snorted in disbelief.

"You asked me for proof of my good intentions…" Andy stared at the Commissioner. "I found two sets of back up discs in the safe. I pushed one set under a chair and gave the other to Call him Jack. Did you find them?"

Kelly stared back at her and seemed reluctant to answer.

"You were there longer than a week," Kelly reminded her. "You don't look ill-treated. I'm convinced that you decided to suck up to this Smith! Were you going to bed with him too? Trading your body for his favours?"

Andy flushed.

"I can't stop you thinking that of me," Andy said trying to control herself. "What you said could be taken as the truth. But it wasn't what I wanted. He said, he'd give the police info about Martin's whereabouts, but only if I pleased him."

"Did he rape you?" Kelly asked bluntly.

"In the sense that it wasn't my choice, and I had no option to refuse – but he …" Andy was nearly in tears. "It wasn't unpleasant. And I let him because I didn't want to be turned loose before you had got to Martin. I didn't want Martin to get me again."

Andy felt a gentle hand on her shoulder.

"Convinced, Sir?" Hayley asked his superior formally. Kelly growled.

"Andy, you are not the first woman that the man you call Smith has victimised in the name of protecting themselves or a loved one. You are a lucky one though. Did Smith say why he was anxious to get Tench's records?"

"No," Andy said in a small voice. "But I gathered he thought it worth a lot to him."

"I'd accuse you of making up another story, Miss Cappell, except for the fact that only a few officers knew about Tench's flat and the break-in there and the discs we found. It was not made public in any way."

"But I read…"

"Someone leaked to the press that we had received information – claimed it was from Tench," Kelly admitted. "We don't know who it was. However, it tempted out the man who wanted him dead. Did you know that we arrested your brother for the attempt?”

Andy nodded. “I saw that in the paper and that he had escaped.”

“Where do you think he might have gone?” Kelly asked sharply.

“Melbourne,” Andy said at once. “If he couldn’t get the money by making me ‘accidentally dead’, he was going to have to come up with the money some other way or hand his businesses over to Smith.”

“What businesses?”

”I don’t know. Smith made him tell his yuppie assistants about them, but I wasn’t privy to that conversation.”

“You are Martin Cappell’s sister, you lived with him...” Kelly insinuated. “If you are so clever – why don’t you know?”

“He didn’t bring his work home,” Andy said coldly. “Yes, I had an idea, more than an idea he was involved in crime, but nothing I could take to the police – even if I dared.”

Andy began to shiver as she recalled Martin’s threats.

“He hit me if I tried to stick my nose in his business. He hit me once when I called him a pimp. I’m damn sure Merryl was one of his prostitutes. He really laid into me when he found me in his room. He didn’t want anything to get around to imply he wasn’t an upright citizen.”

“Surely you can tell us more than that?” Kelly insisted.

“I wish I could. I truly wish I could,” Andy vowed.

“Perhaps you would agree to a session of hypnosis?” Kelly suggested mildly.

When Andy nodded, he looked like he had her where he wanted her.

“Take her back to a holding cell,” Kelly ordered Hayley. “Have a permission slip ready to sign.” To the constable who was acting as recorder. “Type up that report and have a copy on my desk by four o’clock Have a copy ready for Superintendent Lynch when he returns.”

Jason Frost spoke up for the first time.

“I wish to speak to my client.”

Kelly nodded agreeably. “Talk to the constable outside when you are ready to leave.”

Hayley followed Kelly as far as the passage, where he had to wait to take Andy to a cell.

He could imagine what Frost would be telling Andy.

Andy spoke first. "You're going to call me an idiot."

"No," Frost disagreed, though the thought had crossed his mind. "I wanted to be sure you knew what you were doing."

"I've been telling them the truth. I can't tell them any different under hypnosis. I'm not hiding anything and I might remember something that will help them fix Martin for good. And if this will convince them of my innocence – it will be worth it."

Frost simply nodded. "Is there any subject you don't want to discuss under hypnosis?"

"I don't think so," Andy considered. "How bad is everything looking for me?"

"Well, I heard – very unofficially – that Constable Frawley found that false ID you used to get your car – it was in the car that gave you a lift. They have been showing the picture around in Broken Hill and Albury, along with a photo of you. Several people have identified the person in the ID as the person who handed them money. It's a start, and it supports the hypothesis that your brother opened the account. I also heard that she spotted two men out at the property where those people that gave you the lift lived. She identified them as small time crooks from Melbourne – possibly allied to your brother. But that little bombshell you dropped a moment ago is likely to have mixed reactions. Overall, I would say things are starting to turn in your favour, but mainly because Hayley and Frawley are risking their careers on the belief of your innocence."

"I'm ready to go downstairs, if you haven't anything else to say."

Frost spoke to her again after the session of hypnosis. It had been Moore, the psychiatrist who had been working with her, who had supervised the session. That had made it more comfortable doing what she now felt she had rashly agreed to do. Moore had encouraged her and commended her for her progress.

After the session, he had only told her that it had gone well, before he had left with the policemen.

"I agree, Andy," Jason Frost gave his opinion. "I believe that even the Commissioner is convinced of your veracity. He is quite sure now that you and your brother have never worked together. I think he was shocked by what he heard. You have also give Hayley quite a few leads to follow up."

"Good!" Andy stated firmly enough, even though her stomach was cramping from reaction to knowing that she had been talking about Martin.

"What happens to me next?" Andy asked Frost.

"I could re-apply for bail," he offered. "I doubt that it will be refused again."

"No," Andy surprised him. "I have no money and nowhere to go. I don't want to be out on the streets, until I must. With that idea I think I can tolerate being kept in remand."

"Call me if you have problems," Frost told her kindly. "However, thinking about things, I am almost certain that they will want to try and locate the house where you stayed. That bag you found belonged to a woman whose body was fished out of the harbour a month ago. It would appear that she was, like you, one of Smith's hostages – who didn't please him enough."

Andy shuddered, hoping she would never meet Smith again. What if he ever found out what she had done at Tench's place?

"I hope you can wait patiently until the police finish investigating you, your brother and Smith," Frost went on. "The situation is still complicated, but I think things are turning in your favour. Even your admission of guilt yesterday. You were obviously under duress at the time, but you still enabled the police to have information from Tench."

Andy mentally crossed her fingers – walking away from the police charges was only a start. There would still be an angry vengeful Martin – who would eventually get out of prison, if he were ever caught. And there was still Smith.

Andy looked at the large scale map of the area around Epping and considered what she remembered from her flight from Smith's house to the shopping centre. After discussing the points with one of the local sergeants, they settled on a small section of half a dozen streets where they would search first.

Hayley stayed quiet. His job was to keep Andy safe and ensure she didn't run off. Commissioner Kelly had finally allowed that Andy would listen to Hayley and behave and decided to make use of the fact. So when they moved off in the police car he sat next to Andy in the rear seat.

"That one!" Andy said suddenly. "I know it was dark when I left, but that looks like it."

She grew even more certain when the police car drove up the drive and she walked with them around to the side of the house. The door she had left through wasn't even locked.

"I was in a bedroom on the second floor" Andy told the officers who were entering the house.

Hayley kept a gentle grip on her arm, keeping her outside. The lack of activity while they were waiting soon began to get on her nerves.

"Smith had guards with savage dogs," Andy said to break the silence.

Hayley didn't reply, he too was listening intently.

Finally one of the police returned, and had a conversation on the radio. He then came and spoke to Hayley.

"The house was rented out for four months, but is now empty. However we found bodies in the cellar under the kitchen, probably the guards and servants Miss Cappell mentioned. I have requested a car to take Miss Cappell back."

Andy was white faced, but forced herself to ask, "And the dogs?"

"Yes," was the terse affirmative.

Hayley took Andy back to the car they had arrived in, and was aware she was trembling.

"Smith, as you know the man, will have a perfectly unimpeachable alibi," Hayley remarked. "I am still surprised that he let you go."

"Maybe I'm bait for Martin," Andy said without thinking. "He has to know that Martin escaped. Maybe had to go to Melbourne so that Martin wouldn't do a runner."

"Is that likely?" Hayley asked her seriously.

"He's running out of time," Andy said. "The month Smith gave him is almost up."

"Is that what you would do?"

"If I hadn't made a promise to you," Andy said soberly. "If I had money and if I wasn't more petrified than before to be alone on the streets – you wouldn't see me for dust!"

"And now?"

"I'll see this through to the end. Whatever that end is," Andy promised

Hayley nodded, he had come to expect no less.

Chapter 22

When Martin Cappell decided he had to escape, he had created maximum confusion by also liberating the four most dangerous detainees he knew of in the detention facility. Once outside, he had called Clem and they'd fled for Melbourne.

Martin had taken the first opportunity to dress in clothes that labelled him 'successful' and to proceed to empty all the bank accounts that he had used for his businesses. Each had been opened under a different name with false ID's. The money available was not even half of what he needed.

He gave his 'staff' no warning of his impending departure.

Clem had been going around to real estate agencies, getting valuations on the property he owned and an indication of how easy they would be to sell. Neither had gone near Martin's house, which he had also decided to sell. The title was in Martin's name – and it would spite his sister.

Therefore, it came as a major shock, when Martin went to the office that he used as his headquarters, to find Smith sitting in his chair. This was the one place that he had not revealed to Smith's underlings.

"Going somewhere, Mr Cappell?" Smith enquired politely. He drew out from the desk drawer some of the bundles of cash and bank cheques that had been in the floor safe, and displayed them on Martin's desk.

Martin recovered his poise with an effort.

"I have settlement on two of my properties tomorrow," he claimed. I will then have more than enough money to pay you. I will meet you at five tomorrow."

"You won't mind if my associate accompanies you then?"

Martin knew he didn't have an option to refuse.

Martin kept his face neutral, but Smith saw his muscles tense before forcing them to relax.

"That won't be a problem."

"Good. Good."

Smith stood up and walked closer to Martin.

"I would not like it if you disappointed me again. You failed to finish Tench before he talked. Fortunately, your sister helped me to recover all his records before then."

Smith took Martin's right wrist gently and lifted it.

"So tense," he said carefully rubbing it. "I could be mistaken into thinking you were trying to run from me."

"I have been preparing to pay you. Then I am going to find my sister and make her have an accident," Martin snarled and wrested his wrist from Smith's grip.

"Ah, yes. The lovely Andrea," Smith smiled reminiscently. "Such a satisfying bed partner. Most obliging."

"So that's where she was," Martin snarled again. "You promised her to me! He was dead, a week after our deal."

"Ah, but he'd talked," Smith reminded Martin "That meant only that you had to come and find her, instead of me giving her back to you."

"Where is she now?"

"Well, you know what women are like – can't stay out of trouble for long. The police picked her up again, a day or two ago. An informant has told me that they finally believe she is telling the truth. Apparently they had a psychiatrist hypnotise her so they could question her again. I think they will soon be busy down here. Your sister told them so much about you."

Martin's face turned red. "She doesn't know anything!"

"More than you realise, I believe."

"She wouldn't dare!"

"She has."

Smith smiled. He felt sure he was reading this effeminate creature correctly.

If he was telling the truth and intending to pay his debt, not run, his next action would be removing his sister. For sweet revenge and the chance of money to rebuild his piffling empire.

Smith believed in the power of incentive, but he wasn't going to share his own reasons for wanting Andy Cappell out of the picture. He had no sentimental scruples. He had let her go before he learnt that she had left something in Tench's apartment. Something that gave the police what they wanted. And he knew now that Tench had never woken up from that first attempt on his life. So if Andy Cappell was removed by her brother – so much the better.

If however, Martin Cappell was thinking of double crossing him – he'd still go for his sister and he, Smith, would have his own punishment waiting for Martin Cappell.

Martin Cappell maintained an unworried façade as he listened to the woman who managed one of his seven brothels. The police had been there asking for him.

"No Problem, Celia," he said smoothly. "My sister is in some trouble and has run off. They think she is on some kind of crime spree. I hope they have caught her."

The woman accepted his calm explanation and went back to her job. Martin picked up the business 'books' and left the premises.

Smith's guardian followed him like a silent shadow. Martin took the books back to his office and went out again. He had similar news at two more of his brothels, which he contacted by phone, so he arranged for the managers of these places to send their books to a prearranged place and sent Clem to pick them up.

The police hadn't visited his betting parlours or pawnshops yet, so Martin went to those and collected their records too. He intended to remove as much evidence as he could.

All the while he was toying with ways to lose Smith's minder. Smith had appropriated the liquid assets he'd had at his office, fortunately he had twice that much safely in another bank account. But time was getting short. He's told Smith that settlement on the sale of his buildings was at four o'clock, in fact his lawyer was due to attend for him at two o'clock – only an hour away. And, he wasn't intending to pay Smith at all. He was collecting his liquid assets, and disappearing. Smith would be left with bankrupt businesses and heavily mortgaged property. The two he was selling were the only ones he owned outright.

Martin's mobile phone rang. It was so new that only two people had the number. Clem and his lawyer.

"Yes," he answered, and heard Clem's voice.

Clem reported collecting the last of the business books and

stashing them safely. He then suggested a means to remove the minder.

Just under an hour later, in a deserted building in Port Melbourne, Martin straightened up and tidied his appearance. Smith's minder was lying dead at his feet. Clem had injected him with a poison, but the man had fought fiercely and almost succeeded in reaching his gun to shoot him.

"Take him down to the basement," Martin told Clem without remorse.

"Sure, Boss," Clem agreed, knowing that there was an entrance to the sewers down there.

He stalked off, carrying the body with ease.

Moments after Clem had gone off, Martin's phone rang. This time it was his lawyer.

"Trouble, Martin. The other party is a no show. The agent called them – their finance fell through. They are asking for an extension.'

"Give them twenty-one days," Martin instructed. He still needed the money, but now he couldn't pay Smith, even if he had wanted to. He had to run. "Attend to the details. If the money comes through in three weeks, pay it into my account – less your fee. I'll keep in touch."

Martin ended the call thinking furiously. Clem returned, empty handed.

"The building deal fell through." He told Clem, who knew what that meant. "All the records are safe?"

Clem nodded.

"Good. Stan has the deeds to the buildings I own and he knows to keep them safe. Smith can have the others if he wants. We have to leave now."

Andy found, somewhat to her surprise, that she appreciated the solitude of the remand cell. Though she still felt 'closed in' and occasionally found herself crying silently and feeling sorry for herself, she had not felt like she couldn't breathe.

For the last four days, Superintendent Lynch had been questioning her unmercifully about Smith, though there was not much she could tell him except his description and their deal.

She had come to expect the early morning inquisition – only today, he hadn't come. Instead, Frost had turned up as usual and told her that Lynch had gone to Melbourne and taken Hayley with him.

"What else is happening," Andy wanted to know. She wasn't allowed access to TV. Newspapers or radio or anything she might use to escape.

"The bodies have been identified. They worked for an agency and hired through a third party to work at the house. Your brother has been seen in Melbourne, but he hasn't been caught. It looks as if he is getting ready to run. I think that is why Lynch and Hayley went there. Your brother put your house on the market – but the police put a stop on it and have it sealed so they can search it."

Andy smirked slightly then shrugged. "Bastard probably did it to spite me – but I don't intend to go back. Have they dropped any charges yet?"

"No, but whilst they haven't..."

"I'll be safe here," Andy finished. "I know, I know, I know."

"Where are you taking me?" Andy asked Superintendent Lynch as she was handcuffed and told to walk. A constable had hold of her arm and the two men seemed in a hurry.

Her question wasn't answered. She was hustled down to the police garage and into the back seat of a car.

Andy didn't ask again, instead she listened to the police radio hoping that she would hear something that would give her an answer. All that seemed to be happening was a siege involving six pre-school children.

When the police car began to travel faster, with lights and sirens going, and passing all the other cars on the highway, Andy began to worry. She had no idea of where she was being taken until the radio mentioned her brother.

"Is Martin holding those kids?" she asked again, but still met silence.

"You're not going to exchange me for them - you can't."

"No," Lynch told her shortly. "But we may have to let him see you, so he thinks we are. We have to get the kids out – I'm sure you will agree."

Andy did, but she did not want to go near her brother. If he was doing something like this, he was desperate. She settled back into her seat and thought furiously until distracted when the car stopped at a road block. It was the police safety barrier, keeping people back from the scene of the drama. They were allowed through and directed to a safe position to park.

An officer in a flak vest approached the car, opened the door and stuck his head in.

"Miss Cappell, can you tell us what your brother might do?"

"What's happening?" she asked and received a succinct account of the siege. Martin was holding six kids and threatening to kill them one by one unless Andy was given to him.

"I'm sure he's killed before," Andy though of Merryl. "Is he alone?"

"We think there's a second man. A solid chap."

"Clem," Andy said aloud. "If Martin won't kill the kids, Clem probably would. You need to get them out fast."

"Are you prepared to help us?"

Andy glanced at Lynch who was watching her but letting her make up her own mind.

She was feeling cold and trembly. Then she took a deep breath.

"If it's the only way – I'll go in. He wants me; he doesn't want a pack of bawling kids. How does he plan to get away?"

"We don't know, but we have all exits covered. We'll keep you advised."

Lynch maintained a watch on Andy as events proceeded and negotiations were continued.

Andy sat silently, hoping fervently that she wouldn't be needed, but almost sure she would be – why else had she been rushed here.

About an hour later, Andy saw another of the flak-jacketed officers coming towards the car.

He was carrying a smaller vest and a parka.

"Are you sure you can do this?" the officer asked, seeing how pale she was.

"Yes," she assured him, trying to convince herself that if she died it would be no loss to the world.

The handcuffs were removed and she was helped into the jacket and parka, and moved around experimentally. The weight of the jacket was less than she expected and if she had to run or climb, she could.

As she walked between the officer and Lynch, she listened to the instructions she was being given. They didn't want her to be hurt, and if possible, they wanted to get either her brother or the other man into the line of the window. But above all, the children had to be released first.

Martin was barricaded on the second floor of a three story building. It stood between two office buildings so the only windows faced the street or the small rear yard leading to an alley. The back yard was full of trash; loose, dangerous and liberally mixed with scissor wire. The rear windows were barred and boarded up. The third story of the building was booby trapped and the floor of each level was reinforced concrete.

The first floor was deceptively vacant – but the stairway to the second floor had been removed. The only ways up was via a rope ladder or a fold down ladder operated from the second floor.

Clem and Martin were holding off the police with pistol fire and threats to the children. Negotiations were being conducted by mobile phone and the police could hear the children crying in the background.

Andy waited beside Superintendent Lynch, listened to the one sided conversation and watched the windows. The police wanted the children out before Andy went in – but Martin wasn't stupid enough to agree to that.

The whole situation was ludicrous. It wasn't Martin's style. If he wanted her dead, why was he going to all this trouble? Admittedly, he would have deduced, correctly, that she would not want harm to come to children – he probably also expected her to rush in without thought – but why did he want her, presumably alive? For the insurance? If he took her from here and she later turned up dead, he'd never get the money and surely, Smith's deadline had passed? Had he paid Smith off somehow? Had Smith taken over his little empire, whatever it was?

Andy's first thought was that Martin had opted to run from Smith – and that idea felt right. Only desperate men caused situations like this. In her mind that meant he hadn't paid off Smith and Smith was after him. What did he expect her to do about it?

Andy saw that Lynch was also putting on a flak jacket – was he coming in with her?

"Andy, are you sure you can do this?" the negotiating officer asked her.

"I said I would, and if it saves those kids, what happens to me doesn't matter. Any last minute instructions?

"They will not fire at you and the Superintendent as you walk over. You are to go into the ground level and start to climb the rope ladder. Stop when you are half way up. The children will be released down the folding steps. When they are out, I want you to drop and run for the nearest cover.

"Won't he have a gun on me?" Andy asked.

"We'll have a man on the ground floor covering you. You've got the jacket on, remember. Just do as we stay."

Andy reserved her doubts and decided to consider other options once inside.

In spite of the assurances of the officer, Andy fully expected to feel a bullet hit her with every step she took towards the building.

"They are watching us," Lynch warned her.

They paused in the doorway, and saw the rope ladder dangling from the ceiling. It was the only thing in the empty room. Andy spotted the fold up ladder, now seated into the ceiling and then her eyes were drawn to a partly open door on the far side of the room.

"There is a man in the back room," Lynch said very quietly. "He snuck in earlier, during a distraction. He's covering the back entrance. We think they have a way out through the rubbish out back."

"Can they get into adjoining buildings or cellars or anything?" Andy whispered.

"The side walls are solid concrete, there are no floors lower than this."

"Andy, Climb up!" Martin called from above.

"I didn't know you were into doing me favours, Martin. Send the kids out!"

"Climb up half way so I can watch you. Then the kids can go."

"You are an idiot, brother."

Andy walked over to the rope ladder and tested its strength. She saw the gun pointing at her and a new sensation replaced her fear – it was anger. She could hear the kids.

Andy began to climb and stopped half way up. They assumed that she would be no danger to them, clinging to the ladder.

The folding ladder began to be lowered, as soon as it was down, she heard Martin telling the kids to leave or he'd pull their pants down and spank them for being so noisy. It had the desired effect. Even with their hands tied behind them, the six children, all girls, ran down the ramp and over to Lynch who shooed them outside into the arms of the waiting police. Even before they were fully out the door, Andy dropped and ran for the rear room.

There was a man there alright, but it wasn't a policeman. She was caught and gagged, even before she could scream. Her eyes weren't covered, even if her arms were pinioned. She knew the man. It was Clem and he was taking her up another stairway. She struggled as hard as she could, but Clem ignored her efforts. He threw her down on the floor at Martin's feet.

"Look what I found," Clem sneered.

Martin smirked. Andy knew that look. Martin thought he had her petrified with fear; too scared to escape the punishment he wanted to give her.

"I'm here," Andy said to him, hiding her anger. "Aren't you going to run like a frightened rabbit?"

"From you!" Martin laughed. "Get up!"

Andy stared at him without moving.

"I said, GET UP!" his voice rose in pitch.

"Why?" Andy asked in return.

Martin's foot moved to kick her but she rolled out of the way, and sprang to her feet.

Both men had their attention on her, though Clem was meant to be looking out of the window. Neither seemed aware of Lynch, just behind the wall where the third stairway came up.

"You're getting slow, bro," Andy taunted, watching him to deduce his next move. She was thinking of the self-defence training that Frawley had given her.

She wasn't wrong. Martin, predictably, ran forward to grab her. He found himself flying over his sister's shoulder and landing heavily on the floor. He hadn't learnt from their last meeting.

Andy saw him glare at Clem and was ready for a charge from that direction.

Clem's only thought at that moment was to get her, and he forgot to be careful crossing the window. Andy heard the crash of the glass exploding and then blood was pouring from Clem's neck. She turned her attention back to her brother who was erupting off the floor. He grabbed her by the neck and began to squeeze, but Andy had practiced that situation too. Her hands flew up to clap his ears and her knee found his groin. Martin screamed in agony and dropped her.

Andy lifted herself up as Lynch, gun in hand, crossed the floor.

"What kept you! " Andy said rudely. "I saw you behind the wall!"

"I was waiting to see if he was man enough to finish you off, my dear."

Andy's eyes went wide. The voice coming from Superintendent Lynch, was that of Smith and the gun was pointing at her.

"I was right, you can't trust a f... to do a man's work."

Martin was getting to his feet and Lynch nodded his head in the direction of the third stairway. It was only then that Andy realised that Lynch was wearing gloves.

Andy had forgotten she was wearing a flak jacket, but up close, the gun in Lynch's hand didn't have to be aimed at her chest.

"Don't move," Andy was warned. She had no intention of disobeying just yet. The idea of Smith being Lynch, stunned her. It meant that he knew she had put some of Tench's disks under the chair for the police to find. His intentions were quite clear – he'd warned her.

There was a sharp 'thud' from beyond the wall, and a gargling noise that had to have come from Martin.

"Never mind, my dear," Smith/Lynch said carefully. "Your brother won't get far. I promised him his pitiful life if he got you here. I simply neglected to mention his punishment for double crossing me. If he's determined, he'll get out through the secret tunnel I provided. The one I ensured Hayley got to hear about. I think you can be sure he'll be in prison a long time and he'll find it hard to escape with one hand missing. And I even let my police colleagues in Melbourne find out about all of his business affairs."

Smith paused for effect.

"Now you. I was impressed. I didn't think you had it in you to beat your brother. But after all I did for you, you double crossed me too. I warned you about that. What did I promise you?"

"You don't have time to give me a leisurely bashing," Andy stared at him defiantly.

"I said, I would treat you as I treated your brother."

Smith grabbed her hand and pulled her close. He held the gun at her neck and massaged her right wrist. Andy's imagination supplied the options.

"Or you can promise to come with me and continue to amuse me.

Of course, I will have to punish you first."

A mobile phone began to ring, but Smith/Lynch ignored it.

"What's it to be?"

"I'll come with you," Andy decided, staring back at him with loathing. It was the only sensible option at that moment – any other answer and she'd be dead when the police came up and Lynch would have a ready scapegoat in Martin.

Lynch used his phone then to call outside.

"The man Clem, is dead. Cappell has escaped up through the third level," Smith said in Lynch's voice. "Andy is okay. You can come up."

"Are you going to say anything, my dear?" Smith said when he finished on the phone.

Andy shook her head. Smith was still holding her wrist.

"Come on then."

Andy walked down the stairway beside Lynch, hoping for a chance to escape, but she knew how thorough Smith was. Lynch still had his gun out.

They were half way down when they heard a sound behind them.

Lynch spun around, his gun aimed up.

"Put the gun down, Lynch, and let the girl go," Hayley ordered the man who was his superior in the force.

"What's all this about, Hayley. I'll have you disciplined for this."

Hayley's gun never wavered.

"We had a microphone in Andy's jacket."

Andy felt Smith/Lynch become tense and knew he was about to act. She reacted faster. Lynch's gun was no longer on her so she used one of the tricks she had learnt to break the grip of a captor. The man was so sure of his control of her that he hadn't considered her a threat. She twisted Smith/Lynch's arm, put him off balance then pulled him down the stairs. He let go of her, in an effort to save himself but he landed heavily and Andy who had quickly regained her balance, skipped down the stairs and stood on Lynch's gun arm.

More police were pouring into the building and two of them quickly took Smith/Lynch into custody and dragged him away.

Hayley stayed with Andy whilst more police searched the building.

"How are you," He asked her gently.

"Sick," Andy admitted. "Did you get Martin?"

"Yes, we found their secret way out. We had a snitch – Lynch was it? He wasn't intending Martin to get away. Martin is on his way to hospital – they may be able to reattach his hand. There was a really nasty booby trap on the door leading to the escape route."

"I heard it go off," Andy said without emotion.

"You did well, Andy," Hayley told her. "And you faced your brother – he'll think twice about threatening you now."

"Will he? He went too damn far this time," Andy said, the anger clear in her voice. "Kidnapping babies! He'd've known that would get me – but he never even realised that I wasn't scared stiff of him. I was so damn angry that I might have killed him if I had a weapon. I hope they can't sew his damn hand back on. It would serve him right. How did you know about Lynch?"

"We weren't sure," Hayley admitted. "But he implicated himself. Come on, we've got to go back to headquarters."

Andy belatedly remembered the microphone in her parka and decided not to ask any more questions. Time enough for that later.

"Where's the scared child that didn't like closed in places?" Hayley's voice broke the silence in the remand cell.

Andy, who was hugging her knees at the far end of the bunk bed, looked up.

"I still don't like it here," she muttered. "But it's better than being penniless on the streets. At least I get fed here. What do you want?"

It had been a week since her brother's recapture and the scandal of the revelation that Superintendent Lynch was the mysterious Smith, the mob leader police had been seeking for a decade.

The newspapers she was now permitted had been full of it. It eclipsed her own part in freeing the small hostages.

"I have official permission to tell you a few things," Hayley said quietly. He sat on the other end of the bed.

"I would have thought Kelly was too busy washing his dirty laundry to bother about me."

Hayley allowed himself a faint smile of amusement.

"That's true. His reputed anger is focussed on Lynch. He was extremely annoyed that Lynch had taken you to the siege. Lynch didn't clear it with him first. I didn't know about it until Kelly called me and told me what was happening. He was monitoring communications."

"How come Lynch didn't know about the microphone?" Andy asked

"He should have expected it," Hayley agreed. "But it was the leader of the tactical squad that put it in as a safeguard for you. He didn't have a reason to question your presence, because his superior brought you in."

"Has Lynch talked yet?"

"Not a lot," Hayley admitted.

"I've been thinking a lot about last week," Andy said after a while. "I thought all along it wasn't Martin's style. Smith/Lynch set it up to get me, and he hoped Martin would kill me."

"I agree with that analysis. It was too flashy for your brother. He's more into sniping, stealth and poison. I told Kelly that, and he decided that the purpose of the siege was to get to you."

"Brilliant deduction from a man who thought I was in league with my brother."

"We had a hint that there was a leak in the department," Hayley continued. "Only six people knew about the break-in at Tench's place. Kelly sent a four man squad into search as soon as he discovered where the place was. They found the discs under the couch and assumed it was an oversight of the thieves. Having those discs was meant to be highly classified – Lynch found out later after he came back from Melbourne. However, the papers got hold of the idea that Tench had talked."

"And no one would admit to telling the press anything."

"No, but even then we didn't suspect Lynch," Hayley revealed. "Do you have any theory about why he would have leaked the news?"

"I can't make myself consider being this important, but Smith had a deal with Martin – like I told Kelly. He doesn't like homosexuals. I don't know if Martin was one or not, but Smith thought he was. Apart from using me for his own gratification, and to give him credit, it wasn't really unpleasant; I think Smith wanted to have an excuse to make Martin suffer and still lose everything. I wouldn't be surprised if he enjoyed corrupting me. Of course, once he knew what I had done – well, he doesn't like people who double cross him. He probably offered Martin a second chance if he got rid of me. Martin wouldn't have thought twice. And Martin wouldn't have had the means to set up that siege."

"Well, that is quite possible. Lynch doesn't like gay men either."

"Thanks for being there," Andy said looking at Hayley.

"I should thank you for acting so quickly, he was about to shoot," Hayley was truly sincere. "It is the sort of thing your father would have done."

"How?"

"Remind me one day to tell you about a young policeman, a jewel thief and a budding psychiatrist," Hayley said cryptically. "It's the reason I got Moore to help you. He owed me and your father a big favour."

"I wondered why such a big shot was involved with a petty nuisance," Andy admitted, then she fell silent.

Hayley seemed to know what she wasn't asking.

"Your brother has recovered from his operation. His hand was reconnected, but he will never have full movement in it. However, unlike Smith/Lynch, he is busy telling all he knows about anything illegal; Smith, Tench anyone, except himself. At first he refused to admit to trying to frame you, but he eventually decided that an extra ten years for that series of crimes was better than twenty-five for attempting to murder you – on top of the kidnapping charges."

"What about his businesses in Melbourne and Merryl?"

"We haven't got to those yet," Hayley smiled. "We want to get all we can on Smith before we distract him. Never fear, he'll get what's coming to him and he'll be in prison a long time."

"Good!"

"Now, you, Miss Cappell, need to be ready to be discussed at a high level meeting."

"Me?" Andy had a look of hope on her face. "Do you mean they are finally going to drop all charges against me?"

"Just be ready!" Hayley said on rising.

Chapter 24

Andy continued to sit quietly, even after the panel of godlike creatures had left. She had only known Kelly, Frost and the now Superintendent Hayley. The others were state prosecutors, judges and legal experts, plus two Government representatives.

They weren't really discussing her, except incidentally. She was called upon to answer questions about Lynch as Smith, providing knowledge of 'both men'. Then she had sat around outside the main discussion chamber, whilst the analysis of the case against Lynch proceeded.

Frost had requested the state prosecutor to make a ruling on Andy's case. The police had, that morning, dropped all charges except the break in at Tench's office.

Surprisingly, Commissioner Kelly had spoken out in her defence when she was recalled to the room to hear their pronouncement.

"It is the decision of the prosecutor's office that the charge against Andrea Cappell of helping to pervert the course of justice by robbing the office of Corrie Tench, be dropped owing to the fact that she was under duress at the time, and she was responsible for us finding the evidence we needed against Tench. She is free to go with our commendations for her steadfastness in helping to bring several other violent offenders to justice.

"Coming?" Hayley asked, amused by the stunned expression on Andy's face. "Why the look of amazement? You got what you wanted – to be proved innocent. Do you really like this place so much now that you want to stay?"

"NO!"

"Well, come on then. There are some people waiting for you, queuing up to offer you a place to stay."

"Who?"

Hayley merely smiled and led her to collect her few belongings from the impound and took her in his car back to his apartment.

Andy was greeted like a lost friend by Kit Frawley and with a broad grin by Jack Carruthers. She returned both and laughed as she saw all the belongings that she seemed to be forever leaving behind her somewhere, in a neat pile in the corner.

Jack took a wallet from his pocket and handed it back to her. It was her wallet and it still contained eight hundred dollars, but had an added item, a brand new learner driver's permit.

"I can't keep all this money," Andy protested. "Jack said some of it was stolen."

"We recovered almost all of the stolen, non-cash goods," Hayley told her. "The items that were not insured were returned and the owners have agreed that the cash be kept by you as a finder's fee."

"But, I didn't find them," Andy protested.

"The items that were insured," Hayley went on, ignoring her protest, "were also returned and the insurance company paid out on the cash stolen. They have agreed to consider the cash as a finder's fee. It is really only a small fraction of what they would have to have paid to replace the gems and other goods."

Kit Frawley spoke up. "You didn't find them directly, but Martin had planted a lot in the roof of the bungalow where you stayed in Albury and he'd hidden the jewels from Broken Hill in the freight station next to that old silo, before he began to climb up. He probably intended to get them before he left. So indirectly, you did help us find them. We have also unfrozen your accounts. "

"Should I take my money out and put it in a new account?" Andy asked uncertainly.

"I would," Kit said firmly. "We can organise that before we go back to the Hill."

"We?" Andy turned to Hayley. "You too?"

Hayley shook his head. "I'm assigned here for now but I hope to be back there later."

Andy wasn't totally disappointed. She was going to need time to sort herself out and decide on her future.

"I wonder if I could get Kelly to sponsor my application to the police academy," Andy said with a mischievous smile.

Kit Frawley snorted with amusement.

"Didn't think so," Andy shrugged. "I'll probably need to finish High School first."

"That would be advisable," Hayley said gravely. "How about we go out for a quiet celebration this evening?"

Hayley saw Andy's eyes shine and felt his job had been more than worthwhile.

Andy, a more adult and serene version, greeted Hayley with a hug that both surprised and pleased him. She had been living in his house under the care of his housekeeper for the past six months while she studied for her Year eleven and twelve certificates.

Hayley, on leave from Sydney now that the trial of ex-policeman Lynch was over, had come back to Broken Hill. Andy had written to him and promised to show him something when he arrived.

Hayley had thought it would be to brag about her results from school. His housekeeper had told him that they were excellent. So when Andy had led him into the foyer of Broken Hill's tallest building, taken the lift up to the top floor, and then gone out through the fire door and halfway down to the previous floor by the escape ladder – he was full of curiosity. From there she scrambled onto the roof of the neighbouring building and across several other rooves in what was one of the strangest episodes in his life. It was an experience he was to remember for a long, long time, because it tested his head for heights and balance to the utmost.

Andy had almost skipped along the sloping tin and tile rooves and the narrow ledges without any sign of nerves at all. Finally, she stopped.

"You once asked me where I thought the place was that Dad called his Eyrie," Andy reminded him. "What do you think?"

The view alone was worth coming up to see, but Andy wasn't finished. "Come over here."

There was a small shelter between two sloping rooves. The doors were wood, well weathered and ready to fall off rusted hinges. There was an ancient lock on the door, but it wouldn't have kept anyone out. Andy only seemed to touch it and it fell open.

Inside was dark, but where the sun did reach, it seemed full of rotting, rusting junk, mouse eaten cloth and papers. It looked as if it had not been disturbed for over a decade.

Andy moved some of the rubbish and cobwebs from under an old pram, and pulled out a small metal trunk. The lock on the trunk looked new and Andy pulled out a key from her pocket.

"Do you think I can claim a finder's fee on this?" Andy asked as she lifted the lid, smiling in triumph. Hayley looked at the collection of coins, jewellery and small silver ingots with amazement. He smiled at the Magpie's daughter and made a bet with himself that the non-cash proceeds of most of Frank Cappell's robberies was here in the trunk, where only his beloved daughter would find it.

THE END

Other Novels by Margaret Gregory

WANDA: FROM BAD TO WORSE

If she was going to die young, like her mother, Gwen Willard was determined to die rich and she had very few years to do it. Her first step was to leave home. She met Hooch, who taught her some exciting and illegal skills. She was the Draco's lucky mascot until she came to the attention of the police. Then her uncanny knack for predicting trouble, warned her to flee to the city and change her name.

Life wasn't easy. She was 15, had little money and no regular job, but her new skills came in handy. Then she crossed the path of an evil and unscrupulous man and she didn't want him to have his way.

WANDA: CHOOSING CRIME

Wanda was free. She was never going back to jail. But she was homeless, almost penniless and Harrison Franklin had a long and vengeful memory.

Jim Phillips had a long memory too, and Wanda had saved his life. Could he save her from Franklin?

WANDA: RISKING LIFE TO LIVE

The euphoria of successful heists were what kept Wanda Dean alive. At 23, she was crime boss Harrison Franklin's top agent — well paid for absolute obedience. That's all that mattered. Until she met Mike Johnston and her boss ordered him killed. For that, the Franklins were going to pay. In Risking Life to Live, justice conflicts with loyalty and the penalty for betrayal is death.

WANDA: A NEW LIFE - HIDDEN SECRETS

Even before beginning as a covert agent for the US Government, Wanda is abducted by a foreign operative. After being rescued, there are signs that she had been subjected to hypnosis. With an important government gathering imminent, her handler must ensure she is not a security risk.

Can Wanda's psychic extra senses help her recognize and resist the implanted commands and clear her for secret work?

WANDA: A NEW LIFE - FIRST MISSION
On her first covert mission for the US Government, Wanda calls on the skills that made her a skilled thief to convince a revolutionary general that she's an ideal recruit. When her team mates' covers are blown, it is up to her to ensure that two missing scientists and confidential Government documents are not smuggled out of the US.

WANDA: FULL CIRCLE
Three generations after the alien Kumatan left Earth, their own world is suffering from alien invaders. In desperate hope, one returns to Earth seeking help - little knowing they had left one of their own behind.
Wanda, a child of the third generation, answers the call.

ERIN: THE FORCING OF WISDOM
For years, Erin has used the intricacies of cyberspace to banish unwanted emotions. Others call what she does hacking, and her manipulations criminal, but now her skill was exceptional - in, out, traceless. She was wrong. Someone betrayed her.
Travis has dangerous plans. He needs an electronics expert – one he can coerce through fear. Erin was perfect.
With the inescapable threat of prison looming, Erin accepts his offer of sanctuary. When she realises his intentions, she is in too deep. But the terrifying of innocents is unforgivable. She cannot walk away. She is an empath and shares their distress. She has to help them, even if it means prison, and insanity...

ERIN: THE CALL
(including ELISABETH AND TANYA: BLOOD CALLS TO BLOOD.
Elisabeth's sister, Wanda, had been missing for half a year. Multiple authorities had found no trace of her, or her two colleagues. Yet she knew her sister was still alive and had answered a call for help from an alien who had once lived on Earth.
Elisabeth, along with her newly found cousin Tanya, have started to sense things from her missing sister. Enough to know that she is

in dire trouble, but not enough to help her.

While looking for traces of the aliens, Elisabeth makes some unexpected discoveries about her family. Yet even with the help of a second newly discovered cousin, she fears she is not strong enough to help her sister and the others to return.

ERIN: THE CALL

Convicted cyber-criminal, Erin Mason, is startled into awareness in an unfamiliar place, with no memory of escaping and only vague memories of getting there. Voices in her head were urging her to go west, and they were getting more urgent.

After a chance meeting with covert agent, Jim Phillips, when she helped save his mission, he realised that she might be the key to another, more personal quest – to find three missing state department agents.

All he must do is keep Erin safe, and hide her from an intense police search, until he can introduce her to cousins she was unaware of.

However her uncontrolled psychic gifts conflict with a logical mind that prefers the ordered intricacies of computers and electronics. She only wants to shut out the voices and the madness she sees looming.

Can Phillips convince her to help him, before the forces of the law find her?

THE SERPENT'S SHADOW

Three books in one.

Janna consorts with terrorists to protect her friend Prince Ali from assassins.

Former cyber-criminal, Erin, becomes part of the merchandise of stolen tech secrets.

Jim Phillip's team is sent to neutralise the leader of the terrorist Cobra Sect.

KORVU: THE BEGINNING

The prequel to The Wild One

Jai Ansuni was the first female Atapi sorcerer for thousands of years, but she dare not reveal it. However, when tribal sorcerer, Stacion Ansuni escalates the enmity between Atapi and Kumatan to an ominous level. Jai and her womb mate, Con, try to mitigate his atrocities but can two young Atapi, not even a score of years old, win against the powerful sorcerer?

THE WILD ONE

Sixteen year old Jai Cassidy thought she was finally free of her family until she is discovered by her other relatives...the ones that aren't human. Jai uses her natural perversity and cunning to escape their control, but catapults herself into the middle of a deadly feud between two alien races.

ATAPI SORCERESS

The sequel to The Wild One

Jai Cassidy is beginning her mission of reversing the decline of the non-humanoid Atapi. As a sorceress and an Atapi-Human hybrid, she is vehemently disliked by the male Atapi sorcerers and the humanoid rulers of Korvu. Her task is complicated by the treachery of a group of alien engineers, who are inciting insurrection and harsh reprisals.

THE TYMOREAN TRUST BOOK 1 - POWER RISING

The Tymorean Trust - When peace rules Tymorea - Peace reigns in the universe.

Chosen to be the Advocates of the mystical and incorporeal Guardians of Peace, twins Tymos and Kryslie must first learn to control and use the power rising in them - or it will destroy them.

On Tymorea, only the ruling Triumvirate Governors are powerful enough to guide the strong-willed alien-bred twins until they have mastered their power.

THE TYMOREAN TRUST BOOK 2 - GREAT ONES

The peace of the Guardian Planet, Tymorea, is in deadly peril. War there will create ripples of unrest and destruction throughout the settled universe.

Tymos and Kryslie, still adolescents, have barely mastered their power and Llaimos is still less than a year old, but they are the three chosen to be Advocates of the mystical Guardians of Peace, to safeguard the Tymorean Trust.

THE TYMOREAN TRUST BOOK 3 - RETURN TO EARTH
Even before the war on Tymorea, the Elders foresaw that Great Ones Tymos and Kryslie would have an imperative mission on Earth.
But as the Tymoreans prepare to build an Earthbase to support them, they discover that specifications for two vital protective shields are missing.
Now, nearly a century later, Tymos and Kryslie must find his work and build the generator before the base is found.

THE TYMOREAN TRUST BOOK 4 - EARTH MISSION
Just before their graduation from the prestigious WSRA Washington University, Tymos and Kryslie Ward deliberately disappear.
The Great Ones have foreseen the capture and death of the new Tymorean missionaries and discovered that the leader of the Eastern Imperium plans to undermine the United World Nations.
Tymos and Kryslie must protect their kin and prevent a potentially devastating world war.

THE TYMOREAN TRUST BOOK 5 – ALIEN CONTACT
Tymos and Kryslie Ward, hide their Tymorean intelligence and abilities while working as low ranked technicians at the WSRA's lunar base. When an alien ship arrives at Lunar One, pursued by a powerful enemy who will stop at nothing to get what he wants, only the two Tymorean Great Ones have the knowledge and abilities to overcome him, but to do so they must risk their sanity, and their souls.

THE TYMOREAN TRUST BOOK 6 – INVASION
Great Ones Tymos and Kryslie go to rescue the crew of Earth's first deep space mission – and discover that Ciriot space pirates have discovered Earth's location. When the Ciriot invade in force,

the Great Ones reveal themselves so that Earth can gain vital help. However, Kryslie becomes the victim of Ciriot, who want to control her mind and make her betray the people of Earth.

TRICKS

Tom and Jo Dwyer had a reputation for playing tricks – and getting detention. They didn't seem to care about that, so long as they made their class laugh. That was until someone began to turn their tricks against them, and it was no longer funny.